Whiskey Jack Lake

By
Randall Probert

Whiskey Jack Lake
by Randall Probert

www.randallprobertbooks.net

email: randentr@megalink.net

Photography credits:

Front cover sketch ~ Sarah Lane
Bethel Bait and Tackle Shop, Bethel, ME
Author's photograph ~ Patricia Gott

Disclaimer:
This book is a work of fiction. All places and character names are products of the author's imagination.

ISBN: 978-1523803422

Printed in the United States of America

Published by
Randall Enterprises
P.O. Box 862
Bethel, Maine 04217

Whiskey Jack Lake

Chapter 1

When WWI started on July 28th, 1914, German forces were closing in on Belgium and then France. Europe was a flaming boil. England came to the aid of the French and Belgian forces and called on the United States for help.

Many of the President's advisors and military leaders wanted to aid Europe and stop the expansion of the Central Powers. But President Wilson said, "No." The United States would remain neutral. On May 5th, 1915, German u-boats sunk the Lusitania with Americans onboard.

Again the cry went out to join the Allies, but Wilson said the United States would remain neutral.

There were seven merchant vessels sunk by German u-boats. When the United Kingdom intercepted a telegram from Germany's foreign minister asking Mexico to join the Central Powers and attack the United States, this finally convinced the public opinion that the United States should join the Allies.

Anticipating the United States eventually entering the war, young men were being drafted and trained in trench warfare.

The first draft notices were sent via mail and on December 1st, 1916, Rascal Ambrose boarded the Canadian and Atlantic train that ran through the wilderness lumber town of Whiskey Jack Lake, along with three other friends: Sam Dingley, Willie Peters, and Tom Hatfield.

Rascal was married with two children and he was surprised, as was his wife Emma, when the draft notice arrived. The other three were all single men.

Emma, their daughter, three-year-old Beckie, and two-year-old Jasper stood on the cold wind-blown platform watching Rascal board the railcar. "Goodbye, Daddy," Beckie said. She was the twinkle in her father's eye.

Rascal never thought about questioning his draft with a wife and two kids. He simply accepted it. When the train was finally out of sight Emma and her two children walked back to their cabin.

"You know guys," Sam said, "This aint that bad. Leaving this cold hellhole for warmer weather to the south." He was actually excited. Rascal was trying to be excited, but he was concerned about leaving his family behind.

* * *

The weather was certainly warmer, with less snow and ice, but the air always had a dampness to it that would work its way to the bone, and Rascal was often as cold as if he were back home at Whiskey Jack Lake.

For the first time in their young lives the four men were seeing things that they knew had only existed in pictures in newspapers and magazines.

Their training were long days and the four men excelled and became lean, rugged soldiers.

In April of 1916 the four men from Whiskey Jack Lake, along with 10,000 other young soldiers, sailed across the Atlantic, escorted by a convoy of battleships and submarines.

The French and British wanted the Americans for reinforcements of their troops. But General John Pershing refused to break up the Americans to be used as reinforcements. Instead he formed a self-styled Associate Power to fight along with the Allies.

The ship Rascal was on landed at Le Havre, France. It began to rain as the troops were disembarking from the troop transport ship. They set up their four-man tents in the rain in a field outside of town. It continued to rain for another two days. "I guess I had just as soon have the cold weather of home as to live like mud turtles in this soupy mud."

The day after the rain, the entire company was transported near the front lines where they began digging trenches. At least the soil was sandy and the digging was easy. When the trench was dug, underground bunkers were dug out, and a latrine at each end. No one wanted to be stationed near either of the ends of the trench. When it rained the trenches turned into mud wallows.

There was artillery firing a short distance behind them and Rascal found it difficult to sleep.

Two weeks after digging in, the Germans made a push towards the new American troops and were rebuffed time and again. Willie Peters had been shot in the head during the battle, as had three others. But the Germans had come up against troops who were eager to fight; the Germans outnumbered the Americans two-to-one.

After his friends death Rascal came to the conclusion that this warring business was serious and he began to take precautions.

Rascal really didn't understand what the war was all about, other than Germany was trying to control all of Europe. He had had enough after spending six months in the same trench, so near the front. Their position had actually stopped the German advance and they were forced through a funnel-like of landscapes to waiting heavy artillery.

After six months living in the trench, and during another push from the Germans, Rascal caught a piece of shrapnel in his stomach that sent him to the first aid station. Rascal actually walked in on his own and when he removed his coat and shirt, the piece of shrapnel was sticking through his skin.

"Lay down, Private, and let me see what you have here," Doctor Hanson said. "Hum, this piece of metal must have been spent. Usually these shrapnel wounds go entirely inside the body. I'll have to put you under while I remove this, clean the wound and stitch you back up."

* * *

Rascal didn't wake up from surgery until the next day. Dr. Hanson sat in a chair beside Rascal and said, "You were lucky, Private. The shrapnel didn't pierce your stomach, so all I had to do was clean the wound and stitch you back together.

"You might as well enjoy today here inside and out of the weather; tomorrow you'll be back on the line."

"Thanks, Doc," Rascal said. He could use another good night's sleep and hot food.

During that day while he laid in his bed he wrote a letter home telling his family about his wound and that he was okay. There was also a letter there from home. He thought how odd Emma had never mentioned Beckie and Jasper, only that they all wished him well.

* * *

During the summer of 1917 they were moved out of the trench and started pushing the Germans east towards the Russian front. There were rumors that Germany was faltering and maybe the fighting would soon be over.

One afternoon in September they had been trying to take a hill the Germans were using for an artillery base. The fighting had been heavy all day and finally a retreat was ordered, and as Rascal was picking his way through the debris on the hill he was shot and fell forward and screaming for a medic.

* * *

Rascal opened his eyes but he couldn't see anything. Everything was in total darkness. He tried to move his head and he couldn't. *That's strange,* he thought. Next he tried to move his arms and those wouldn't move either, then his legs, then he remembered he had been shot in the right leg from behind, as he was retreating down the hill. "But my leg doesn't hurt."

He was awake and he was lying on his stomach, he thought. The air smelled fresh and clean. Not like an old latrine. He laid there on his stomach, he assumed, totally confused. He couldn't see anything, nor move and there was no pain when certainly there should have been.

His mind was conscious and aware, but that was all. The last thing he could remember was falling face down and screaming for a medic.

Panic started to creep across his thoughts and he struggled to move, with no avail. Then he heard someone moaning and he thought for sure he was in hell.

His eyes began to water and run off the end of his nose. He had accepted the fact that he must be dead. There was just no other reason to think otherwise. He was unable to see or move and he knew only the awareness of himself. There were others in the same predicament, as he could hear someone moaning.

He was scared and he closed his eyes. This wasn't at all what he thought hell would be like. He tried to forget about his current circumstances and he started thinking about his family and Whiskey Jack Lake. Oh how much fun he used to have there. But he guessed that was all gone now.

Then he began to wonder if he was in some kind of an intermediary place. "But this, wherever I am, can't be an intermediary place between home and heaven. Heaven wouldn't be this cruel or scary." He had convinced himself that he was in some place between his earthly life and hell. "Oh woe-is-me. What did I ever do to deserve this?"

Just then, to make matters even worse, he could feel himself turning over. He stopped breathing, trying to hear something, anything. There wasn't a sound. This position was more comfortable though. But still he couldn't move or see. He was in total darkness. And now even the moaning had stopped.

He was passing through eternity and all he was aware of was the memories of home and his family and he was feeling unusually sleepy, and tired of all these thoughts in his head. He closed his eyes as if that would be any different; he just couldn't keep them open any longer.

Rascal didn't want to close them, because he was afraid he would not exist anymore, anywhere, not even as awareness only. But close them he did.

* * *

For the rest of that night Rascal drifted in and out of consciousness. Even when he was aware of his consciousness he refused to open his eyes. And see what? Nothing but total darkness? He felt as though he was in a huge black void where nothing existed but his memories.

There was no concept of time and he had no idea how long it had been since he had changed his position to now lying on his back. Then, much to his surprise, he began to hear voices. But he was still too scared to open his eyes. Maybe now he would actually find himself in a fiery hell.

Little by little Rascal was able to distinguish words that were being spoken and then conversations. Little by little he began to open his eyes. At first there was only a little light. Then he recognized that there was a woman standing beside him looking at him and then she said, "Well good morning, Private Ambrose." Her voice was so tender and sweet to his ears.

He just laid there looking up at this woman. Then he realized she was a nurse and asked, "Where am I?"

"He speaks. I thought maybe the cat had gotten your tongue," and she laughed.

This certainly was no hell. "Where am I?"

"You're in a field hospital, Private."

"How long have I been here?"

"It'll be three weeks tomorrow," she answered.

"Three weeks!" he almost hollered. "What about my leg?"

"Your wound was more serious than the medic first thought.

Oh, here's Doctor Langford now. I'll let him explain things to you."

"Well good morning, Private Ambrose."

"Doctor, the nurse said I have been here for three weeks. But I only woke up during the night."

"Yes, Private, that is correct. Your wound, that is your more recent wound, was more serious than anyone first thought. The bullet passed through your right butt muscle, at a rather steep angle, and through your femur or your thigh bone, about two inches below the hip socket. It was a complete break and then the bullet lodged in your thigh muscle. You were shot by friendly fire. Someone close behind you shot you. Someone in your own outfit.

"I cleaned the wound and removed the bullet and reattached the bone. You have been kept on morphine and in a subconscious state so you could not move. The bone needed to heal, fuse back together. So you were strapped into this bed to keep you from moving and you were routinely turned over so your blood would not pool in one place."

"Boy, does that explain a lot."

"How do you mean, Private?"

"Continue, Doc, about my wound."

"Actually that bullet saved your life."

"Come again, Doc. What are you talking about?"

"Your earlier wound. The one in your stomach had become infected. Enough so, so I had to reopen that one and clean out the infection. My guess is you were sent back on the lines before your stomach had properly healed. It opened and infection set in. If the infection had gotten into your bloodstream, it would have killed you. So as I said, this leg wound was a Godsend, actually. However painful it might have been.

"At midnight last night we started lessening your morphine and we'll continue to do so every four hours. Bring you off the drug slowly."

"How long will I have to remain tied up in his bed, Doc?"

"I'll have the nurse remove the restraints. But you'll have to remain in bed. Then in two weeks I'll remove the cast and then after a week, you'll be sent to a stateside hospital for therapy. The fighting is over for you, Private, and after your therapy you'll be discharged from the Army, with I am presuming total disability, so you'll be receiving a disability check each month. How much that'll be I'm not sure.

"Oh, I forgot to tell you, there are rumors that the war will soon be over."

"That is good news, Doc. Too many young men have died fighting in this damned war."

Doc Langford left and nurse Belle returned and started removing the straps from his arms and legs and the one holding his head in one position. "That feels better already, Belle. I'll be glad when I can get out of bed."

"Don't get any ideas, Private. You are here for another two weeks and if I find you trying to get out of bed, I'll strap you down again." Boy did she sound forceful.

"Now I'll put your bed up in a sitting position for you and after a light breakfast, I'll change the dressing on your stomach."

Rascal was feeling a bit foolish now for being so scared earlier. He had no intentions of ever saying a word about it.

Breakfast was one hard boiled egg, one piece of toast and a cup of black coffee. It had been a long time since he had eaten a real egg and the coffee was much better than he ever had in the trenches.

Nurse Belle returned soon after he had eaten and changed the dressing and only washed the wound. "This will be okay now without any bandage." Then she shaved his whiskers and gave him a tooth brush.

He was feeling much better now. But as the morphine dosage was lowered every four hours, he was feeling the pain from his leg wound. He decided he would have to live with it.

That afternoon another wounded soldier was put in the bed beside him. "What happened to him, Ma'am?" Rascal asked.

"It's Lieutenant Belle, and he was shot in the shoulder."

"Serious?"

"Not really, the bullet went through without hitting bone. You two will probably be discharged from the hospital at the same time."

By late afternoon the new patient was alert enough to carry on a conversation. "You okay?" Rascal asked.

"Yeah, but the pain killer is beginning to wear off. At least I'm alive. How long you been here?"

"As near as I can tell, three weeks," Rascal replied.

"Don't you know?"

"I was kept in a subconscious state so I wouldn't move. My leg needs to heal properly."

"What's your name?" Rascal asked.

"Leroy—Leroy Kessel."

"Ain't that a German name?"

"Sure is. My grandparents came to America and my grandfather fought in the Civil War. My dad was born in America and so was I. That makes me an American. Just like you."

"Don't you find it difficult fighting against your own nationality?"

"Not really, my friends and family are all Americans. What's your name?"

"Rascal Ambrose."

"Huh, huh! What kind of a name is Rascal?"

Rascal bristled up and wanted to punch Leroy, but instead he replied, "My grandmother gave me that name. My real name is Reuben Francis Ambrose. I have always hated the names Reuben and Francis. Growing up I was always getting into mischief and my grandmother started calling me Rascal. It stuck and I like it better."

"Where you from, Rascal?"

"Maine, a lumbering village in the woods. There are no roads in or out, but the Canadian and Atlantic railroad goes through the village. It's called Whiskey Jack Lake."

"Huh, huh, huh, that's an odd name, Whiskey Jack Lake. There's a bird called Whiskey Jack."

"The village wasn't named after a bird. Before there was a village at the lake there was an old hermit who lived there alone and he made the best whiskey that has ever been brewed. One day his still blew up and he died. The lake and the village was named for him, Whiskey Jack. His name was actually Jack. No one ever knew what his last name was. Maybe that's why he became a hermit in the woods. . .running away from something."

"How did he get his supplies, and his whiskey to markets?" Leroy asked.

"The railroad had a water tower there and it would stop each way for water. He'd ride the train to Canada for his supplies and some of his whiskey, and the rest went out to the other train stops."

"What was his secret to making the whiskey?" Leroy asked.

"No one knows. It is said he couldn't write, so the only recipe would have been in his head."

"Did you ever drink any?"

"Once. It was strong and had a wood flavor. Trouble was my hangover lasted for two days.

"Where are you from, Leroy?"

"A small town near Pittsburg. My family have all worked in the steel mills. And I suppose that's what I'll do when I get back home."

They talked all afternoon. Rascal was enjoying Leroy's company. He was interesting to talk with.

The next day there was a lot of commotion outside and then it began to move throughout the hospital. There was loud shouting and suddenly Lt. Nurse Belle came in and said, "Boys! The war is over!" Everyone shouted hurrah.

"We're going home!" Belle said still excited. She kissed every solider in her ward.

Many in the hospital were already being discharged and shipping home. Rascal was still on his back, or his bed cranked up to a sitting position. Leroy was being discharged early, since the fighting was over. He spent much of his remaining hours either walking around the hospital or talking with Rascal.

Leroy shipped out five days after the armistice was official and Rascal felt like he'd lost his best friend. The cast was eventually removed from Rascal's leg, "And you are to stay off this until you start therapy stateside. And to make sure you do, Private Ambrose, you will be accompanied by Lieutenant Belle. She has orders to return state-side also. Oh, and by the way, she has my authorization to use whatever means or force is necessary to see that you follow my orders."

"Yes, Sir."

Rascal was allowed wheelchair use now and he took advantage of it. He was tired of lying in bed and the only activity he had was reading magazines. There were only a few patients left in the hospital now as most had gone stateside. Only the more serious remained, who needed more recovery time.

"Private Ambrose," Lt. Belle said, "Our departure has been delayed for a week. We won't be leaving until December 15th."

"Lieutenant, I'd prefer it if you'd call me Rascal, like everyone else does."

"Okay," and she smiled when she turned and left.

If only I wasn't married, Rascal was thinking as he watched Belle walk away.

Even though there were only a few patients left in the hospital the place was a hubbub of activity. Orderlies were busy packing supplies that would no longer be needed and it seemed to be a central command post for the post war effects.

On the 14th Rascal, along with the remaining staff and patients, were told they would be leaving, ". . .at 0600 tomorrow. A bus will take everyone to Le Havre where they will immediately board a troop transport ship already tied up in Le Havre. After tomorrow this building will be empty. I want to personally thank all of the staff for your services here and your devotion to the injured troops. I will not be shipping back with you. I have orders to staff a new hospital near Berlin Germany.

"Again I want to thank each and every one of you," Colonel Winthrop said and they left the building.

There were only six other patients besides Rascal now and they all had nurtured a special fondness for Lt. Nurse Belle.

Belle spent as much time as she could with Rascal. She wanted to know how he came to be called Rascal. She asked, "I see you wear a wedding ring, so are you married?"

"Yes, her name is Emma."

"Tell me about her."

"Well she's two years older than me. She won't admit it though. We have two kids, boy and girl. And I really miss them. Em is quite pretty. So pretty in fact I could never understand why she agreed to live in a backwoods lumbering village."

"She sounds like quite a woman," Belle said.

"She is."

"Does she work while you're over here?"

"She works as an accountant for The Hitchcock Lumbering Company, there in Whiskey Jack. Only three days a week though. The other two days she stacks lumber from the green chain.

"What about you, Belle, are you married?"

"Me? No, almost, but I volunteered to come over here instead. That was the last I heard from him.

"What did you do, Rascal, for work before you were drafted?"

"I guided fisherman and hunters and I trapped. I actually made a pretty good living guiding and trapping. Now I'm not sure how much of that I'll be able to do now."

"It'll take months of therapy, Rascal, but you will slowly get full use of your leg.

* * *

The day finally came when everyone climbed aboard a bus for Le Havre Harbor. Rascal and four others were still in wheelchairs, but with help everyone was onboard.

It was a day's trip to Le Havre and they were not on board the troop transport until 2200 hours. Everyone was tired from the trip and Rascal was asleep before the ship left Le Havre.

That first day out Rascal slept well but the North Atlantic in winter is rough sailing at best. The water was dark slate-gray and the twelve foot swells also were breaking white water. Thereafter, sleeping was like trying to sleep in a rocking chair while someone rocked it.

Belle was constantly sick until Rascal said, "There's a reason why sailors are called salty sailors. Eat a lot of salt and soda crackers. It'll keep your stomach quiet and you'll be able to eat."

At sixteen knots they were a little more than eight days sailing to New York. By the time they arrived, the decks were covered with six inches of ice.

The recovering patients were taken immediately to Fort Hamilton. The base was still under construction but the hospital area had been completed first.

While still two days out from New York, Rascal wrote another letter to his family explaining where he would be and he wasn't sure how long he would be in therapy. That as soon as he knew something for sure, he'd send another letter when to expect him home.

Before Dr. Thwistle would let Rascal stand up on his own he said, "Private Ambrose, before you even try standing on that leg, you need to put some strength in those muscles. Remember the bullet tore muscle tissue as well penetrating the femur bone. Toning your muscles will help to support the bone. So for the first week you will exercise in the swimming pool for an hour in the morning and another hour in the afternoon. Each day for a week. Then we'll work on letting you walk while you support your weight on the parallel bars. Depending how long it takes you to walk with some weight on that leg, will determine how soon we'll let you walk with a pair of crutches and then a cane.

"Lieutenant Belle will always be in charge of your therapy. Don't make plans of being home for Christmas, because that won't happen. I would say maybe the middle of February. But we'll see. Just don't start making any plans."

The next morning Lt. Belle wheeled Rascal out to the swimming pool. She had to help him into his swimming trunks. "Don't be bashful Rascal. I'm a nurse remember. I've already seen what you have, so let's get by any embarrassing remarks." Rascal never said a word; he didn't know what might happen if he did.

Once he had his trunks on Lt. Belle wheeled him into the shallow end of the pool until the water was up to his chest. Then she took his hands and helped him out of the wheelchair. "I'll swim beside you in case you need help. There's no hurry, take your time."

Rascal was swimming, but he wasn't sure if his bad leg was working or not. "I can't tell if my bad leg is even working, Belle."

"Not surprising really, Rascal. Once the blood starts to circulate better you'll begin to feel what your leg is doing."

Before he reached the end of the pool, he could feel his leg working along side his good leg. And he was now swimming a bit faster.

At the end of the first workout he was exhausted, "But I feel good," and he grinned when he looked at Belle. She smiled back.

With each day Rascal was getting stronger and stronger and swimming fast. He was also happier than he had been for a long time.

After several days of therapy Rascal so wanted to try walking. His leg was feeling that good. But as much as he wanted to try, he decided to follow Dr. Thwistle's advice.

* * *

The day came when Lt. Belle wheeled Rascal to the parallel bars and helped him to stand while supporting his weight on the bars.

"Are you okay, Rascal?"

"Yes, it seems a little strange to be standing up."

"Okay, let your bad leg support some weight. A little at a time until you can stand on both legs without supporting some weight on the bars. That's good. Now walk, but hang onto the bars, just in case. Walk to the end and then back."

Belle waited until he had returned and then said, "How does your leg feel now?"

"Tired. But it feels great to walk." He walked back and forth for an hour before stopping.

"You tired?"

"Yeah, and my leg hurts some now."

"That's good. It should after your first walk. This afternoon we'll walk for only half an hour and then I'll massage your leg. "

Sundays were just another day of therapy. Rascal was doing fine. He had regained lost weight and toned his muscles and strengthened his leg. He was now beginning to practice using crutches and at first those hurt his shoulders.

"After a day or two your shoulder muscles will adapt and feel better.

Rascal's progress was remarkable, even with a limp. "How is your stomach, Private Ambrose? Have you had any problems after Doctor Langford reopened the wound and cleaned it?" Dr. Thwistle asked.

"Once in a while there is a little tightness, but that's all."

"That's to be expected. Lieutenant Belle tells me you are progressing quite will with your therapy."

"Yes, but I still limp."

"That'll get better with time, but you'll probably always have a slight limp," Dr. Thwistle said.

Rascal was so glad to be up and moving, even if with crutches, he felt like running. But he knew enough not to push it. He would continue with the therapy.

Christmas had come and passed and so too had New Years. Rascal knew the snow would be piled up high now and day time temperatures would fall below zero. He wouldn't be able to do too much walking with crutches on ice and snow. So he decided to take advantage of his time in rehab.

When Lt. Belle wasn't working with him, he would walk the corridors on his own, and if there was no one around he would practice running down the corridors.

Finally on January 31st, Rascal was summoned to Col. Beckworth's office. "Sit down, Private," Beckworth said.

Rascal sat. "I understand you prefer to be called Rascal. How an unusual name."

"Yes Sir, my grandmother gave it to me." Then he retold the story.

"You have progressed well with your therapy, according to Lieutenant Belle."

"Yes Sir. She is an excellent nurse and therapist. She has helped me greatly."

"That is good to hear, Rascal. In February you will be discharged from the hospital and your inscription in the Army. Because of the seriousness of both wounds you will be classified as total disability. And you will receive a check of $80.00 each month for the rest of your life. And for the first year you'll receive $100.00 a month to help you put your life back together.

"At some point you may be able to return to light duty work. But for the first year you should not even think about returning to work. Your femur bone will need that much time to finish healing and mend properly."

Col. Beckworth stood up then and handed Rascal two Purple Heart Awards. "These awards, Rascal, are for your two wounds. Wear them proudly and thank you for your service." Then Col. Beckworth saluted Private Reuben Ambrose.

Rascal wrote a letter and posted it telling his family he would be leaving there on February 7th.

For the last two days of his therapy Belle gave him a cane and said, "Give me your crutches Rascal and use this cane."

He just balanced himself at first with the cane. "I can feel the weight on my leg."

"That's to be expected, Rascal. I'll walk beside you—just in case."

Using the cane for balance Rascal started walking, slowly. "It really feels odd not having the crutches to support my weight."

"You'll get use to it soon enough. I just wouldn't try running," and she looked at him.

The next day Col. Beckworth's assistant gave Rascal his back wages. "Sit down please, Private Ambrose. You have had us send a portion of your monthly pay home to your family and you have not drawn on your account at all, so here is what the Army owes you, $817.79."

"Thank you."

"I understand you will be discharged tomorrow morning and traveling home."

"Yes."

"Good luck to you."

"Thank you."

* * *

That evening after supper Rascal decided to go for a walk outside in the fresh air. The weather was unseasonably warm with only a gentle breeze blowing off the ocean. He put on his coat and with cane in hand began walking along the base sidewalk.

Lt. Belle had had the same idea and she noticed Rascal only a little ahead of her. She caught up with him and said, "Would you like some company?"

He stopped and turned to face her. He had recognized her voice.

"Are you excited about leaving tomorrow, Rascal?"

"Yes, I have been away from home and the woods too long. What will you do now?"

"I'm taking thirty days leave and going to my parents.

I'm thinking about resigning from the Army and working in a hospital near home."

They found a park bench and sat down for a few minutes. "I need to rest my leg some."

They talked for several minutes and then they kept walking. On their way back they rested at the same bench. "Is your leg giving you much trouble?"

"No, the muscles tire easy and the bone is sensitive."

"It'll still take time, Rascal, but don't try to hurry. Do only a little extra each day."

As they were walking back to the hospital Belle said, "You are the only patient, Rascal, that didn't ask me to get in bed with them or hit on me. I really appreciate you not asking."

"I didn't want to embarrass myself or you. I'm not saying the idea never crossed my mind, because it did. But as I said, I didn't want to embarrass you or me."

"As I said earlier, Rascal, Thank you."

They stopped and Belle kissed him and then opened the front door for him. "I'll see you off in the morning, Rascal. Good night."

Rascal found it difficult to sleep his last night in the Army and this hospital. His thoughts of home and seeing his family after more than two years kept him too excited to relax enough to sleep. And to be honest with himself, there were thoughts floating around in his mind of Belle. She was, he had discovered, a remarkable woman.

When daylight finally came Rascal breathed a sigh of relief. In his waking hours he would be able to shut off the thoughts of Lt. Belle.

There was a bus waiting to take Rascal and four others to the train station. As he was walking towards the bus carrying his crutches in his arm, he heard a familiar voice.

"Rascal."

He turned to see Belle walking towards him "You're a civilian now," and she kissed him as others were watching. She was in uniform but Rascal was officially discharged. "I wanted to see you off, Rascal."

He hugged her and said, "Good-bye, Belle."

Chapter 2

Rascal boarded the train, excited about going home finally and seeing his family. How much had Beckie and Jasper grown? Would they even know him? Jasper had been so—well, only a baby when he left. But with all this excitement, little by little, thoughts of Belle started lingering in his head, not just passing through.

Not wanting to disrupt his family, he tried to push thoughts of Belle aside and began wondering what his life would be like now. Dr. Thwistle had said that heavy strenuous work would be out. Would he be able to hunt, guide and trap? These were his livelihood. He would find a way. He was sure he could sit in his canoe and fish.

Fishing reminded him of a close call with Game Warden Jarvis Page. Beckie was only a year old then.

He started chuckling as he saw in his mind that glorious caper. Thoughts of Belle had disappeared.

* * *

It was a warm day in the middle of July and Rascal was getting restless. Emma was nursing Beckie. So he decided to canoe up to the muddy shallows at the head of the lake. His fly rod and fishing gear were already in the canoe. "I'm going after some frogs, Em."

"Okay."

His .38-55 Winchester was hung over the door and he took that and one cartridge and his sharp knife. "I thought you were going frogging. Why do you need your rifle?" she asked.

"Just in case." That's all he said and closed the door and walked down to his canoe.

As he paddled towards the shallows his mouth began watering, thinking how good a feed of frog legs would be, with fried potato and dandelion greens cooked with a piece of salt pork. Of course a nice fat trout would go down very good also. But he figured it was too warm and late in the season to find trout near the shallows. Even if there was a cold spring somewhere in all that black muck.

The more he thought about eating a supper of frog legs the hungrier he became. He paddled faster.

He paddled the canoe into the thick of the lily pads. There were huge bull frogs everywhere and filling the air with their crocking. He dangled the fly in front of the frog's nose and they'd take it every time. He had to move the canoe a couple of times to find more frogs. There was only a couple of inches of water.

One time as he dangled his fly a huge brook trout jumped out of the water and took the fly. Rascal played the trout for several minutes before pulling it in the canoe. "Here's breakfast." He saw something move out of the corner of his left eye. Without making a sound he picked up his rifle and turned his head just enough to watch a nice spike horn deer feed at the water's edge.

The spike horn sensed something wasn't as it was supposed to be and turned and started walking slowly up the incline through the bushes and trees. Rascal spotted a little opening in the direction the deer was going. He brought the rifle to his shoulder. The deer was about a hundred feet away from shore now and Rascal took a fine bead on the back of the deer's head and squeezed the trigger. The repo was deadening. The deer dropped.

Rascal put the rifle down and continued catching frogs. Twenty minutes later he could see a canoe and one man coming towards him. "Damn, I don't want to go to jail."

His response was to go ashore and run. But he had heard

stories about Jarvis and he knew he'd catch him. An idea flashed through his mind and he pushed his rifle into the muck. Then he continued frogging and trying not to look too suspicious.

"Hello there." Jarvis pulled up along side of Rascal. "Never thought anyone would be foolish enough to spend much time fishing in these shallows."

"Well, look at this," and Rascal held up the brook trout.

All the time Jarvis was looking for a rifle and he didn't find one, he was disappointed. "I actually came up here for frogs." This was the first time he had been confronted by Jarvis and he was larger in person than his reputation. All 6 foot 6 inches of him.

Jarvis didn't know what to think now. Rascal didn't even have a rifle. "Rascal would you mind opening your pack for me?"

"Certainly, what are you looking for?" As he pulled everything out of his pack.

"Actually I was hoping you'd have a handgun in there."

"Why?" He knew full well why.

"Well, someone fired a rifle or handgun thirty minutes ago, and it came from this end of the lake."

"Now that you mention it, I did hear a single shot. But I thought it came from the lower end. One shot is difficult to pinpoint and the echoes around might fool you."

"Maybe, but I was sure it came from here."

"Maybe someone was up the track somewhere," Rascal said.

Jarvis only grunted as he pushed off from Rascal's canoe.

Rascal caught a few more frogs and decided to canoe home. Jarvis had gone ashore and Rascal knew what he was looking for. Any signs of tracks that he had gone ashore. Jarvis was stumped when he didn't find a rifle in Rascal's canoe.

When he didn't find any evidence that Rascal had been ashore, he pushed off in his canoe and paddled to the opposite shore where he pulled his canoe on shore and out of sight. Then he hiked around the end of the lake and down where Rascal had been.

He wasn't long finding the dead spike horn and he knew Rascal had killed it. But where was his rifle? He hadn't gone ashore and there was nothing in his canoe. Maybe Rascal didn't shoot the deer, but he'd bet money that Rascal did. If he could only find the rifle.

He cleaned the deer and waited to see if Rascal or whomever would come back after it.

Jarvis had not brought anything to eat with him, so he kindled a smokeless fire and roasted the heart. While it was roasting he cut off small pieces of liver and put it on a stick and roasted it over hot coals.

As Rascal paddled for home he didn't dare turn around to see if Jarvis was watching him. He didn't have to, he could feel it.

As he pulled his canoe ashore at his home, he looked up towards the shallows. He couldn't see Jarvis. He cleaned the trout and the frog legs and took them inside.

"Wow, Rascal, you had some pretty good frogging. There's enough for three or four meals and a big trout besides. Where's your rifle?"

When he told her where he had hidden his rifle she started laughing. And laughing until her sides hurt. "How are you ever going to find it?"

"I'll have to wait until Jarvis isn't around and I'll go back. It's about thirty feet in front of a dead white birch tree."

"You keep it up, Rascal, and Jarvis will have you sitting in jail."

Rascal didn't reply. He went out and sat in his rocking chair on the porch. Watching the lake.

The next morning Rascal went into the village and inquired if Jarvis had left yet. No one had seen him. He checked with the ticket agent to see if Jarvis had left. "I haven't seen him since he stepped off the train yesterday morning."

Since the train was the only way out Rascal figured Jarvis was still around. Probably still up at the shallows.

He'd have to wait until he was sure Jarvis had left. Rascal

stayed close to home and on the porch that day and the next. On the third day he canoed across to the village and learned Jarvis had gone out on the morning train. That's all he wanted to hear.

He canoed back to the shallows and checked first to see if the deer was still there. It wasn't and he found where Jarvis had had a fire.

After locating the birch tree he waded out in the muck to retrieve his rifle. He waded out about thirty feet and the muck was up to his chest. He searched round and round, back and forth for two hours before he hit something with his feet. He felt around the best he could with his feet and finally decided it had to be. And the only way he was going to be able to get it would be to go under in that foul smelling black muck. But he did and he brought his rifle up with him

He put his rifle in the canoe. "I smell worse than an outhouse." But the water was too shallow to submerge and wash off the stink. So he canoed home.

Emma wouldn't let him close to the house until he had washed off all that stinking mud. He was three days taking his rifle apart, cleaning it and trying to put it back together.

* * *

He started laughing out loud then and remembering those days. He was feeling sorry for Jarvis Page, but if Jarvis had known what he had gone through to retrieve his rifle he would have had a good laugh. Besides, he got to take home some fresh venison.

Everybody in the car was looking at Rascal as he sat there laughing. After a while he fell asleep until the train stopped in Boston. There was a forty minute wait and the next stop was Portland, Maine. He was soon back to sleep.

It was 2 a.m. when the train pulled into the Portland terminal. Rascal was tired and had been cramped up in a seat for fourteen hours. He now had to use his crutches to walk over to the Canadian Atlantic (C&A) Terminal.

When people noticed his two Purple Heart awards they all offered to help him. The C&A engine wasn't as big as the New York Line locomotive and Rascal wasn't sure how long it would take to get home. Or how many stops along the way.

As daylight started to filter through the trees Rascal began to recognize a few landmarks. He knew he was getting close to home and excitement began to surge through him like a rolling wave on the Atlantic. He would also be glad to get off the train. He had been onboard one train or the other for twenty-four hours now.

When the train finally stopped at the neighboring town of Beech Tree, Rascal knew he was almost home. He even recognized a few people walking beside the rails. As much as he would have enjoyed getting off and talking with people he knew, the train was only there ten minutes. Long enough for the mail to be dropped off and some passengers to board for Canada.

Once the train started moving from Beech Tree to Whiskey Jack Lake, Rascal recognized every turn in the tracks, every stand of spruce trees, every pool in Jack Brook. Yes, he was finally home. Tears ran down his cheeks, he was so overcome with joy.

The weather was always colder at Whiskey Jack Lake than at Beech Tree because of the higher elevation. So it was by no surprise that no one was waiting on the platform for the few passengers who stepped from the train. A cold wind was blowing down from Canada and everyone hurried inside the terminal building.

Rascal saw his wife Emma right off. She was standing to one side and no kids. She looked up and saw him walking towards her. He was thinking how haggard and worn-out she was looking. That girlish prettiness wasn't there.

They hugged and kissed and Emma said, "Hold me Rascal— hold me tight."

Rascal was thinking how nice it was to feel his wife in his arms again. He had forgotten just how nice she felt.

"Where is Beckie and Jasper, I had hoped they would be here to greet me."

"I'll tell you when we get home."

The train was pulling out and Rascal turned around to look across the cove at their log cabin. Their home. "Is the road packed hard?" The one going from the village and up behind their cabin.

"Yes it is. Will you be alright?"

"I'll make it. I might have to switch to using the crutches if my legs get tired."

Emma carried the crutches while Rascal used the cane. "Is there anything I can do to help you?"

"Not unless you can carry me."

It was a slow trip to their cabin and Rascal's leg was throbbing. "Will you be okay, Rascal?"

"I'll sit down in the rocker. I'll be okay soon."

Emma took his coat and saw the two Purple Hearts. "What are these medals?"

"They give them to you when you get wounded."

"Where are your wounds?" she asked.

Rascal lifted his shirt so she could see his stomach wound. "The other one is in my butt." He then told her all about it.

"You mean someone in your own outfit shot you? Who?"

"They wouldn't tell me, only that it was someone behind me while we were retreating down the hill."

"Now what about Beckie and Jasper?"

"Rascal—," she hesitated and then continued. "Rascal, the village was hit by the fever in the spring of 1917. Beckie, I think, was infected while in school and she brought it home to Jasper. Beckie died three days after she contracted it and Jasper three days later. Two other school age kids contracted the fever and they both died before Beckie."

"Couldn't the doctor do anything?"

"A telegram was sent and he replied that he would come as soon as he could. He had several kids with the fever in Beech

Tree also. By the time he arrived, Beckie, Jasper and the two Smith kids were gone."

"Why didn't you tell me about this, Em?"

"You were off fighting in the damned war and I thought worrying about the kids might get you killed. I figured you had enough to worry about trying to stay alive over there," she began to cry, then it wasn't long before Rascal was crying too. Now he understood why Em looked so haggard and tired.

After a while Emma asked, "Are you hungry, Rascal?"

"Yes and a cup of coffee with a shot of whiskey, too."

"When Beckie and Jasper died I threw out all those bad spirit drinks, Rascal."

"Okay, some coffee then."

The coffee was good and Rascal didn't eat much. The news about Beckie and Jasper kinda took his appetite away. They stayed up talking until it was time to go to bed. They stayed away from the subject of their children. They had shed enough tears.

"The doctor said that not to think about going back to work for a year and if I do, it should not be anything strenuous. And maybe some fall trapping and hunting, but no long treks and not to carry anything heavy."

Rascal gave Emma the money he had been given and she said, "This will certainly help. Mr. Hitchcock gave me today off because you were coming home, but I have to work my regular hours from here on. I work in the accounting office all week now and not stacking green lumber."

"Did Sam and Tom make it back? I lost contact with them after I was wounded the first time."

"Sam died in the same battle where you were shot in the butt. Tom came home, stayed a month and went back. He wanted a career in the Army," Emma said.

* * *

The next morning at 6 a.m. the mill's steam whistle blew its wake up call and would blow another blast at 7 a.m. telling workers it was time to start work.

Emma went off to work after a cup of coffee and a slice of toast. Rascal put wood in the stove and had another cup of coffee. If the temperature would warm he'd go outside and walk for a spell, to keep his muscles from becoming weak and slack.

He wished Emma hadn't thrown out the beer and whiskey. But then again he guessed he could understand it. As he sipped another cup of coffee he was listening to the C&A train coming into the station. How he had missed all of this. The sounds of the train, the saws and planers in the mill, the smell of spruce and fir in the air and the comfort of his log cabin. It wasn't fancy, but it was comfortable and warm. There were three bedrooms and gravity-fed running water. A hot water heater built into the back of the wood stove provided hot water. The bathroom was fifty feet behind the cabin in an outhouse.

The temperature had risen enough so Rascal put on his coat and with cane, walked out to the snow packed road. The walk to the village was more than he wanted, so he walked back and forth to the road and cabin until his leg was tired. But he was feeling good.

A knock came on his back door in the afternoon and before he could get to the door and open it, the door opened and Jarvis Page, in uniform, walked in carrying a quarter of a moose over his shoulder.

"Hello, Jarvis."

"Heard you got back yesterday." And he had heard about his wounds. "How is your leg?"

"My leg is slowly getting better. The doc said it might be a slow process."

"Train hit a big bull moose a mile north of town and I had to go up and take care of it this morning. I brought this hind quarter back, thinking you could use it."

"Thank you. What did you do with the rest of it?"

"I quartered it and left them beside the tracks. The train will stop on their way down and pick it up. I saved the back straps and heart for me."

"I really appreciate it, Jarvis. But that must have been a heavy carry all the way from Ledge Swamp."

"Not bad—did have to swap shoulders once. Hey, you ain't offered me any coffee yet."

"Sorry. I'll make a pot."

They talked and drank two pots of coffee like two old friends. With Jarvis bringing him a hindquarter of a moose, he was beginning to think differently of him. Maybe he wasn't such a bad guy and certainly not what folks were saying about him.

The mill whistle blew, signaling it was the end of the work day, 4:30 p.m. "I guess it's time for me to leave if I want to catch the 5 o'clock train to Beech Tree." Jarvis stood up and pulled on his coat.

"Thank you, Jarvis, for the meat."

"If you need anything until you're back on two good legs, let me know."

"I'll do that. And thanks again."

Rascal sliced off enough for supper for he and Emma and peeled potatoes and opened a jar of dandelion greens.

"I met Jarvis on the road, what was he doing here?" Emma asked.

"He brought us a hindquarter of a moose. It was hit by the train up near Ledge Swamp. We spent the afternoon talking and drinking coffee."

"He isn't such a bad fellow, is he?" Emma said.

"Not like the stories told about him."

"Goes with the job I guess," Emma said.

Rascal spent the next day taking care of the moose meat and canning most of it. Emma had plenty of Mason jars. "How long do I boil the water, Em, after it starts to boil?"

"An hour and forty-five minutes."

"How is your accounting job at the mill?"

"The Hitchcock brothers are shipping more lumber every week and if it keeps up I'm going to have to have me an assistant."

"That good, huh."

"Yes, four new workers were added to the mill crew yesterday and the woods boss is looking for more crews to cut lumber."

Rascal worked all day taking care of the meat and he was feeling good to think he had been able to do something. And his leg wasn't bothering him. . .too much.

He had only been home for a week and a nor'easter snowstorm brought the lumber business to a halt until they could get dug out and twitch trails broke out for the horse teams.

The mill yard was full of wood and the crews started piling down the saw logs on the ice, to be sawn during the summer.

Snow was piling up on the cabin roof, but the cabin was sturdy and Rascal didn't think there would be any problem. Some of the other buildings had to be cleared off of snow. Once the path to the road and the road was once again packed down, Rascal would walk down to the village and have coffee with friends and read the newspaper.

"Hey, Jesse, what is all this women suffrage stuff? I have never heard of it," Rascal asked.

"Women all across the country want the right to vote," Jesse replied.

Jesse was an old retired logger who had to quit early because a horse had stepped on his foot and broke it. His foot was never right after it healed.

"Mark my words, young fella, if'n we give 'em the right to vote you can guarantee they'll vote in this damned Volstead Act."

"What's this Volstead Act, Jesse?"

"Where have you been, Sonny!" Jesse exclaimed. "I figured everybody knew about Volstead. If it passes there won't be no more drinking. Alcoholic drinks that is. This country of our'n going right into the garbage can, I tell you."

It was clear to see that Jesse was agitated as he stood up and stormed out of the cafeteria without even so much as a goodbye.

Before going home, Rascal bought two half gallon jugs of whiskey. There was a neat place to hide them in the woodshed where Emma wouldn't find them.

Rascal tried to have supper ready when Emma was back from work. Then she would clean up the kitchen and wash the dishes. This evening as Emma was doing the dishes Rascal stood on the porch, which during the summer months would be screened in, looking at the village lights.

The Hitchcock brothers, Rudy and Earl, owned the mill, the forest land and some of the buildings in town. They had a diesel-driven generator for the mill and a steam-driven generator for all the lights throughout the village and any small fixtures used in the office and main buildings. And each home had electric lights, which cost each homeowner fifty cents a week.

As Rascal stood on the porch looking at the village lights, he couldn't help but think how lucky he was—even with a bum leg.

March came in with the coldest temperatures Rascal had ever experienced. With both woodstoves going the cabin was cold enough so they had to wear a shirt over their already-winter shirt. The extreme cold did harden the packed snow in the path and road which made walking easier. At night as they lay in bed the lake was making ice and rumbling, cracking and echoing through the valley, sounding like a huge, giant groaning. Sometimes the cracking ice would be so severe that the vibrations would actually rattle the dishes in the cupboard.

When the cold weather broke, warm air blew in from the south. By April the snow was too soft and slushy for the crews to continue cutting. Everything that was already down was twitched to the lake and the men who were only there for the winter work returned to their homes in Beech Tree.

The soft snow was more tiring for Rascal to walk in, but he manage to make his daily trips to the cafeteria and twice a week Jesse would join him for coffee and they would talk mainly about how things used to be.

This morning someone new showed up for coffee and sat down with Jesse and Rascal. "Good morning, Jesse."

"Morning, Jeters. Sit down. Jeters, this is Rascal Ambrose, Rascal, Jeters."

"That's a funny name—Rascal. Somebody playing a joke when they named you?"

"My grandmother gave me the name. Jeters, is that your whole name or first or last?"

"Asbau Jeters. Everybody just calls me Jeters. I prefer it."

"Do you work here, Jeters, or are you passing through?" Rascal said.

"I work here—I keep the fires going in the boiler room for the steam generator. I have the night shift. Trouble is there ain't nothing to do here during the day. Maybe when this ice and snow is gone we can do some fishing."

"Sure thing."

As Rascal was working his way home it suddenly occurred to him that he was having less trouble with his leg now. Although he still would have to stop some to give it a rest. But he was feeling stronger. And that day he began clearing the snow away from the cabin and out buildings.

It rained the last two weeks of April and this opened the ice on the lake early and most of the snow was gone. But the road to the village was too muddy for either Emma or Rascal to use, so he took her to work every morning in the canoe and picked up her again.

* * *

Buds were turning red on the hardwood trees and flocks of geese flew overhead every day. Some stopping to rest a night at the head of the lake.

Jeters and Rascal fished the lake often; Rascal would not show him his special spots. One day, Jeters brought a bottle of whiskey with him and when the fish weren't biting, they'd have a sip of whiskey.

After a while, because of the whiskey, they each thought they were getting hits on their line when they actually were not. Jeters cast his fly out and no more than the fly hit the water and he snapped the fly rod to set the hook. Of course there was no trout. The fly came whipping back and stuck in his ear, "Yeow!" he screamed. "That damned trout spit that fly out and stuck me right in the ear with it."

Rascal started laughing and he recast his line and fly and landed it near where Jeters had been. He started working the fly back and he snapped his rod to set the hook. And again of course there was no trout. The only trout near them was only in their stupor imaginations.

Rascal's line came back over Jeter's head and then he snapped the rod forward again to recast and his fly—streamer actually—a gray ghost and caught the back of Jeter's head. "Yeow! Damn you, Rascal, you caught the back of my head!" He yeowed when Rascal brought his line up taut. "Damn you, Rascal, watch what you're doing! I'm no damned pin cushion." When he pulled the streamer from his scalp he yeowed again.

"What you doing using this big streamer and trying to fly cast?"

"It didn't look big to me, besides it casts out there nice-like," Rascal said.

"Hand me that whiskey bottle. I need a drink."

Rascal handed him the bottle. "It's empty."

"Yeah, been that way, Jeters, for a while now. You want to head back?"

"Might as well. You keep fishing and you'll have me by the nose." They both started laughing then.

Half way down the lake the mill whistle blew signaling the end of the work day.

"Oh damn, Rascal. We'd better hurry. I'm suppose to be at work."

"Yeah, and I'm suppose to pick Em up so she doesn't have to walk that muddy road."

Rascal was in the stern and he was having a hard time keeping the canoe in a straight line. But they finally made it to the village and Jeters jumped out before the bow had hit the bank. "How many fish we catch, Rascal?"

"Two, one each."

"All that work for two fish. I could have sworn we'd have twenty or thirty. Thanks for the trip, Rascal."

Emma was nowhere in sight and Rascal knew she'd be upset for having to walk the road. He canoed across the cove and pulled the canoe ashore and walked up to the cabin with one ten-inch brook trout. Emma saw Rascal canoeing across the cove and went out to the porch to greet him.

"You were late, Rascal; you and Jeters must have had good luck," Emma said.

"Not really," and held up the one trout.

"Then why were you not here to get me, so I didn't have to walk up that awful road?"

"Time just got away from us and before we knew, the whistle blew and we were only halfway down the lake."

"Well come in and get washed up and I'll start supper."

After Rascal had cleaned up he hugged Emma and said, "I'm sorry I was late." Then he kissed her.

"Your kiss tasted like whiskey and your breath reeks of whiskey, so you and Jeters couldn't make it back in time because you two were drinking whiskey. Where did you get it?"

"Jeters brought it."

"I don't care which one of you brought it. I will not put up with a whiskey-soaked husband. Nor will I share my bed with a whiskey rat. Nor will I cook and keep house for a whiskey rat. Get out! You can sleep on the porch tonight."

Rascal grabbed a quilt from one of the other bedrooms and headed for the porch. "And if you want to sleep in my bed tomorrow night, you'll agree right now to go to church with me on Sunday."

"You don't give me any alternative, do you, Em?"

"Well, what is it?"

"Yes, I'll go to church with you—this one time."

* * *

It was a cool night, but that wasn't Rascal's biggest problem. He hadn't had anything to eat since breakfast and he was hungry. He had experienced hunger in the trenches in France—but here he was in his own house.

He slept, but pitifully. Then as the sun was brightening the morning darkness he heard his wife say, "Breakfast is ready; are you hungry?"

This sweetness caught him off guard. He wasn't sure what was going on. But he was hungry. As he ate his breakfast he kept thinking she was going to lower the hammer any minute. *What is she up to with all this sweetness?*

Emma was acting as if nothing at all had happened the day before.

"Are you going for coffee at the cafeteria today, Rascal?"

"I thought I might," he replied.

"While you're gone, I'm going to take a bath and then do some spring cleaning. Don't forget about church tomorrow."

"Maybe I'll buy some vegetable seeds for the garden before ole man Douglas sells out."

As Rascal canoed across the cove to the village he was more concerned now than the day before about how Emma was acting. And this made him nervous. He wasn't quite sure how to respond to her just now.

When Rascal arrived at the cafeteria he found a hubbub of confusion. Everyone was talking and apparently not listening to anyone. Finally Rudy Hitchcock raised his arms and said, "Folks, folks can we have it quiet so we can get something done." That lasted for about five seconds. Rudy gave up and as he was walking for the door he saw Rascal.

"Rascal, come with me outside, please. I'd like a word with

you. I can't talk with you inside here; no one will shut up."

Rascal followed him outside. "Phew, I'm glad to be out of that hubbub. Now, the cook Minnie came in early this morning, before the sun was up to do some baking. She had laid out three pies and a cake on one of the cafeteria tables and went back in the kitchen. Apparently she had opened the windows to let in some cool air. While she was grinding coffee beans a bear had crawled inside through one of the windows. When she came out from the kitchen a bear was sitting on the table and had already eaten the pies and was now eating the cake. Minnie grabbed a broom and drove the bear off the table and back through the window." Rudy was laughing so hard now he had to wait until he could stop so he could finish the story. "I always knew Minnie was a tough woman, but chasing a bear with a broom? It's a wonder the bear didn't turn on her.

"But what made Minnie even madder, that bear crapped on the table and floor when Minnie swatted it with the broom.

"You're probably the best hunter and trapper in Whiskey Jack, Rascal, and I'd like to hire you to get that bear. How, is up to you. Do you think you can handle it with your leg and all?"

"My leg won't be a problem, Mr. Hitchcock. I'll get right on it."

Before going home, Rascal walked around the village looking for bear signs.

From the window the bear came and went, he found where the bear had dug up the thin soil exiting from that mad woman with the broom. He was able to follow the trail through the grass, looking for bent or folded over patches about the same size as his hand. The bear had made a beeline behind some of the other buildings heading in a northwesterly direction. The direction of the village dump.

There was nothing any worse than a dump bear. There was always the smell of rotting food and the bear had lost their fear of people because there was so much human scent around. He gave up following the bear trail and headed for the dump.

There were bear tracks in both directions in a muddy spot in the road and he figured it was the pie eating bear. Just before rounding the corner to the dump he could hear quite a commotion.

As he eased around the corner he could see three bear pawing in the garbage. When they saw him the three took to the woods and then three yearling cubs followed close behind.

If all three of the adult bear came into the village at the same time they would dishevel folks and cause a lot of problems. He followed the bear into the woods and found a well-worn trail the bear had been using, probably for years. About a hundred yards away from the dump he found a natural covey for a trap.

Rascal returned home and told his wife all about the pie eating bear and the six bear he had seen at the dump. "What will you do, Rascal?"

"I'll set a trap on the trail I followed into the woods and bait it with an apple pie. I don't suppose you could make me an apple pie while I check my traps over?"

While the pies were baking Emma made venison stew with some of the moose meat Jarvis had brought. "Hum, that pie sure does smell good. Maybe I'll only use half for bait and eat the rest."

"I'm baking two, one for us."

As Rascal was putting the pie and other tools in his backpack Emma was noticing quite a change in her husband. He seemed happier now that he had something to do that required his skills.

Instead of canoeing across to the village he went above it and then put ashore. He didn't need any curious onlookers knowing where the trap would be.

This time he brought along his favorite rifle. His .38-55 Winchester. Maybe he'd get lucky and get a shot at one. He walked silently up the road to the dump, but there were no bear.

He found the natural looking covey and put the pie on a piece of wood so the wind could pick up the smell better. Then he dug out enough sod so the trap would set flush with the ground. Then he narrowed the entrance with wood lying on the ground, so to guide the bear into the trap. When he had finished he brushed the ground with a spruce bough. "There, that spells bear." Satisfied he canoed back to the village to see Mr. Hitchcock. He was in his office.

"I have found the real problem, Mr. Hitchcock."

"Oh, and what is that?"

"The dump—it attracts the bear and it is too close to the village."

"I'll get someone right on it. That's a good point."

"I'd ask that you wait until I've gotten rid of the bear. I have a trap set just behind the dump and any activity there now might make catching a bear harder."

"Sure thing."

"You said you would pay me, Mr. Hitchcock, but you never said how much."

"How about $50.00, and you can turn in the ears for the reward. I believe the state pays $25.00 a pair."

"That seems fair, Sir, thank you."

* * *

Later as he and Emma were sitting on the porch he said, "I don't know if it is legal to kill a bear on Sunday."

"It's a nuisance bear isn't it? Then I don't see any problem," Emma said.

"I hope Jarvis has your logic."

They went to bed that night, the whiskey drinking day before now forgotten.

The next morning a pair of loons started calling out front and that was signal enough to get up. The sun was already above the horizon.

Emma fixed bacon and pancakes. "This is the last of the bacon. We're needing other supplies too and we should make a trip to Beech Tree."

"Maybe you should Em, but I've got this bear. And I don't

think the problem will stop with only one bear caught. I'm going to have to spend some time."

"I can't go until next Saturday now."

"Can we get along with what we have until then?"

"We'll make out."

When they had finished eating Rascal donned his hat and brought his rifle down off the rack.

"Where do you think you're going?" Emma asked.

"Check the trap and scout around some."

"Maybe later, but you are going to church with me this morning. Remember?"

"But, Em, I have important work to do," he pleaded.

"Do you want to make the porch your permanent bedroom and cook your own meals?"

"No."

"Then you're going to church."

"Ohh, you're a hateful woman, Em."

"Well it wasn't me who came staggering home smelling of whiskey."

Rascal made no reply. He knew when he was beaten.

There was no church building. The cafeteria substituted well enough. The minister from Beech Tree came up once a month. Today's sermon was about vices of men and the moral depravity of drinking.

Rascal had convinced himself that his wife had set this whole thing in motion. But how did she get Jeters involved? If and when he ever found out there'd be hell to pay. He looked at his wife and she was smiling. Serenely happy. He thought to himself, *You're a despicable woman, Em.* He couldn't wait for the service to be over so he could tend to the bear business.

As he and Emma were leaving, "Nice to see you here, Mr. Ambrose," the minister said.

"Reverend."

Rascal paddled with strong strokes across the cove and almost ran up to the cabin. Emma watched and began giggling when she was sure he wouldn't see her.

By the time she reached the cabin Rascal had already changed his clothes and with rifle in hand he said goodbye.

"My, that didn't take long."

Racal almost ran up the dump road. He didn't want to leave the bear or any animal in a trap any longer than was necessary. There were no bear at the dump and he followed the trail into the woods quietly. He could hear some thrashing about and he knew he had a bear.

As he came closer, the bear stopped struggling and turned to face him. Rascal had no idea if this was the nuisance bear or not. He shot it and after it lay quiet he removed it from the trap. It was a female and no signs of cubs. She was probably alone and would have mated soon. If this had been fall when the temps would be cooler he would have taken the entire bear to the cabin for meat. But now in this warm weather the meat would soon spoil and he didn't care for canned bear meat, so he cut off one hindquarter and put it in his backpack and headed for home, carrying his rifle and trap. Before he reached the canoe his leg started aching, only a little though, nothing he couldn't handle.

"Rascal, when can you plant the garden?"

"As soon as I get some free time. Maybe this evening I can do some work with the soil."

Before doing that he skun the hindquarter and deboned the meat. "Save what fat there is, Rascal, and we'll have fried potatoes tonight fried in bear fat."

"You know the fiddleheads will be ready to pick soon. I'll check tomorrow.

"When I came home I never realized I'd be this busy."

That evening after everything else was done, Rascal started turning over the garden soil with a spade. Before he quit because of darkness he had half the plot turned over.

"I'll sleep good tonight."

"How's your leg, Rascal?"

"You know it doesn't hurt, only tired."

About 3 o'clock the next morning, Rascal and Emma were rudely awakened by a yowling, screaming bear beneath their bedroom window. It sounded like a woman screaming bloody murder. "What in hell is that, Rascal?" She was clutching his arm as hard as she could squeeze.

"A bear, and it's right outside our window."

He climbed out of bed and with rifle in hand he stepped out onto the porch. There was moonlight, but not much. But he could see the bear run across the garden plot.

He stood there watching where the bear had disappeared to. Trying to understand why it screamed beneath his window? Was it intentional? How did it find him? This was eerie. Was it intentional after all?

He went back to bed but couldn't go back to sleep. Emma was still shaking. She had never heard a bear scream. Let alone beneath her bedroom window.

"Why do you think that bear came here, Rascal?"

"That was a female in my trap and bear breed this time of year. Maybe he smelled my scent at the trap and followed the scent here. I don't know, but I can't think of anything else."

* * *

They had an early breakfast and while Emma was making it Rascal went out to the garden to look at the tracks. The tracks were of a big bear.

As they ate he said, "I'll have to set more traps now. While you're getting ready for work I'm going to see if I can find how the bear got here. It would have left a trail."

Rascal took Emma to work and before he could push off from shore Rudy Hitchcock came running. "I'm glad I caught you, Rascal, another bear was back again last night. Maybe you should come see for yourself. The bear went through the same window as before, only this time it broke out the glass first. Then it climbed in and ransacked the kitchen."

"A bear visited us this morning also. Probably the same one. I'd better get to work, Mr. Hitchcock."

Rascal thought it would be a waste of time to use the same covey so he searched for another trail. He didn't find it until he looked behind the dump. This trail actually paralleled the other trail through the woods. About two hundred feet from the dump he found an old pine tree that the trunk had been charred in a forest fire years ago and now the center of the tree was hollow, which would make a nice covey. This time he used a loaf of bread that he had hollowed out and filled with jam and honey. He wired that to the tree above where the bear's head would be. He put the trap inside the tree and flush with the pulpy covered ground. He liked this set up better than the first one.

As he walked home he had an idea and went to the mill's saw shop. "Hello, Harry."

"Hi, Rascal, you looking for a job?"

"Got one. I'm trying to take care of the bear problem."

"How can I help you?"

"Do you have any old two man crosscut saws?"

"Yeah, I do, but what in the world for?"

"I'm going to spike'm across the cafeteria windows to keep the bear out. I'll take six."

"Sure, but you'd better wear gloves."

"How about a hammer and spikes?"

When folks saw him spiking the saw blades across the windows they didn't understand what he was doing. "This is to keep the bear out. When he reaches up to the window, he'll catch his pads on the teeth and he'll jerk his paw back. The teeth will stick in his paw, like you grabbing a pin cushion. One attempt should keep the bear from trying again and he probably will leave the area.

"Minnie, when you leave this evening make sure all the food stuff is put away and close both doors to the kitchen and lock the back door."

"You sure the bear will be back, aren't you."

"Yeah, I'm pretty sure."

At his own cabin he put saw blades across the two side windows, and under his bedroom window he set another trap without bothering to bait it.

At the bottom of the porch steps he laid down a board with nails driven through the board and the sharp points sticking up an inch. And then the same kind of board on each step.

He stood back and looked at the steps and checked out both windows. "This should take care of him, if he comes back."

After eating lunch at the cafeteria he canoed up to the head of the lake where Jack Brook enters the lake. There was an abundance of big fiddle heads along the right side of the brook. He filled a five gallon bucket in no time.

All while he was picking fiddleheads he kept thinking of Emma's tirade of he and Jeters drinking whiskey, and as part of the punishment promising to go to church with her. But he had a hard time understanding that Em could be that scheming and devious. When this bear problem was settled he'd have to go see Jeters.

* * *

Rascal was so busy cleaning fiddleheads he forgot about picking up his wife. That is until she walked through the door. "Well I'm glad to see you have a good reason for not picking me up. The road is okay now so I don't mind walking."

"They're all cleaned. Now to can'em."

"Why don't you sit down and rest your leg while I fix supper. How's fiddleheads in a cheese sauce on warm bread sound?"

"Do we have any canned trout left?"

"Go check, will you?" There was one jar left.

While they ate supper he told her what he had done to their cabin and then the cafeteria. "So you think he'll be back?"

"I'm sure. He has a taste for sweet bakeries. I'm going to have to leave you alone here tonight, but with nails and saw blades, if he does come here he won't get far. But I'm almost certain he will go to the cafeteria first. I'm going to be there if he does."

They worked together until 10 p.m. canning. "That's the most fiddleheads we have ever canned."

"Yeah, but they sure are good. I need to leave now, Em. I hate to leave you alone."

"Go on, get. It's not like I haven't been alone before. I'll be okay. . .now go on."

There was no moon tonight and Rascal didn't know if he would be able to see a black bear in the darkness or not. The more he thought on it the more convinced he became that he surely wouldn't. Besides, there was a heavy cloud cover. As he sat on the front steps mulling it over, he wondered if he should go home. There was no way the bear could possibly get inside the cafeteria again. And he was feeling uneasy about his wife being alone.

He walked back up the road to home. It was so dark the only way he could stay on the road was to stay between the tree tops. And hope the bear wasn't around.

Emma was sound asleep when he walked in and the noise startled her. "I thought you were staying at the cafeteria tonight?"

"It's so dark out I couldn't see my hand in front of my face."

"Well, I'm glad you're home."

They went to bed and Rascal kept his clothes and boots on in case. He lay on top of the bedding. Emma rolled over and lay her head on Rascal's chest. He put his arm around her and lay awake, waiting for the bear to return.

He knew if the bear was caught in the trap he'd have to shoot it immediately or it might wreck the side of the cabin. His rifle was loaded and standing next to the bedroom door.

Some time after midnight he heard the trap spring closed and the bear screamed a blood-curdling yowl. And right behind that, another scream from the front of the cabin. Rascal jumped out of bed and grabbed his rifle. Emma woke up with the first scream. He turned on the electric lights so he would have some illumination outside. Then he lit a lantern and went out the back door and around to the trapped bear. The bear was fighting so vigorously against the trap and chain, it never knew Rascal was there.

He set the lantern down and shot the bear. As he walked past it he saw that it was a really huge bear. Probably a male and the one causing all of the ruckus. Then he walked around to the porch steps and three of the boards with nails had blood and hair on them. "Well, this bear won't be back."

Back inside Emma had gotten out of bed. "Well that bear won't be bothering anyone again and the other one has sore feet and probably will go deeper into the woods."

"Well, I'm glad that is over," Emma said.

They went back to bed and Emma was asleep again in minutes. Rascal stayed awake for an hour or so, thinking about the bear.

In the morning while Emma was making a big breakfast of the last of the bear meat, eggs and bear-fat fried potatoes, Rascal went out to look at the bear. He took the trap off and looked at both front paws. There were deep cuts in both. That told him the bear had first tried to get into the cafeteria and couldn't get past the saw blades.

He opened the mouth and the front teeth were worn down to nubs. There were gashes about his head and front shoulders also. He cut off the ears for the bounty. He would have to borrow a work horse to drag this fellow far off some place.

"It's no wonder, Em, that that bear was breaking into the cafeteria; his front teeth are worn down to nubs and there are gashes on his head and shoulders. He had been fighting with another bear. There were saw blade cuts in both paws, so he tried to get into the cafeteria before coming here."

"I don't understand how he thought he could find any food here. I don't leave anything out. Unless he was after you again, Rascal."

"That kinda makes me paranoid."

"You don't have to canoe me across the covey now, Rascal, the road has dried up and I just as soon walk."

"Are you sure, because I have to go down to the cafeteria anyhow."

"That's okay, the walk will be good."

Chapter 3

There was blood and hair on both saw blades and Rascal doubted if the same bear would attack two windows barred with saw blades. Then that would mean there is a second bear with cuts on the front paws.

As he walked out to the dump road he was sure what to expect. There were no fresh tracks in the drying mud. No sooner had he started out along the trail behind the dump and he could hear a bear thrashing about in the trap.

As he came closer he walked slower and quieter, not wanting to spook the bear. He could see the humped back of the bear. It looked like another big one. He didn't want to shoot it in the back. He wanted a good killing shot. He began inching his way to one side trying to bring the bear's head into view.

The bear must have scented him. He stopped struggling and looked squarely at his pursuer. Rascal shot him in the throat and the bear fell to the ground and suddenly all was quiet.

This bear also had cuts in the paws and battle scars about the head and shoulders. "I wonder which one was the victor." Because this bear had been struggling so, the meat would be tougher than boiled owl. He removed the trap and cut the ears off. "This should be the end of the bear problem."

"Mr. Hitchcock, I think I've taken care of the bear problem. How do I apply for the bounty? I have three sets of ears."

"Give 'em to me and I'll pay you and send the ears and application to the department. I owe you $50 plus $25 three times. $125 total. Not bad for a few days work."

"And nights and my wife being scared out of her wits."

"Well you did a good job."

"Thank you. It felt good to be useful again."

"How is your leg?" Rudy asked.

"It's okay, only the muscles aren't as tough as they used to be."

* * *

With $125.00 in his pocket Rascal was feeling like a rich man. He went back to his cabin and put his trapping gear away and then he remembered he had to borrow a work horse. He went back to see Rudy and he told him to go to the stables and take any horse he wanted and harness and chain.

The horse didn't like the smell of the dead bear and it took a lot of coaxing before Rascal could get the horse close enough to hook the chain to the bear's leg.

He went out to the road behind the cabin and dragged the bear to the end, about a half mile away.

For the rest of that day he finished turning over the garden soil. By the time he stopped in the evening he had half the vegetable seeds planted. And he was tired.

"It isn't any wonder that you are tired, Rascal, how much sleep did you get last night?"

"Not much I guess."

* * *

After breakfast the next day and Emma was at work, there was a question that had been plaguing him for days. And Jeters was the only one who could answer it.

He stopped at the cafeteria first for a cup of coffee and visit with friends. "Hello, Silvio, what happened to your foot?" Rascal asked.

"Hello, Rascal, this is the first I've seen you since you've been back. Oh, my foot. Two years ago I slipped on the ice when the train pulled up for water. I was lowering the spout and slipped. Doctor in Beech Tree came up and set it, but it ain't never been right."

"So, are you still working, Silvio?"

"Ain't worked for two years. The railroad gave me a small pension, damned small. Just enough to keep me and Anita from starving."

"Maybe I'll drop off a mess of brook trout sometime or train-hit deer or moose."

"It would be appreciated, Rascal, let me tell you."

Silvio wanted to know all about the Great War, as it was being called. They drank coffee and talked for an hour and Rascal said, "I have to leave now, Silvio, but you tell Anita I'll be around soon for some of her brownies."

"Come up anytime, young fella."

Rascal left the cafeteria and went in search of Jeters. He had a small shack that set way back from the village.

He knocked on the half opened door and no answer. He pushed the door open and Jeters was lying on the sofa. "Hey! Jeters."

Slowly Jeters opened his eyes and recognized Rascal. "Hey, man, what you doing? Don't you know I work at night and sleep during the day?"

"Yeah that's what you told me before, Jeters. But what about that time we went fishing and you had to work that night?"

"Huh, what you talking about, Rascal?"

"You know, Jeters, the day you brought a bottle of whiskey."

"Oh yeah, that day. What about it?"

"Well, you weren't too tired that day to go do a little fishing and drinking. Why, Jeters? Why was that day any different than today?"

"What do you mean, Rascal? What are you getting at?"

"Well, Jeters, you are concerned today that I awoke you from sleeping because you worked all night."

"Yeah, that's right."

"But what is so different from today and the day we got drunk? You didn't seem to mind too much not being able to sleep that day. Why?"

"Don't do this to me, Rascal. I don't feel so well all of a sudden."

"You're going to feel worse if'n I can't get a straight answer from you."

"Okay, okay, I'll tell you. But you ain't gonna like what I have to say."

"Don't stop now, Jeters, you were doing so good. Tell me the rest of the story."

"What makes you think there is anything? Can't two friends spend a day fishing and drink a little whiskey?"

"The pain in my ass tells me there's more to it. And Jeters, whenever you're nervous or lying your left ear twitches!"

Jeters rubbed his right ear. "That's the wrong ear, Jeters.

"Fess up Jeters or I'll keep you here long after you're suppose to be at work. If you're late again what do you think Mr. Hitchcock is going to do?"

"He told me I would be fired. Damn you, Rascal, you have me wedged between two trees. I gave my word I wouldn't say anything." He was almost crying now.

"Jeters, do you want to look for another job, instead of one that keeps you so warm in the cold winter. Fess up Jeters."

"Alright! Damn you. It was your wife. You happy now?"

"I thought so. Tell me, Jeters, why did she want you to get me drunk? I think I know the answer, but you tell me so I don't have to guess."

"She said if you came home drunk with whiskey on your breath she could use your drinking whiskey to coerce you into going to church with her." Jeters was pouting like a scolded child.

"So that's what she was up to all along. And I'll bet she asked the reverend to do a special sermon on the vices of man, especially drinking. Oh, Em, you are a devious woman."

"You mean, Rascal, she set this all up to get you to church to listen to a sermon about drinking?"

"That's what it looks like. Don't say a word about this, Jeters, to anyone. Promise me."

"Okay, but what are you going to do?"

"I don't know yet."

He left Jeters and went back to his own cabin. The first thing he did was to pour himself a drink and then he hid the bottle again. He took a sip and then sat in his rocking chair on the porch. He really didn't know what to do about it. One thing for sure, his wife was a lot more cunning than she had ever let on. As he thought about that, he broke out laughing, until tears filled his eyes.

After finishing his whiskey drink he made a bacon sandwich. And ate that out on the porch. His whiskey glass he washed thoroughly with soap and made sure he had not spilled any on his shirt. In the two and a half years he had been away the bushes were beginning to grow up around the cabin.

It was a warm day and he spent the afternoon cutting bushes and pulling weeds out by their roots. He picked up old and rotting wood and carried it into the woods. He split cedar kindling wood and then he chinked logs where the old caulking had either been pulled out by squirrels or just had fallen out.

And the last thing he did was to put the summer screens in about the porch so they could sit out in the evenings without being chewed alive by insects. Emma came walking in from the woods road just as Rascal was finishing. He hoped the smell of whiskey was gone. He drank a dipper of water just in case.

"Wow you've been busy today. You cleaned up around the cabin and put the screens on. I'm afraid I didn't have much time for all of that. I'm glad you did it. How is your leg?"

"Whenever I do any work or am on it for long, it begins to hurt. But it never gets any worse. I think it has gotten as good as it's going to. If it never gets worse, I guess I can live with it."

* * *

The next morning at breakfast, "I'm going up the tracks tomorrow, Em, and I might be late. After dark maybe. I won't be leaving here until the afternoon."

"Is Jeters going with you?"

"No I'm going alone, and I'm not going to be drinking whiskey."

"Can't you tell me what this is all about?"

"I'd rather not, but I don't want you to worry either. Silvio and Anita Antony don't have much since he was hurt. He gets a small pension from the railroad, but that's only enough to buy groceries. I'm going to get them some meat."

"Why be so secretive about it?"

"Well, because it will be illegal and I don't want anyone to know about it."

"I won't say a word."

Rascal walked down to the village with his wife that morning. Emma was a little suspicious why he was being so nice and accommodating, especially so since her tirade about him drinking whiskey. She didn't feel at all guilty, she was simply curious.

Rascal said goodbye to his wife and went to the cafeteria for coffee and a donut.

For what he intended to do there was no hurry. He went back to the cabin and walked around the garden plot. There were deer and raccoon tracks. Both animals would be detrimental to the vegetables later in the summer. Raccoon hides were worth two or three dollars. But they required a lot of handling to flesh 'em and comb out the snarly fur and stretch'em. But two or three dollars was more than most men's daily pay. He really wanted to wait for cold weather before trapping them, but one coon would destroy more than two or three dollars a night in crops. So he set two traps between the garden and the woods. What he needed was page wire fencing to keep the animals out, but that was expensive.

After he had eaten lunch he found two gunny sacks in the shed and with his rifle and one cartridge, he canoed up to the head of the lake. From there it was only a short walk to the tracks and he'd only be a short distance below Ledge Swamp. He pulled his canoe ashore and hid it in a thicket of jack fir and spruce.

The mouth of the Jack Brook was full of brook trout. "Wish I'd brought my fly rod. Tomorrow maybe. I could catch enough to can for winter."

When Rascal and Emma sat on the porch this morning finishing their coffee there wasn't a cloud in the sky. Now it was overcast with a thin layer of white clouds. Not the ones that might be threatening a storm. A good day to hunt actually. Before stepping out in the clearing on the tracks, he waited to see if he'd hear maybe a track crew working, or an unscheduled train. All was quiet, except for the constant shrieking of blue jays.

Rascal walked between the rails happy to be where he was and doing what he knew best. The majority of the swamp was to his left. He had hunted here many times and knew of a natural saltlick near the further end of the swamp. Deer are naturally drawn to salt in the spring to replace the sodium their bodies needed which they couldn't get in the feed they ate in the winter. Usually he wouldn't shoot a deer before the 4th of July, but this was a special cause. The Antonys needed food.

It was a beautiful walk on this side of the swamp. The other side was so thick with hazel bushes only a rabbit could navigate through them. Before he reached the saltlick he saw movement up ahead. He waited and eventually a doe with twin lambs stepped into view. He had allowed he would shoot nothing but a deer with antlers. Before continuing on he waited until the doe and lambs had left and were out of sight. He didn't want to spook the doe and have her raise the alarm and signal every deer in the vicinity. He sat down behind a short fir tree and leaned back against another.

Blue jays and red squirrels were making quite a racket. Eventually, though, they accepted his presence and shut up.

Everything was so peaceful and serene. His head kept bobbing, trying to stay awake. And then he saw it, a slight movement to his left. He froze. As much as he wanted to turn his head and get a clear view of it, he resisted. He only took shallow breaths of air. He could tell it was a deer but he was unable to tell yet if it had any antlers. As long as it had even short nubs that would be good enough. After all, even a big stag this early would only have short nubs.

The deer was pawing at the ground at the lick and so far he had not seen the head. Anxiously he waited as this was the size he wanted. It wouldn't be too heavy to carry back to his canoe. The deer heard something and lifted his head and he had antlers, albeit short nubs, but it was a buck. He raised his rifle to his shoulder and with a fine bead behind the head he squeezed the trigger. To Rascal the report was deafening. The deer dropped and did not even twitch. Rascal knew it had been a good shot.

Without dressing the buck, Rascal began skinning, being careful not to get too much hair on the meat. As he was removing the hide he could hear the train south bound. He skun the deer, so when he finished, the body was laying on the hide. He removed the two gunny sacks and began carrying away the meat. From the time he pulled the trigger he was an hour deboning the meat. It wasn't as if he had never done this before.

He figured the deer was probably only two or three years old. He hefted the gunny sack and figured he might have sixty pounds of meat.

He kindled a small smokeless fire using snapping dry fir limbs and then he cut out the heart and found some water to wash it out. Then he cut off a small piece and roasted it over the fire. It would have taken hours to roast the heart intact. Small pieces cooked through quick and besides he had worked up an appetite. "Oh man, this is good. It's been a long time since I've had roasted deer heart."

If he didn't have to get back to the village and home he would have liked to stay right where he was.

With his stomach full, he thoroughly extinguished his fire, shouldered his pack and started back for the tracks. It was still daylight—not much left—when he stepped on top of a knoll where he could see in both directions of the tracks. He would wait there until almost dark before stepping out into the clearing.

There was something coming down the tracks and it wasn't loud enough for a train. "Must be a track crew on a handrail car." He didn't have long to wait and three men on a handcar came into view. The three men were talking excitedly and as they went past him he recognized all three: Freddie Blair, Stenson Jones and Ralph Bubar.

But more surprising, the three had a deer with them. Field dressed and all. He hadn't heard any shots and it was too dark now to see a rifle. "Maybe it was struck by the train. But it sure didn't look like it had been. Oh well, as long as they don't bother me."

When they were out of sight he climbed down off the knoll and checked again to make sure he was in the clear.

As he walked around the turn he could still hear them talking and laughing, but he could not see them. It was dark by the time he turned off the tracks. He didn't need a lantern to see his way. He had made this trip enough so he was sure he could find his way with his eyes closed.

Even though he knew he could find his way through to his canoe, he was a half hour reaching the lake. He dragged the canoe to water and loaded his pack and started paddling for the village. Still being quiet, just in case Jarvis was about. He stayed close to shore and in the shadows all the way.

He put ashore above Antony's cabin and when he was satisfied no one was around he proceeded towards their cabin. The bedroom light was still on, Rascal had intended to simply leave the gunny sack on the front step, but the air was warm and the meat might spoil. So he knocked rather loudly on the door several times until he was sure someone was coming. Then he set the sack down and stepped away from the cabin and into the shadows.

Anita opened the door and when she didn't see anyone she said rather loudly, "Who's out here? What do you want?" Then she noticed the gunny sack and she opened it. "Oh my word. Silvio! Silvio!" She picked the sack up and went back inside and closed the door.

Rascal could still hear Anita exclaiming over the gift of meat, as he walked away.

* * *

As he pushed off from shore in his canoe the moon was beginning to peak over the treetops. "Damn." He didn't want to be caught out on the water in the light of the moon. He paddled faster with heavy strokes.

Emma was still up, sewing. "How did it go?"

"Like clockwork. I left the deer meat on their doorstop and they have no idea where it came from."

"You'd better hope so or Jarvis will be after you again."

He told her about all of the brook trout he had seen in Jack Brook. "I'll go back tomorrow and we should be able to fill enough canning jars to last the winter."

During the night a thunderstorm blew in from the northwest following the valley down from Canada. The lightning strikes were close and with each flash the inside of the cabin was lit brighter than daylight. Emma had always been terrified of loud noises and the thunder claps were sharp and deafening. She clung to Rascal and buried her face in his neck and shoulders.

She couldn't even think about sleep until the storm had passed. Rascal had fallen to sleep before the storm had stopped. At first light in the morning the air was clear and the sky was blue.

Rascal walked with Emma to her office and then went to the cafeteria for coffee and donut and to talk with friends.

Silvio was sitting in the corner and saw when Rascal entered. "Hey, Rascal, come sit a while and talk." Rascal got a cup of coffee and a donut and sat down with Silvio.

"Good morning, Silvio. That was some storm last night."

"Sure was—lightning, she hit pine tree behind me cabin. Splinters of wood everywhere."

Silvio lowered his voice and said, "I got me some venison yesterday."

"Silvio, you'd better be careful; if Jarvis catches you, he'll take you to jail in Beech Tree. And where will you get the $50.00 for shooting a deer in closed season?"

"That's just it. I didn't."

"What are you talking about, Silvio?"

Rascal didn't want Silvio to know who left the deer meat.

"No, no, I didn't shoot any deer. Someone left it on the doorstep last night."

"Who?"

"No idea. A knock on the door and when Anita went to see who was there there was no one, only a sack full of boned out deer meat."

"Well, Jarvis brought me a hindquarter of moose right after I was home. Or maybe the train hit a deer and one of the linemen left it."

"Perhaps, I don't know."

"Do me a favor would you, Silvio?"

"Sure thing, what?"

"Keep this to yourself. Don't spread it around someone left you some deer meat. It might attract Jarvis's attention and now and again I like to have some fresh venison."

"Sure thing, young fella. I know what you're saying."

Rascal walked back to the cabin and checked the two traps he had set for raccoons before heading up the lake. There was nothing there.

He put his fly rod and tackle box, gunny sack and his axe in the canoe. As he paddled up the lake a few clouds were blowing from the north. That was a good thing. The trout would take a fly better if the sun was not so bright. All the way up the lake he kept thinking about his wife and Jeters.

There was a breeze out on the lake, but in the cove at Jack Brook the water was calm like ice. He sat still in his canoe for five minutes before making his first cast, just in case the school of trout had been scared off. He tied on a red wolf fly and with his first cast he hooked into one that was about a pound. Then he sat quiet for another few minutes before making another cast. He wasn't in any hurry, he had the rest of the day.

His next cast brought in another trout about the same size. The blue sky and sun were gone now and replaced with clouds. And the fishing began to get better. He caught a brook trout with every cast and they were somewhat larger.

He took a break and went ashore and kindled a small fire and put a trout over the fire to cook, while he cleaned the fish he already had. When those were cleaned, he put them in the gunny sack along with green grass to keep the fish from drying out and spoiling.

The trout cooking over the fire smelled good and this made Rascal even hungrier.

Food was always best, Rascal thought, when it was cooked over an open fire. He put another trout on the spit and went back to fishing. When coming into a school of brook trout like this one often catches the smaller trout first. Rascal caught several trout that would go two pounds or more.

The fly was about chewed up so he decided this would be a good time to go check on his spit. It was toasty golden brown. After eating that trout he tied onto his line a grasshopper fly. Theses always seemed to work good. He only needed five more trout to make it an even fifty to take home. And he had those five with five more casts.

He cleaned them and put more green grass in with everything. He pushed off in his canoe and checked his watch. If he hurried he might be able to get to the village to give Emma a ride across the cove.

Out in the lake the gentle breeze had turned into a wind and luckily it was to his back. He knew then that he would be on time.

Just as he was pulling up to the public wharf he saw Jarvis walking towards him. His first instinct was to push off away from the wharf. But that would look as guilty as all get-out. Now he'd have to play along and try to outwit the old fox. Jarvis was cunning as all get-out and he didn't want to get on the wrong side of him. But maybe he had gone too far this time.

"Hello, Jarvis, nice day if'n it don't rain," Rascal said trying not to look guilty.

"How's your leg anyhow?"

"I can do pretty much as I want. I guess there will always be some pain."

"Are you going to trap any this fall and winter?"

"I plan to."

"Good, there are several nuisance beaver colonies along the tracks between here and Beech Tree."

Jarvis was toying with him now and Rascal knew it. He wanted to know in the worst way what Rascal had in the gunny sack and right now Jarvis was only making Rascal more jittery the longer he talked.

"I understand the church is putting on a picnic a week from this weekend. I'll have to bring my wife Rita up.

"The south bound train should be through shortly," and he stood up and Rascal thought he was going to leave.

"What's in the gunny sack, Rascal? I hope it's a moose," he said jokingly.

"Now, moose wouldn't fit in that sack. But a nice deer would," and they both laughed. Rascal knew Jarvis wasn't leaving until he saw what was in the sack.

"Been fishing. Didn't do as well as I had hoped."

"Well let's have a look at'em Rascal," and he bent down to lift the sack. "My, this is heavy enough to be a hindquarter of a moose."

Jarvis turned the sack upside down and emptied it. "Wow,

nice catch, Rascal, but I think you have too too many. Where did you get these?"

"I'd sooner give you my wife, Jarvis, than tell you where my fish hole is."

Jarvis laid out and counted Rascal's limit of twenty-five and counted out another twenty-five. "Two limits Rascal."

"Yeah, one for Em. I thought I could give her a limit."

"You can, but you can't catch two limits in one day. I'm going to have to take you for the second limit."

"How much will that cost me, Jarvis?"

"Oh, it might be a dollar a fish."

"You going to take me to jail?"

"For a few fish, no."

Jarvis gave Rascal a summons and said, "Be in court Monday morning. You should be able to be on time by taking the morning train."

Jarvis put Rascal's limit and grass back into the gunny sack and gave it to him. "What about those?"

"I'm going to take them with me Rascal."

"Thought as much."

Jarvis put the brook trout in his pack and said as he walked off the wharf. "Have a good day Rascal—what's left of it."

Rascal wasn't upset with Jarvis, but now he knew he should have been more careful if he was going to poach. Instead of being careful, he was thinking about picking up his wife, so she would not have to walk home.

She was just coming out of her office and she saw Rascal. "I thought I'd canoe you across the cove so you wouldn't have to walk."

"That's thoughtful of you, Rascal. Did you have any luck fishing? Why are you looking so gloomy? I would think you'd be happy."

"The fishing was great. I caught two limits. One for each of us. Jarvis met me at the wharf and now I have to be in court Monday morning for that second limit of brook trout."

"You said he met you on the wharf. How did he know you were fishing or coming to the wharf?"

"I don't know, unless he was up there and saw me. If he was, then he would have had to run all the way back on the tracks. I just don't know, Em."

"I think you should be careful of Jarvis. He may be watching you more now since you are getting around easier."

Emma was correct there, he'd better be more cautious in the future.

* * *

The next day, after Emma left for work he began canning the brook trout. He kept two of the larger ones out for supper. While the water was boiling in the canner he decided to check on tracks in the garden and his traps.

There were no new tracks and a raccoon in one trap, which he dispatched and the other trap was gone. Just then he could smell skunk. "Just what I wanted." He followed his nose to the trapped skunk. He didn't know whether to kill it or take a chance of being sprayed and try releasing it.

"Maybe this wasn't such a good idea."

He found the skunk. The chain, which he had forgotten to secure, was now caught up in some bushes. The skunk was back-to, to him. If he jumped or scared the skunk, the skunk would spray. He walked around in front of it so the skunk could see him. "So far so good."

He started talking to the skunk to calm it and to show it he meant it no harm. "Okay, fella, I mean you no harm. I'm going to get on my hands and knees and I'll let you out of the trap if you promise not to spray me."

Rascal wasn't liking this at all. But if he shot him, then the skunk would spray anyhow. He kept talking and moving slowly towards the skunk. The skunk was actually calm. As long as the skunk was facing him he knew he was safe.

He had the trap by both sides and began compressing the spring, trying not to jerk the trap. The spring was fully depressed and the jaws dropped down. The skunk was free, but he stayed right there. "Hey you the trap is off you. Move it will you so I can let go of this trap."

Maybe this was the skunk's way of getting back at him. His hands, arms and knees began to hurt. Rascal knew if he suddenly jerked the trap away it would scare the skunk and it would spray. But something had to happen PDQ or there was going to be a big stink in the air. Instead of jerking the trap, he tried pulling it towards him, carefully, the skunk felt movement and picked its leg up. Rascal had the trap in his hands. "Whew." Rascal stood up. And when he did the skunk turned around, raised his tail and sprayed.

Rascal with trap in hand tried to out run the stink. But he was already covered with it. His eyes were red and watering and he had all he could do to breathe.

As he was taking his clothes off in the woodshed, Emma came walking in from the road. "What are—oh my gawd! Rascal, what have you done?"

Rascal explained to her about the trap and skunk. She began laughing while holding her hand over her nose. "You might want to stop laughing, Em, and take the canner off the stove. The jars will be sealed now."

"Don't you come in the cabin, Rascal. As soon as I have the canner off the stove, I'll bring the wash basin out for you and you can start scrubbing. But I think I'll have to go to the village and get all the tomato juice Mr. Douglas has. That's the only thing that'll get rid of the smell."

Emma brought out all the warm water there was, which wasn't much. While Emma went after the tomato juice, Rascal began scrubbing and scrubbing. Some of the stink was gone, but he didn't think he'd ever be able to eliminate it from his nostrils. The water had turned cold and he was cold.

An hour later Emma returned with a case of tomato juice.

"You empty the water, Rascal, while I open these cans." Emma found a brush and began scrubbing Rascal's head, shoulders and back.

"It's remarkable how well tomatoes cut the smell," Emma said.

Rascal didn't think he'd have any skin left after all the scrubbing. When he was scent free, Emma washed his clothes and boots in the juice. It was almost dark when they had finished.

As they lay in bed that night Emma said, "I bet this is the cleanest you have ever been, Rascal."

"I learned a good lesson about skunks."

"Maybe you should get some chicken wire from Douglas's store and put it around the garden."

"Good point."

The next morning Rascal bought some fencing from Mr. Douglas and spent the rest of the weekend putting it around the garden. And he made sure no rodents or rabbits were able to crawl under it. When he finished Sunday afternoon he stood back admiring his work. "There, that looks good and it should keep out the deer too," he said to Emma.

"Promise me one thing, Rascal."

"What's that?"

"No more trapping skunks."

"You can count on it," they both laughed and then sat on the porch with a cup of coffee.

"You know, Rascal, I really enjoy sitting out here in the summer with the screens in. At least the blackflies can't get in."

"When I get back from court I'll see if I can wash some of the dirt off the screens."

Chapter 4

Rascal and Emma were up early and after a good breakfast Rascal walked with Emma to the village. It was too early for Emma to start work but the train was already at the station. She kissed Rascal goodbye and said, "Hope the judge doesn't put you in jail."

"No, he wouldn't do that. He would if I had shot a deer or moose in closed season or at night, but I don't think so for having a few too many fish."

Emma left the platform and Rascal found an empty seat in the first car. No sooner had he sat down and the train blew its whistle and lurched forward.

The big engine had pulled into the station earlier and connected four cars loaded with sawn lumber and two cars with four foot pulp. The engine was huge and in no time at all the train was up to speed at 25 mph.

Rascal saw the beaver colonies that were a nuisance to the railroad. Maybe he could use a handcar to come down to them.

The train pulled into the station and he had fifteen minutes before court started. He tried running but that aggravated his leg so he walked. If he was late he was late.

The courthouse was further from the train station then he remembered. He was ten minutes late.

Jarvis saw Rascal enter the room and stepped over to speak with him. "The judge already called your name. I told him you would be here, so he put your case at the bottom."

There were more people in court than Rascal thought would be. Finally the judge called his name and Rascal stood and walked down front. "So you decided to come after all Mr. Ambrose."

"I had every intention of coming, Sir. There was no way I could have been here sooner."

Jarvis smiled, pleased to see Rascal stand his ground.

"Mr. Ambrose you are in court today because Game Warden Page says you had two daily limits of brook trout. To whit fifty trout or twenty-five more than you should have had. How say you, Mr. Ambrose?"

"I did have an extra limit."

"I'll take that as a plea of guilty and fine you $1.00 for each fish."

When Rascal turned around Jarvis had already left. The next train wasn't until 5 p.m. He had several hours to wait.

It was almost noon and he was hungry. He remembered passing a restaurant on his way from the station. After a bowl of soup, a club sandwich and coffee, he bought a new dress for Emma, and a pair of boots for himself. He asked the salesman if he would throw his old ones away.

Much of the rest of the day he spent wandering around Beech Tree. It hadn't changed much since he was last here three years ago.

Finally he heard the train whistle blow which meant the train would be departing in thirty minutes. Right on time. He found an empty seat on the opposite side of the tracks and suddenly he was hungry again.

He saw two more nuisance beaver colonies. He figured he could probably trap at least six beaver from each colony. And since they were nuisance beaver he would take even the small ones. Usually he left those for seed, but these were nuisance beaver. Rascal was already figuring up what these beaver hides would be worth.

By the time the train arrived in Whiskey Jack, Emma had already gone home. He noticed bear tracks in the road to the cabin and when he stopped at the path to his cabin the tracks— small indeed—continued on.

"How much did the fish cost you?" Emma asked.

"$25.00. The judge was awful surley. I didn't like him at all. I bought you something."

Emma unwrapped it and exclaimed how much she liked it. "And you knew my size. I'm surprised. Oh, by the way, you have a letter on the table."

Rascal picked it up and saw the return address Belle Patience of New York. "Must be Lt. Belle. It's been opened."

"When my husband gets a letter from some woman I don't know—you betchya I'm going to read it. Was she pretty, Rascal?"

He wasn't going to lie, "Yes she was."

"Did you like her?"

"Yes. I thought a lot of her. She was my nurse in France and therapist in New York."

"Did you kiss her, Rascal?"

"No," not exactly a lie—she kissed him.

"Did you go to bed with her?"

"No, and in fact she said I was the only patient of hers who didn't ask her into bed. Any more questions? Now be still while I read this."

After he had finished reading it she asked, "Are you going to answer her?"

"Yes." That's all that was said.

* * *

The next morning after Emma had left for work, Rascal wrote a letter to Belle. He was actually happy to hear from her, and happy that she had found work in one of New York's hospitals.

By Thursday night, Emma finally had cooled off about her husband receiving a letter from, as he had said, a pretty woman. She snuggled close to Rascal. No more was ever said about Lt. Belle Patience.

Come picnic Sunday, Emma put on her new dress. "You look beautiful in your new dress, Em." Emma hadn't said anything about Rascal going to church with her; maybe she was feeling guilty about the letter from Belle. Rascal didn't have any fancy clothes but he put on some clean clothes, shaved and combed his hair.

"You don't have to go, Rascal."

"I know, but this is a special occasion for you, so I'll go with you."

She kissed and hugged him. "But don't expect me to go every time with you."

Emma had made a large potato salad with just a touch of vinegar to spice it. She held the bowl in her lap while Rascal paddled them across the cove. Everyone had brought a dish and there was enough food to feed an army. Jarvis and his wife Rita were there as were several other people from Beech Tree. All but two people from Whiskey Jack were there. The station master and the telegrapher. Those two positions had to be manned always.

After the sermon everybody gathered down to the lake shore where picnic tables and benches had been set up. There were four horseshoe pits for the men and several quilts on display for the ladies.

There was chicken, pork and bear to eat, many potato salad dishes and Emma's was emptied first. There were bushels of corn which the children had fun shucking, biscuits and baked beans, and the favorite pie was venison mincemeat.

After eating, Rascal and several of the men, including Jeters, Jarvis, Silvio and Rudy Hitchcock had disappeared. Emma figured they were just off somewhere engaging in manly talk. And they didn't reappear again until it was almost time to go home.

There was so much food left over it was decided to divide it up amongst the most needy. Anita had a large box filled with food to take home.

When the men did return it was obvious to Emma that they all had been drinking. Even Jarvis. She wanted to grab Rascal by his ear and scold him, but she would wait until they were home. None of the other women seemed to care much that their husbands had been off drinking.

Emma never said a word until they were inside the cabin. Rascal was feeling a little sheepish. "You drinking whiskey again." Not a question.

"No, I was not."

"What were you drinking?"

"Cider, hard cider and it was good."

"Who brought it to the picnic?"

"Silvio brought one jug, Jarvis brought one and Mr. Hitchcock had one. Jeters didn't bring anything to drink."

"What else were you doing?"

"What do you mean? We were talking and drinking cider. And I ain't about to sleep on the porch tonight. If you don't want to sleep with me—well, you can have the porch."

Rascal was surprised when Emma didn't reply and she walked off. He had never talked back to her before. Maybe because he still was holding an ace in the hole.

Rascal didn't think Emma would sleep on the porch. He went to bed early and just like he thought, Emma came to bed. But she wasn't talking to him.

By the next morning, Monday, all was forgiven and Emma was her usual self. After she had gone to work, Rascal weeded in the garden. Most of the seed was up and there were no tracks either.

Business had picked up at the mill because of an overseas contract, and to keep up with demand, Earl Hitchcock, who was in charge of the lumbering and getting the logs to the mill, went to Beech Tree to find more help. A mile and a half behind the knoll was the huge Hitchcock Farm, with five hundred acres of cleared fields of hay, oats and a variety of vegetables. What the farm couldn't produce for the timber company crews, was shipped in by rail from Beech Tree.

Earl hired four more teamsters and their own crew. They

would be housed at the company's lumber camps. Rascal was at the station the day the extra crews with their work horses arrived. That evening Emma said, "Mr. Hitchcock has hired me another woman to help with accounting. The company is doing that well."

About once a week Rascal would go fishing at the mouth of Jack Brook. He would eat two while there and then he would count and recount to make sure he had only twenty-five to bring back. Once he had to throw away two, so he wouldn't be over the limit. So once a week Emma would bake trout and Rascal would can the rest.

He was really wanting some fresh deer meat, but he was a bit antsy about Jarvis's whereabouts. He decided to change his tactics. One day after Emma had gone to work, he cut off about eight feet of telephone wire, which every cabin in the state had a coil of, and slipped a pair of pliers in his pocket and took the road behind the house and followed it away from the village. This area was lumbered in the winter because the ground was too wet and soft for summer lumbering. The ground needed to freeze first.

This was ideal deer country. Clover and raspberry bushes growing alongside the road. The cedar thickets had game trails through them, but he was looking where the deer were currently traveling.

He was quite a while before he found what he wanted. A deer trail coming from the left side of the road, across the road to the other side. At first he thought about hanging a snare on either side, but then if the deer were crossing from side to side, all he would need would be one snare. Besides he didn't want to have to take care of two deer.

The newest tracks indicated the deer had traveled to the left. So Rascal decided to set his snare there for when the deer came back through. He didn't have to go far when he found what he wanted, the trail went between two small cedar trees. He broke off enough branches to make an opening and secured the snare to one of the cedar trees and made a slip loop on the other end with an opening of about eighteen inches then he hung it so the snare was about twenty inches off the ground.

After he had finished with the snare he decided to walk out the road and see what the crews had done last winter. The further he hiked the more deer signs he saw. He was confident though that even though there seemed to be more deer further along on the road, that his snare would catch a deer. When he came to the end of the road, he explored the cutting. The crews had left the smaller fir, spruce and pine, taking only the larger trees. This area would soon grow back with second growth and in ten or fifteen years the crews could come back and harvest what they had left. "Pretty good conservation planning, yes sir, and it'll be ideal for deer and moose too."

It was almost lunch time so he hiked down to the cafeteria and Jarvis was sitting by himself at a corner table. Rascal sat down and ordered a cup of coffee and two ham and cheese grilled sandwiches.

"How's your garden growing? Trap any more skunks lately?" Jarvis asked and his way of telling Rascal he was keeping an eye on him.

"That darn skunk was alright until he realized he was free of the trap. I have to weed the garden about every three days, but everything is growing good."

"Are you going after moose this fall?"

"I would like a small moose but I don't have any way of twitching it out of the woods or a place to hang it. A couple of deer will see us through the winter. Of course Em will have to shoot her own. You know for a woman she's a pretty good shot."

"What about the nuisance beaver along the tracks. Are you going to be able to get to them?"

"As soon as there is enough ice to support my weight."

"After you have the beaver cleaned out the C&A will send someone down with dynamite to drain the ponds."

Silvio came in and sat down with them.

"Hey, Jarvis, I could sure use some venison if the train ever hits a deer or moose close by."

"I'll keep you in mind."

As the three men drank a pot of coffee and talked socially, Rascal tried not to be nervous. But it was clear from what Jarvis had said that he was keeping an eye on him. Why else would he be up around the cabin and garden. He was beginning to think that he had been underestimating Jarvis Page.

On his way home he was thinking he would from now on be more careful of Jarvis and more elusive. Jarvis was taking all the fun out of his poaching ways.

He sat on the porch for the rest of the day thinking and worrying about Jarvis. Did he already know about the snare? If he hadn't been so worried that Jarvis might, right now, be watching to see if he will return to the snare... "Nonsense, Jarvis just has me paranoid."

By the end of the afternoon he had decided that Jarvis could not have already known about the snare, since he was already at the cafeteria. When he had entered, he had come straight to the village after setting the snare. No, he was probably just feeling guilty after what Jarvis had said.

Rascal was still on the porch when Emma came home from work. She was surprised that Rascal did not have supper ready. When he's home he usually did. "What did you do today?"

"I took the road behind the cabin to the end where they lumbered last winter and set a snare for deer. Then I went to the cafeteria for lunch and sat with Jarvis, and then Silvio joined us. There was something Jarvis said that makes me think he's watching me. I sat on the porch most of the afternoon thinking and worrying."

"Well what are you going to do?"

"Be careful. I'll get up a couple of hours before daylight and pick up the snare or deer if there is one in it."

Emma started laughing jokingly and said, "You keep messing around with Jarvis and you'll end up in jail. I like deer and moose meat as well as you do. But Rascal, this isn't a game you're playing."

"I think Jarvis looks at it like it is a game."

* * *

Rascal didn't sleep much during the night and as he lay there thinking about Jarvis, he began wondering if Jarvis had done this on purpose. Saying just enough to make him start thinking and worrying.

Rascal was up at 3 a.m. and he stumbled around in the dark because he didn't want to turn on a light in case Jarvis was watching the cabin. He found a gunny sack and his knife and headed out back. There was just enough light to see his way along the path to the road.

When he was close to the trail that went through the cedar trees, he could hear something thrashing about. More than likely a deer in his snare.

As he followed the trail the thrashing became more violent. There was just enough light to see a crotch horn deer caught by the antlers and the wire was wrapped around the trees. He couldn't afford to let the deer die in the snare, especially since it was caught only by the antlers. And he wanted to be on his way home before daylight.

There was no alternative, he would have to get close enough and cut the deer's throat. He dropped the sack and unsheathed his knife and came in from the rear. Just as he was reaching around to the throat, the deer lurched and kicked out knocking Rascal off his feet. He landed on the deer's back and the deer really began thrashing and kicking out. Rascal was getting the living hell beat out of him. He was kicked in the ribs, behind the head, both legs and one antler prong in the cheek. He was finally able to bring his knife across the deer's throat and slowly the deer stopped fighting.

After he skun the deer, he began slicing off the meat from the four quarters and the backstrap. There wasn't time for the heart and liver and he felt bad for having to leave them. He would have liked to bury the carcass and hide, but he didn't have time. The horizon was trimmed with a golden glow.

He shouldered the gunny sack and started for home. He walked as fast as he could without running. The lake was covered with mist and as he reached the door of his cabin the first rays of sunlight were shining through the treetops.

Emma was just getting out of bed. When she looked at Rascal she began to laugh and said, "Who have you been fighting with?"

"A crotch horn deer. It wasn't dead."

"You need to clean up, Rascal, and look in the mirror."

He washed up and changed his clothes. While Emma fixed breakfast Rascal started cutting the meat into small pieces and putting them in to mason jars. "When you leave I'll start the boiler and get this canned."

"If I were you, Rascal, I'd stay away from the village until that bruise on your cheek is gone. What else did he do to you?"

"He kicked me in the ribs, which still hurts, on the back of my head and both legs. There are cuts on both my legs."

"I'd say you better stay away from the village. If Jarvis sees you he is going to want to know what happened."

Emma went to work and Rascal spent the rest of the day canning all that meat. When he had finished he had twenty-four quart jars sealed and put away. He breathed a sigh of relief when he had finished.

When Emma returned from work, Rascal had worked himself into a bundle of nerves, worrying about Jarvis, and Emma could see his nervousness and laughed and said, "My word, Rascal, you're so paranoid you're a bundle of nerves, and so tense. Why don't you go for a walk while I fix supper."

As he closed the door Emma watched and shook her head and laughed. Emma had been wanting some fresh venison steak and Rascal, in his paranoia, had canned everything. So she opened a jar of meat, with boiled potatoes and fiddleheads. A good country meal.

That night Rascal had nightmares all night that Jarvis had found where he had snared the deer and came knocking on his door.

That morning as Rascal and Emma were finishing their morning coffee, a knock came at the kitchen door. Rascal choked and spit up his last bit of coffee. Emma saw the strained look on Rascal's face and she stood up and opened the door.

"Why, good morning, Jarvis. What brings you out here so early?"

Rascal knew, he just knew, Jarvis was there to arrest him.

"Is Rascal here Emma? I need to speak with him."

"Surely, won't you come in. I'll fix you a cup of coffee."

There were many things going through Rascal's mind just then. Was Emma being so corrigible because she had set him up again and told Jarvis he was snaring deer again.

"Good morning, Rascal. I don't have a lot of time, I need your help today if you're not busy."

Rascal swallowed and breathed freely and said, "Sure thing, Jarvis, what do you need?"

"The Douglas girl, three-year-old Susy, wandered away from home late yesterday afternoon. At first her parents thought she must be with the neighboring friends. But by dark no one had seen her. I received a telegram last night and took the early train here. I know with your bad leg you won't want to do much hiking in the woods, but I'm going to need someone in a canoe searching the shoreline."

"Certainly I'll help, Jarvis."

"Good, I thought you would. Do you have a pistol, you can use to fire a signal shot if you find her?"

"No, I only have a rifle and a shotgun."

"Okay, bring your rifle. I'll canoe back to the village with you."

As Emma walked to work she couldn't help but think of the varied nature of Jarvis's job. Chasing poachers one day and the next looking for a lost three-year old. She wondered if he ever had time to spend with his own family.

A group of people had gathered at the cafeteria, all wanting to help. "Rascal, you take Jeters with you. If you find the little girl, fire three shots. And that goes for any who might find her. No shooting at all unless you find the girl. You two can leave now, Rascal. I'll have to organize the search of the woods."

Rascal and Jeters climbed into the canoe and started paddling along the shore, and hollering for Susy; Jarvis was busy organizing the rest of the volunteers. "I want three people to search everything within the village. Look in every nook and cranny. Any place where a three year old could crawl into. Every house, building and shed. Look at everything." Jarvis took the rest of the searchers and set up a hasty line between the lake shore and the railroad tracks. At first the searches were bunched up but as the area widened everyone spread out.

Rascal and Jeters were very conscientious about finding the lost Douglas girl. There was no tomfoolery, no story telling. This was serious business. "Jeters, my throat is getting hoarse; you holler for a while and then I will." They had canoed all the way around the lake once and now they were going back and forth along trackside.

Suddenly Jeters stopped paddling and cocked his ear towards the shore. "Stop paddling, Rascal, and listen."

"Did you hear something?"

"Shh, there it is again."

"I can't hear anything, Jeters."

Jeters hollered, "Susy!" and then they both could hear a small child crying. Rascal brought the bow around pointed towards shore and they both with two powerful strokes ran the bow of the canoe up on a grassy tuft of shore. Jeters stepped out and held the canoe steady for Rascal. They both could still hear the little girl crying. Jeters followed the sound into the bushes and the little girl was laying on the ground with her knees pulled up and under her chin. He picked the little girl up. "It's okay now, Susy. I'm Jeters, you know me and Rascal, and we are going to take you home now."

Rascal fired three shots with his rifle and then the three canoed back to the village. Everyone was so happy to see Susy. Except for being cold, fly bitten and scared, she was okay. Rascal and Jeters waited in the cafeteria for the rest of the searchers to return.

When all of the volunteers had returned and were all accounted for and out front of the Douglas's store, Mr. Douglas offered cold beer to all the searchers. Jeters grabbed two and handed one to Rascal. "They're good and cold, here."

They were each thirsty and in two swallows the beer was gone. "I'll buy us two more Rascal." Jeters was trying to make amends for helping Emma get Rascal in trouble. The second beer went down just as quick. "Another?" Jeters asked.

"No, not for me, Jeters."

"Hey man, who hit you in the cheek? I just noticed it."

Rascal felt his face. It was still a little sore, but he had forgotten all about being beaten up by a deer. He wondered why Jarvis hadn't said anything. Probably because of the concern for the lost three-year-old girl.

"Ah, I was cutting bushes around the cabin and one slapped me in the face."

Jeters didn't believe it, but he decided not to push it any further. "Well, I need to get some sleep, Rascal. Talk with you later."

Rascal went home before someone else asked him about the bruise on his cheek. And he wanted to get clear of Jarvis.

* * *

Rascal didn't go anywhere except on his side of the lake. He scouted out a new fall trap line and brushed out a trail to make the hike each day easier. He checked the garden several times each day to see how the vegetables were growing. And one day he saw a skunk digging for grubs outside the fence. He spoke to it so it would know he was close. He'd rather do three days in jail then get sprayed again.

"People are asking about you Rascal, wondering why you haven't been down for your morning coffee and donut."

"What are you telling them?"

"That you fell down."

"As long as Jarvis doesn't get suspicious."

"I think you're still a little paranoid, Rascal. Why don't you go up to the head of the lake tomorrow and get us some frog legs. I'd like to try canning a couple of jars."

* * *

Before canoeing up to the lily pad cove near the head of the lake Rascal went and walked down to the village with Emma. "Have a good day, Rascal, and stop worrying so much." She kissed him and walked into the accounting office.

Silvio was sitting with Jeters. "Sit down, Rascal."

Rascal sat down and Silvio was looking at the bruise on Rascal's face. "Who hit you, Rascal?" Silvio asked.

"My leg gave out and I fell in the woods."

"That's not the story he told me, Silvio. I think Emma hit him."

Rascal and forgotten that he had earlier told Jeters something different.

"Let it alone, Jeters," Rascal answered.

Silvio and Jeters just looked at each other.

Rascal left the cafeteria after only one cup of coffee. Silvio and Jeters looked at each other again and shrugged their shoulders.

Rascal took his fly rod and two gunny sacks and his rifle he left hanging on the wall. If the fishing was good at all, he would have enough for lunch and a sack full for the Antonys.

* * *

While on the search for three-year-old Susy Douglas, Jarvis

had overheard a conversation of two men talking about the goings-on near the farm. So after he was clear of the search, he found a place in the nearby woods to spend the night.

He intended to work his way through the cuttings after breakfast. But as he was leaving the Douglas store he saw Rascal canoeing towards the head of the lake. This piqued his interest more than the conversation he had overheard.

The easiest route to where he wanted to be would be to walk the rails and then cut through the woods to the lake.

As he walked along he kept thinking about the last time. About this same time in July before Rascal went into the Army, when he was up to the head of the lake and after frogs. He had had frogs alright, but Jarvis had also found a freshly killed deer. It had been shot, and Rascal didn't have a rifle. He had sat on the deer for two days waiting for Rascal or whoever to come back for it. No one had and the deer went to waste.

If Rascal had indeed shot the deer then where was his rifle. It hadn't been in the canoe and he had not gone ashore. He had always been puzzled by that. And now Rascal was heading back to the same lily pad cove.

He began to hurry as the thoughts of that time passed through his mind. A short distance below Ledge Swamp, Jarvis left the tracks to the north and Whiskey Jack Lake.

When he reached the shore he was almost out of breath. "I'm getting too old for this. But ain't it fun."

He stayed back in the shadows and leaned against a spruce tree. Rascal was just getting into position amongst the lily pads, just like he had done before. Jarvis found a spot where he could sit down and watch Rascal with binoculars. And just like before he was catching frogs. He watched as Rascal was dangling his fly about four inches above the water. "What in hell is he doing." And then a two pound trout jumped for the fly and cleared the water. "Well I'll be damned."

Then he watched Rascal go back to catching frogs. About every fifteen or twenty minutes Rascal would dangle the fly above the water again, and again he would catch a nice fat trout. "Now there can't be more than three or four inches of water there. On top of black muck. I'd learn a lot, Rascal, if I spent more time watching you."

There was movement to the left of Rascal and he turned to see what it was. A nice spike horn deer had come down to the shoreline to feed on the aquatic plants.

Rascal saw the deer, but paid little attention to it. This isn't how it was suppose to happen. He expected Rascal to shoot it. But Rascal didn't seem to be at all interested with the deer.

Rascal was hungry and the frogging had petered out here. He went ashore to roast a couple of trout and then he set over and caught a few more frogs.

When Rascal went ashore Jarvis was sure now that Rascal would go after the deer that was now standing on a knoll, not far from shore. But instead, Rascal kindled a fire and it was obvious he intended to cook a fish or two.

Rascal leaned back against a tree and slowly turned the trout over the fire. The smell of roasting fish made him even hungrier. Jarvis could smell fish cooking as well.

While the fish were cooking, Rascal laid back on the ground staring up at the blue sky and thinking how lucky he was to be living at Whiskey Jack Lake, and with a good woman like Em. But he hadn't forgotten either about staging the scene to get him to church. He just hadn't figured out yet how or what needed to be done.

Jarvis was hungry enough to gnaw the bark off a poplar tree. He kept watch on Rascal with increasing anticipation with each passing hour. He just knew Rascal was up to something no-good.

Rascal ate both fish and made sure the fire was out and then went back to frogging and catching an occasional nice trout who had swum under a lily pad for shade. Rascal counted twelve nice brook trout and enough frogs to half fill the gunny sack. "All those frogs is going to take a lot of work to clean them." He put his fly rod up and started paddling leisurely for the village. Once out in the lake he let the gentle wind push him along. All he did was guide the canoe.

Jarvis saw that Rascal was about to leave so he started back for the village. He wanted to get there before Rascal. It was a good thing Rascal was in no particular hurry.

Jarvis was exhausted as he reached the outskirts of the village. Rascal was just turning his canoe in towards shore, and not to his cabin or the wharf. This was good for Jarvis. He went down to the shore to greet Rascal.

"Hello, Rascal."

"Jarvis."

"Been frogging again?"

"What would make you say that?" Rascal asked, wondering if Jarvis had been watching him.

"Well, it's too warm and the sun is too bright for good lake fishing."

Rascal handed him the sack with the brook trout. "Oh yeah, look at these."

Jarvis looked at each trout and laid them on some grass. "Nice catch. I was hoping to find a deer in there."

"I'm afraid I can't help you there. I intended to give these to the Antonys."

"How many frogs do you have?"

"I'm not sure, but it's going to take a while to skin all the legs. But they sure are good."

The train whistle just blew. "Hope you weren't intending to take that train out, Jarvis."

"Well, I was. Guess I'll wait until morning now."

"Tell you what Jarvis, you help me clean these frog legs, then you can stay for supper."

"That sounds like a good deal."

Jarvis walked with Rascal over to the Antonys and Silvio was really surprised to see Jarvis with Rascal. "What did you do, Rascal, shoot a moose? You going to take him to jail, Jarvis?"

"No moose, no jail, Silvio. Here's some brook trout if you

and Anita would like them."

"Sure thing. Won't you come in?"

"Can't Silvio, we have a long job ahead of us skinning frog legs."

Emma saw Rascal canoeing across the cove with Jarvis, "Oh my word. He's going to jail this time."

Trouble is they were talking sociably like two old friends. "What's going on," Emma said aloud. "What did you do this time, Rascal?"

"Jarvis here has offered to help me skin these frog legs for supper. How about it, Em?"

"Okay with me. You look like you could use a good night's sleep, Jarvis," Emma said.

"I could, believe me."

"You two skin the frogs outside and I'll get you both some coffee."

Once inside the cabin and out of ear-shot Emma burst out laughing. "The cat and mouse playing together. But who's the cat and who's the mouse," and she laughed some more.

Emma made some fresh biscuits and opened a jar of fiddleheads. Rascal and Jarvis were an hour before they had finished, and talking like two old friends.

"Supper is ready boys. Would you like water or coffee, Jarvis?" Emma asked.

"I'd like a cold beer, but water will do." Rascal smiled and looked at his wife. She turned trying to make believe she didn't understand Rascal's look.

"This is all so delicious, Emma. I have eaten frog legs before, but never have I ever had my fill of them."

They all three kept talking through supper. Just like good friends and not the law and poacher sparring at each other's throat. Emma was just as talkative and enjoyed Jarvis' company.

The sun had set and Emma excused herself and said, "You two sit out here on the porch and talk, will you? I'm going to bed."

The air was now cool for this time in July and the lightning bugs were putting on quite a show. They reminded Jarvis of kids in Beech Tree running around the park with sparklers on the 4th of July.

A loon out front of the cabin called and another loon answered at the head of the lake. "I envy your life here, Rascal. Even in the darkness you can feel and hear all the beauty that surrounds you."

"You know Jarvis, some day there won't be a village called Whiskey Jack. This is a company town and the Hitchcocks own all the land around here. I expect when the timber is all harvested that'll be the end. First the mill will close and it'll be dismantled and shipped out. Douglas' store will go, the school, the blacksmith shop; hell everything will have to go because there won't be any way for anyone to earn a living."

"What would you and Emma do, Rascal?"

"As long as the train runs through and will stop, so we can get on and off, I'd like to stay. I can make a good living trapping."

"If Whiskey Jack is still here when I retire, I just might convince my wife to move here."

Eventually they both fell asleep in their chair. When Rascal woke up just before daylight Jarvis was gone. Rascal thought he had had to go to the bathroom so he waited a bit to see if he would come back. When he didn't Rascal got undressed and crawled into bed with Emma. "What time is it, Rascal?"

"Not quite daylight yet."

"And you're just coming to bed? Where's Jarvis?"

"Don't know. When I woke up he was gone."

"Hum." They went back to sleep.

* * *

The end of summer was drawing near and Rascal spent some time every day in the garden harvesting vegetables. And because Emma worked every day, he did most of the canning.

But every morning he went to the cafeteria for his coffee

and donut, and sometimes breakfast. Most of the time Silvio and sometimes Anita would join him. But mostly it was a time for the men to socialize and find answers to all of the world's problems. Rascal wouldn't leave until he had the day's newspaper. The headlines every day were either about Women's Suffrage, their right to vote, or the Volstead Act, Prohibition, which would curtail alcoholic beverages, brewing and drinking.

"Women are going to be the damnation to this country. Ever since this suffrage movement got started in 1840s they have tried to close down saloons and brothels, and I'll bet everything I have, this here suffrage movement is behind Prohibition," Silvio was red in the face.

"I don't see anything wrong if a man wants a cold beer or a stiff drink, once in a while. I'm divided, though, whether women should have the right to vote," Jeters said.

A newcomer to the group, Jeff Daniels, said, "I agree with Jeters. There ain't nothing wrong if a man wants to drink. I think women should vote, but I'm afraid of the changes it'll bring."

"What about you, Rascal?" Do you think women should have the right to vote?" Jeters asked.

"They make up half of this country's population. They have gone through hard times just like we men have. I think they should have the right to vote. As far as Prohibition goes, I don't know if there are places where drinking has become a problem or not. It's like any law, it'll hurt those folks that aren't any problem. Those of us who like a cold beer or an occasional stiff drink will be affected more, I think, than anyone else." Then as an afterthought he added, "My wife has me on *Prohibition* already." He looked at Jeters and Jeters turned away.

"It's going to happen and there ain't one thing we can do about it. Me, I think I'll start making some home brew and hard cider. Even my wife Anita likes a glass of hard cider occasionally," Silvio said.

"Have you ever made home brew before, Silvio?" Jeters asked.

"Before I hurt my ankle and foot, I used to make five gallons every summer. I can't afford it now."

"Well, when the time comes, maybe we four can do something about that." Everyone nodded their head in agreement.

The morning social hour broke up and Rascal walked home. Along the way he kept thinking about what had been said.

He went into the kitchen for a coffee mug and went out to the woodshed and half-filled the mug with whiskey and then put the whiskey jug back. He put a little water in the mug and sat on the porch. The drink was more for him to feel he could have a drink if he wanted, than him actually wanting a drink. He nursed his drink for a long time and never finished it. He threw what was left over the porch railing.

* * *

By the time Emma came home from work, the whiskey smell on his breath was gone. He had even forgotten about it.

The next morning he asked Rudy Hitchcock if he could borrow a work horse and wagon so he could haul some of the dried wood slabs from the pile to his cabin. When he had finished his wood pile he would make sure the Antonys had enough wood for the winter.

"Sure, Rascal, tell Smitty that I said it was okay to loan you a horse and wagon for as long as you need it."

"Thanks, Mr. Hitchcock."

As he was walking across the mill yard, Sam Grindle, C&A superintendent, hollered to Rascal, "Hey! Rascal!"

Rascal stopped and turned to look at Sam. "Yes, what can I do for you, Sam?"

"At mile nine between here and Beech Tree there is a nuisance beaver colony and the water is almost up to the rail bed. I need the beaver, all of them, removed and then we'll clean the bridge. Can you trap, shoot—or however—and remove the beaver?"

"Yes, but it'll have to be this weekend, if that'll be soon enough."

"That'll be okay. Are you up to walking there and back?"

"That will be a problem, with all the gear I'll have to take."

"What if I give you one man and a two-man rail car?"

"That would make a difference."

"Good, I'll tell the station master, Greg, to assign one man to you for this weekend."

If he had not talked with Mr. Hitchcock earlier and Rudy being so kind to lend him a horse and wagon, he would much rather go after the nuisance beaver at mile nine. So he worked for the rest of the week filling his own woodshed and Antony's.

"You have been working all week on firewood, Rascal, is your leg okay? I'm afraid you might be over doing it," Emma asked.

"It hurts, but I've gotten use to it. I know when I need to rest."

"Well, I'm glad you won't have to walk to mile nine and back again, two miles round-trip, carrying your backpack and gear. I'm also glad to see you working. It's good for you. You know the saying about idle hands."

"Yeah, I know the saying."

With each load of wood to the Antonys Anita would bring out a cold glass of milk and a brownie. "You keep feeding me like this Anita, I'll never get your woodshed full."

"I don't know how we'll ever be able to repay you, Rascal."

"Just keep making those brownies, Anita."

Silvio's woodshed was full now and Rascal hauled one more load to his cabin. He worked it up and split it to fit the kitchen cook stove.

The next morning he met Elmo Leaf at the crew shed. "As soon as the northbound goes through we can put the handcar on the rails. We might as well have us a coffee while we wait," Elmo said.

Silvio and Jeters were already in the cafeteria and still talking about Women's Suffrage and Prohibition. Rascal tried to steer the conversation away from either topic.

"I've noticed the beehives are about twelve feet off the ground this year," Rascal said.

"That usually means how much snow we'll get this winter," Silvio said.

"If we get twelve feet, that's surely going to put a crimp on lumbering. I wouldn't want to be cutting trees and having to wade through that much snow. Not even for twice the pay. My job in the boiler room is beginning to look good," Jeters said.

"It'll be a tough job for the train to plow snow too. C&A will have to have an engine and plow purposely just to keep the tracks open."

The train whistle blew, signaling it was approaching the village, at mile ten. "I guess that's our cue, Rascal. Time to go to work."

Elmo moved the junction arm and Rascal pushed the car onto the main rails, then Elmo moved the junction rails back. "This is a slight downgrade all the way to mile nine. It'll be an easy ride down. Coming back up we'll have to work at it."

This was the way to travel Rascal thought. He wished there was a car he could use to Ledge Swamp. The ride only took them ten minutes. "We'd best get this car off the rails, just in case."

The water was within two feet of the rail bed. "This ain't so good, Rascal. This water can soften the ground under the bed and cause a lot of problems."

Rascal went right to work. The trapping laws had changed making it illegal to tamper with a beaver dam or set traps on the dam. But these were extenuating circumstances. So Rascal made a trough on the top of the dam allowing a good flow of water. Then he placed a beaver trap in the trough. Then he did the same thing about ten feet over.

"Now what do we do, Rascal? Sit and wait or go back?" Elmo asked.

"We ain't done yet. But it would be my guess that when we

come back we'll have at least one beaver here, maybe two if we're lucky. We'll walk around the pond and look for another dam up stream. There is always another dam."

"If you didn't have to take the beaver and if C&A didn't destroy the dam, this pond would be some good fishing come spring," Elmo said.

"I understand what you say Elmo, but what if this steam is a natural spawning bed for brook trout? The trout left in the pond will eventually die because of lack of oxygen in the hot summer months. Removing the dam now then the trout should be able to make their way to the spawning beds."

"If you say so, Rascal."

"The beaver has skid trails for their wood to the dam, and they are still wet. Beaver had just used this first trail. But look at all the trails. There must be more beaver here than we first thought."

"Rascal, come here?"

"What is it, Elmo?"

Elmo pointed to some black mud at the edge of the beaver pond. "Look at that, Rascal. That is fresh."

"That's a big bear track. He might have been here when we stopped. He's a big brute, too."

"Doesn't this make you a little concerned?"

"Why? Bear are just as afraid of us as we are of it. You see, Elmo, he must have heard us and he left, although we were quite a distance away."

"If you say so, Rascal. But I'm keeping watch."

Rascal laughed. "Here's the inlet and there's peeled wood all over the bottom and stream banks."

"This means what, Rascal?"

"That there is beaver up stream and this peeled wood floated down here from another colony."

They only had a short distance to hike. "There probably won't be any houses here. This is probably only a cofferdam." Rascal pointed to a trail going up the dam to the water. "We set our first trap here."

91

It didn't take him but a few minutes to dig out a trough and set a trap. And then he set another trap to one side of that one.

"Rascal, look," and Elmo pointed to a beaver swimming up the stream.

"Let's get off the dam." He led the way to a small hillock and they sat down to wait. "Let's see what happens."

The beaver stopped to chew on an alder stick in the stream. He peeled the bark off and ate it and then continued his journey to the cofferdam. Once the beaver reached the top of the dam, he didn't hesitate at all. He walked right into the trap and Rascal and Elmo heard the commotion.

When Rascal just sat there Elmo asked, "Aren't you going down to see?"

"Yeah, but we'd better let the beaver drown first. If we both grabbed ahold of a live beaver we both would take a licking. They are really strong. There's enough chain on the trap to allow the beaver to swim to deeper water where it'll soon drown.

"Are you hungry, Elmo?"

"Yeah, but we didn't bring anything to eat."

"We do now. You build us a small fire on top of that rise and I'll get us dinner."

Elmo had no idea what he was talking about, but he started a fire and then Rascal came walking up carrying a beaver.

"Two-year-old." Then he began skinning and fleshing the hide as he went. He made sure to take the castors too. When he had finished there were hot coals in the fire and he cut off both hind legs. "Get us some roasting sticks, Elmo."

They cut off small pieces of meat instead of roasting the entire leg. "Cooks faster in small pieces."

Rascal propped his sick up so the meat was over the coals and he cut out the heart and put another stick through it and suspended that over the coals.

Elmo took a bite of his and said, "This is delicious, Rascal. I have never tasted sweeter meat." He ate that and started roasting another.

As Rascal was eating his piece the trap went off again. "That sounds like another beaver, Rascal," Elmo said.

"You keep cooking beaver and I'll go get this one."

Elmo made a shish-kabob with the pieces of beaver meat. Then he put some more wood on the fire and Rascal came walking back. "Another two-year-old."

While skinning and fleshing that one he would chew on a piece of beaver meet. "This meat is done to perfection, Elmo. I'll make a trapper out of you yet."

Elmo was still keeping a watchful eye for that wandering bear. "Rascal, isn't the smell of this meat cooking going to attract that bear?"

"Elmo, he's probably long gone by now." He told Elmo about the bear during spring that he was sure was hunting him.

Rascal rolled that hide up and put it in his pack with the first. They sat back and ate their fill of roasted beaver. "Can we take any of this beaver meat back with us, Rascal?"

"I was intending to. Cut the legs off that beaver. I'm going to walk around and have a look see."

"Sure. If you see that bear—holler."

Rascal saw moose and deer tracks around the edge of the flowage.

"We'd better go check the other traps. We probably have beaver there too."

There they had two super large beaver. "These are the older adults. Although in a colony this big there are maybe two more. And probably four more two year olds and a bunch of kits."

Rascal reset those two and put the beaver on dry land and began skinning. While he was skinning Elmo was cutting off the meat and storing it in his pack. After the two beaver were finished they moved back away from the water to wait.

"Are these hides worth much?"

"They'll be worth a couple of dollars. More if this was winter. Now the guard hairs are too short. The castors will be worth almost as much as the hides."

"What do they do with the castors?"

"They make perfume."

"They make perfume from beaver scent-glands?" Elmo asked.

"Yep."

Nothing was happening at the first dam, so they moved back to the cofferdam. They had two more two year olds. Rascal skun them and cut out the castors and Elmo cut off the meat.

Rascal reset those two traps and they went back towards the tracks. There they had another super large beaver. "I'll reset this trap and after we have it skun and cut off the meat I think we can leave today. Come back tomorrow morning and it wouldn't surprise me if we have a beaver in each trap."

They packed everything and their packs were heavy. Once they had the handcar back on the rails they loaded their packs and climbed on. Because the tracks were on a downhill cant, they started to slowly roll downhill. They each grabbed their handle and began to slowly move the car forward.

"Rascal!" Elmo screamed. "Rascal, bear!"

"What are you talking about, Elmo?"

"Bear! Damn it! Pump harder!"

"Where's the bear?"

"He just came out of the woods and right now he's running up the tracks at us."

Rascal turned just enough to see a bear running up the tracks toward them. "Hey!" He hollered, "Hey!" The bear kept coming.

"Pump that damn handle, Rascal, or we'll be bear food!"

They were both pumping the handle as fast as they could. The bear was now about fifty feet behind them. "What was all that you were saying about bear being more afraid of people than we are of them?"

"Something is wrong here." Rascal hollered at the bear again and the bear kept running after them.

"He's getting closer, Rascal! Come on man pump!"

Both of their faces were covered with sweat. Elmo's maybe

a little worse as he could watch the bear running after them.

"The only thing saving us, Rascal, from becoming supper is that it isn't easy for him to run on the uneven ties."

"I can't believe he is still following us," Rascal said.

"Maybe he can smell the hides and meat in our packs."

"I don't think so, Elmo. If he was hungry, we left the remains of five beaver that I'm sure he already has scoped out."

"Then what is it?"

"He acts like the bear I caught at my cabin. If'n I didn't know better, I'd say he is hunting us. Or running us out of his territory."

"Well damn it, he's doing a good job of it."

"How close is he now, Elmo?"

"Oh, maybe thirty or forty feet."

"He's gained ten feet on us in what—a half mile?"

"We just passed the nine and a half marker. What happens if he chases us right into the station?"

"Maybe he'll get tired before we get there."

"I'm already tired, Rascal."

"Me too."

The bear was tired too and froth foaming around his mouth. For some strange reason the bear suddenly put on more speed.

"Pump, Rascal!! He just started running faster! He might be less than thirty feet now."

Rascal and Elmo looked at each and began pumping the handle as hard and fast as they could and still the bear ran after them. "I can see the station house, Elmo. Maybe he won't want to enter the village."

"Don't stop pumping, Rascal. He's not slowing! I wish that damn steam whistle would blow!"

They were so close to the edge of town now they could see people on the train station platform. They could hear people talking. "That bear isn't going to break off, Rascal. What do we do!?" Excitement clearly in his voice.

"Keep pumping, Elmo. We can't stop. Maybe the noise in

town will cause the bear to break off."

"You're full of maybes, Rascal! And I think the noise is making him run faster. He's only about twenty feet behind you now! Pump faster, damn it!"

Almost everybody in Whiskey Jack heard the noisy chatter of a bear chasing two men on a hand railcar, and they were gathering trackside to see.

Emma was on the porch hanging out some wash and she stopped and her mouth gaping open, watched as the bear chased Rascal and Elmo up the tracks through the village.

Someone threw a rock and hit the bear and the bear ran faster. "Don't throw rocks at the bear! Please!" Elmo hollered.

The whole village was a clamor of laughter and whooping. Silvio and Anita came out to see what all the excitement was.

"Well I'll be go-to-hell! Look at that, Anita. That bear is chasing Elmo and Rascal up the tracks."

"Why ever for, Silvio?"

"I don't know."

"You boys better pump faster, he's gaining on you." Silvio began to laugh, "hah, hah, hah. Maybe all he wants, boys, is to hop on and ride with you. Hah, hah, hah!" Silvio laughed so much he began coughing and had to sit down.

"Hey, Rascal, he's a big one! What did boys do to him?"

"We ain't done nothing to him! He's chased us now from mile nine!" Rascal hollered.

"You'll have a difficult time getting through Canadian Customs with that bear!" Silvio hollered as the boys were going out of sight around the bend.

"Damn it, Rascal I'm getting tired!"

"Me too! But do you want to stop?"

"Not hardly."

"Then we'd better keep pumping. I can hear his huffing for air now. How close is he, Elmo?"

"He's closer than twenty feet. I never knowd a bear could run this far."

"Me neither," Rascal said. He was beginning to get worried. Almost as worried as when he had first awakened in the hospital after having been shot.

"We're really going to be in a pickle if a Canadian southbound comes down the tracks," Rascal said.

"Usually on a weekend nothing comes out of Canada. Only between Beech Tree and Whiskey Jack."

"I hope you're right, Elmo."

Emma stood on the porch watching long after they were out of sight. She couldn't even begin to imagine why that bear was chasing them. "Hope you boys will be okay." Eventually she went back to work.

"We just passed mile eleven, Rascal, and this idiot is still chasing us, although he has dropped back a little."

"What's the mile marker at the border?"

"Mile sixteen is just before the crossing."

"I don't know if I can go another five miles without a rest," Rascal said.

"Me too."

They were coming to Ledge Swamp. "Oh damn!" Rascal exclaimed.

"You see something Rascal?"

"I say, I saw something! Another bear!"

"What!"

"Another bear was standing on his hind legs between the rails."

"How far away?"

"Hundred or hundred fifty yards. It's down on all fours now, looking at us."

"I knew I should have stayed home today," Elmo said.

"Okay, that bear just walked off the further end towards the swamp. I can't see it now. What's our bear doing?"

"He's closing in again, running faster—pump, Rascal, pump!"

When they passed where the second bear had run off, their

bear abruptly turned off the tracks in the same direction as the other bear.

"We'd better go a little further before we stop," Rascal said.

"To hell you say, Rascal. I'm stopping this car now and we get the hell out of here!"

They stopped and then started rolling in the opposite direction. After a short distance they both relaxed and let gravity take over. They both sat down on the leading edge with their feet hanging over the end. "We probably could roll all the way into the village with this down grade," Elmo said.

"I'm all plum tuckered out pumping that handle."

"I'm just glad to be rid of him. I still don't understand why he chased us and for so far," Elmo said.

"Well, he was a male and my guess is that second bear was a male and the first one chased him out of his territory. There probably was a fight at the end, but I think that second bear left the area."

"But why us, Rascal? Was he only trying to chase us out of his territory?"

"I'd like to think that and not that he wanted to kill and eat us. The whole thing was strange, I'll admit."

"I just never want to see another bear as long as I live," Elmo said and stood up. "Let's get the hell out of here, Rascal."

* * *

They chattered continuously all the way back. It was one way of relieving the stress of being chased by the bear and how close that the bear had come.

"Let's stop at Silvio's first, Elmo. Maybe he and Anita would like a couple of beaver legs."

Silvio heard the car grind to a stop and when he saw who it was he began laughing all over again. "Huh, huh, huh, how far did that brute chase you two?"

"Just to the other side of Ledge Swamp. Another bear was

standing between the rails and our bear took off after it. "

"Why do you suppose that bear was chasing you?" Then in the same breath— "Would you boys like a cold beer?" There really wasn't any need of asking.

Rascal told Silvio all he could about the bear, "And your guess is as good as ours, Silvio."

"I've never heard or seen anything like it. To think he chased you two through the village. If I were either one of you I'd be mighty careful in the woods here after. He undoubtedly has your scent and if he smells of you again he just might come after you again." That was all Elmo needed to hear. For the rest of his life he'd always be looking over his shoulder for bear.

Emma saw Rascal coming across the cove and she went down to their wharf to greet him. "Why was that bear chasing you?" The most obvious question.

They sat out on the porch while Rascal told her all about the bear. When he had finished she asked, "Have you been drinking?"

"Silvio gave us a cold beer when we stopped to give him and Anita some beaver meat. And don't think for a minute, Em, that I'm going to sleep out here tonight."

She decided to change the subject. "How many beaver did you get?"

"Five this trip but I'll have to go every day until I have them all. Even the kits. The water is so close to the track bed it could wash the bed out. C&A wants the beaver gone so their crews can dynamite the dam."

"Are beaver worth much, this time of year?"

"Not as much as winter beaver, because of shorter guard hair. But C&A is paying $50.00 to remove them and Jarvis said earlier I could sell the hides. Not a bad deal really."

"Tonight we have fresh beaver and this morning I went out back and found some mushrooms. I picked some early corn and potatoes. What beaver we don't eat tonight, I'll can tomorrow."

"I'll probably have some beaver meat to bring back tomorrow too."

After supper Rascal put the hides on drying boards and stretched them in an oval shape. The Canadian fur buyers preferred them oval instead of round. When he had finished he was ready for bed.

* * *

Rascal met up with Elmo at the cafeteria the next morning. Seems as though most of the village people were there too. All wanting to hear the story of the bear.

As they were loading their gear onto the handcar Elmo said, "I'm glad you brought along your rifle. I wouldn't go back there again without one of us having one."

"Emma wouldn't let me out of the house unless I agreed to take it."

"Good ole Emma. Remind me later to thank her," Elmo said.

At the first dam they had two more super large beaver. "This is probably the last of the supers," Rascal said. "We'll pick up a couple more two year olds, and then the kits."

He reset those traps and skun the beaver before they got stiff. Elmo cut away the meat.

At the next dam, just like Rascal had said they had two more two-year-olds. While Rascal was taking care of those Elmo built a fire and started some meat to roasting. Then he stood with Rascal's rifle surveying the woods around them. He wasn't taking any chances.

"Chances are, Elmo, that ole bear is up to Ledge Swamp."

"Maybe, but I ain't gonna take no chance of being chased by him again."

When they left mile nine in the afternoon Rascal had two more super beaver, three two year olds and two kits. "There might be another two year old here or two, and maybe four more small ones. We'll have to keep coming back until I'm sure we have them all."

"At least the water isn't any closer to the top of the track bed," Elmo said.

Rascal had a shed full of drying beaver now. He hoped he'd get enough for the fur to make the effort worth it.

When he was satisfied that he had all the beaver, he had taken five super large, six two-year-olds and six small ones. He also had three pounds of castors. He wasn't sure if he'd be able to sell the small ones or not. It would really depend on the demand.

Rascal and Elmo reported back to the superintendent, Sam Grindle. "Mr. Grindle, Elmo and I have taken out all the beaver at mile nine."

"Good job. Elmo, tomorrow morning take a crew back there and dynamite the dam and make sure the bridge is clear of all debris."

"Yes Sir, as soon as the morning northbound goes through."

The next morning Rascal was working in his garden harvesting what was ready and he heard an explosion. The sound at first took him by surprise. Then he remembered Elmo and crew were dynamiting the beaver dam at mile nine.

One day while Rascal was canning vegetables while Emma was at work, Jarvis knocked on the door. "Hello, Jarvis, come in. How about a cup of coffee?"

"That would be good. I see you trapped the beaver at mile nine. Heard quite a story too. About a bear chasing you all the way to mile eleven." He began laughing. "I wish I had been there to see that. Chased you and Elmo right through the village." He laughed some more. Rascal wasn't yet able to see all the humor in it.

"Seems like that bear had it in for you and Elmo."

"Well, that wasn't the only bear either." He told Jarvis about the bear outside his window.

"If I were you, Rascal, I'd carry a revolver with me in the woods. But that could get you in trouble too. If, let's say, you happened into a nice spikehorn while frogging. There'd be an awful temptation there."

Rascal knew what Jarvis was alluding to and he tried not to show any understanding.

"I'm surprised to find you so domesticated, Rascal. I never figured you for housework."

"Well, it needs to be done and Emma is working. And besides, I like to eat."

"I hear you there."

After visiting for an hour, Jarvis excused himself and said, "I've work that needs my attention. Have a good day, Rascal, and thanks for the coffee."

With the coming days the garden and vegetables were taken care of. "We have a good stock of food now, Em. All we need is a deer or two."

"I would like some ham and bacon and salt pork. We also need flour, sugar and coffee and two bushels of apples."

"I'll go to Douglas' store tomorrow and see if I can get everything there. If not we might have to take a trip to Beech Tree."

"The day time temperatures are cool enough so I think everything will keep okay in the root cellar."

The cooler day time hours and the gradually changing foliage colors and no humidity was Rascal's favorite time of year. They were almost ready for winter. Their food stores were in except for a deer or two. Trapping season would soon be here and Rascal laid out all his trapping gear and inspected them. The traps he boiled to remove human scent and oils. He had made a special lure mixing beaver castors and scent glands with bear fat.

When that was done he banked the cabin with spruce and fir boughs to insulate the cabin floors from winter wind and cold.

He didn't know if anyone else would be trapping or not, or even if anyone but him had the time. Three years had passed now since he last fall trapped. Even if there might be one or two others, he was sure they wouldn't be where he intended to run a line.

Partridge season opened and he wasn't long each day coming back with his limit. He bird-hunted mostly along the road behind his cabin. He and Emma were eating partridge morning and night until one day she said, "Enough, I've had enough partridge for a while, Rascal. Start canning some or give some to the Antonys."

Rascal was getting anxious to start trapping. He knew he could probably start a couple of days early and Jarvis would never know. *But what if while skinning an early caught animal, Jarvis stopped by for a visit and a cup of coffee.* Jarvis' reputation, at times, kept Rascal paranoid and legal. As legal as legal could be.

He had already laid out his line, along the deer trail where he snared the deer. Just so he wouldn't have to hunt for the trail he scarfed trees with his axe. He traveled north for a distance before turning southwest towards the lake and then back home. He figured this line was two or three miles.

The night before the season opened Rascal was besieged with disturbing dreams all night. First he began reliving that moment when he was on his stomach in the hospital and regaining consciousness, when he wondered if he had awakened in hell. He woke up and bolted upright. Drenched in sweat. Emma had been awakened too. "What's the matter, Rascal?"

"Bad dream. I was remembering the scare when I first regained consciousness in the hospital." He never told Emma about that morning or how scared he had been. Or anyone else.

He slept pitifully after that, seeing the animals in his traps, and in the last dream Jarvis had somehow gotten himself caught in one of Rascal's traps and was asking him for help. When he awoke from that he laid on his back refusing to even close his eyes. Eventually Emma woke up and got up dressed and started breakfast. While she was doing that, Rascal put more wood in the stove and then made himself lunch to take with him.

Rascal had packed his pack basket the day before. He put in his lunch and shouldered it and Emma came out with his rifle. "You'd better take this, Rascal, after two bear incidents. I won't take no for an answer." He grinned and took it. Emma was all bundled up in her winter coat.

Rascal set three traps for fisher, or pine martin, or red fox by the time he turned off the road on the snare trail. The deer remains he had left there were all gone. The head, hide and all bones. The work of a bear. He set another trap about a quarter of mile from there. Then he had an idea. This was an area that should be conducive to both fisher and martin. So he looked for a hollow log on the ground. There was one, however rotten, but it was what he wanted. He baited it and set the lure and trap and then with a spruce bough he brushed out the area. He really expected both traps to be full when he returned.

At noon after eating his lunch, he turned towards the lake which he guessed should be about a half mile away.

He set three more traps along that line and then he turned for home. Between there and home he set only two more.

He was home before Emma and he was exhausted. After cleaning up he lay down on the bed to relax and he was soon asleep. When Emma arrived home he was still asleep until she closed the door and he jumped up.

He hadn't realized before he lay down how tired he was. "I should sleep better tonight. Tomorrow I'll canoe up to the head of the lake and set up along Jack Brook for a ways and then cut through the woods to Ledge Swamp."

"Isn't that where the bear broke off from chasing you and Elmo?"

"Yes, but I don't believe he'll still be around."

"Mr. Hitchcock said their business is increasing and C&A has put another train on specifically for the run from Whiskey Jack to Beech Tree. Right now the harvesting crews are supplying adequate timber to the mills to provide for the increase in sales. And I think the Hitchcock Company will be giving all of the employees a Christmas bonus."

"That does sound encouraging. Have you heard anything from Jarvis?"

"No. What have you done now?" she asked.

"Oh, nothing. Just wondering, that's all."

* * *

The next morning started out foggy and cold, but Rascal loaded his canoe and started up the lake. The air was cool and the fog was wet. He had to keep wiping the moisture from his face.

He pulled his canoe ashore at his usual spot and started up along Jack Brook. He found an ideal spot to make an otter set and a little further upstream he found two more likely otter sets. Then he set two ground blinds and cut through the narrow stretch of woods to the tracks and he came out on the lower end of Ledge Swamp.

He set one trap for fox on the bank beside the track right of way. Then paralleled the edge of the swamp, staying back about seventy-five feet.

There were obvious game trails leading to the swamp. He had high hopes for this area. At the upper end of the swamp he found a small beaver colony. Probably only a pair of two year olds. But he found otter scat in one of the beaver trails and he went out in the shallow water and made an otter set.

He was five hours making the loop around the swamp and back to the tracks. He sat down on the bank over looking the tracks and ate lunch. When he had finished eating he crossed the tracks and he hiked down to Jack Brook. He was a little above where he had stopped setting traps, and since he had three traps left he set those, too, before hiking back to his canoe.

As he canoed down the lake he was feeling good about this line. He expected this line would probably outproduce his earlier line behind his cabin.

As he paddled he began to think in the past how he used to dispatch an animal caught in his trap and never felt comfortable with it. He took along a hard maple billy-stick with which he would hit the animal on top of the head. But sometimes he would have to hit it twice or even three times. Once when he thought a bobcat was dead, it had come back to life as he was resetting the trap and it ran off. He knew some trappers would use a .22 caliber handgun. It was quick and effective.

So he turned his canoe into the village wharf and went to see what Mr. Douglas had for .22s in his store.

"Hello, Rascal, can I help you find something?"

"Hello, Ethan, yes do you have any .22 caliber handguns?"

"Surely do. Came in last week. Over here in this case."

Ethan Douglas laid a new colt .22 six shot revolver on the cabinet top. Rascal handled it and liked how it fit his hand. "I'll take two boxes of .22 long rifle bullets and a box of .22 shorts."

As Ethan was getting the ammunition another handgun caught his eye. "What is this other revolver, Ethan?"

"That's a colt .45."

"Would that kill a bear?"

"Within fifty feet it would be deadly."

"I'd like to look at that also."

As Ethan was handing Rascal the .45 he said. "What is, that ole bear chasing you again?"

"It's a thought. How much for both handguns, two holsters, a box of .45 ammunition and three boxes of .22?"

Ethan did some figuring and said, "That comes to $149.00. You give me $145.00 and they're yours."

"Okay. I'll have to go withdraw some money."

Rascal returned fifteen minutes later with the money. He counted out $145.00 into Ethan's hand. "Thank you, Rascal."

As he was leaving Douglas' store he saw Emma. She chose to walk home as the wind was now blowing and it would be cold out on the water.

At home she asked about the two handguns and after Rascal explained she felt a little better about him trapping alone. "And I guess I can understand that it will be more humane to kill the trapped animal by shooting it in the head than having to hit it with a stick. But at that same time it's a lot of money."

"Yeah, it seems like it, but I bet I'll get enough with my first tend to pay for them."

As they were eating, Emma said, "Word is that Jarvis has been seen around the choppings near the farm."

"Well, as long as he stays over there."

That evening he sharpened his skinning knife. A small pocket knife. It was now as sharp as a razor.

The next morning he put the .22 on his belt and the .45 in his pack. "If I'm late tonight it'll be because I have had a lot of skinning to do."

"Be careful."

The morning air was cold and there was hoarfrost on the ground. He had a fox in his first two sets and a raccoon in the next. In the cedar thicket he picked up a fisher and one martin. The next two traps were untouched and when he came to his double set there was a bobcat in the hollow log set and another martin in the blind set.

So far the day was going pretty good. He took the time to skin these and he rolled the hides up and put them in his pack. He would put them on stretchers once he returned home.

By the end of the afternoon he had picked up two more martin and a white ermine. They weren't worth much, but he put it in his pack. Nine pieces of fur on his first tend wasn't bad. He was looking forward to his check the next day at Ledge Swamp. That night he didn't get to bed until almost midnight. But he had everything drying on stretchers.

"How is your leg, Rascal, with all of this hiking you're doing?" Emma asked.

"It didn't bother too much until I turned back toward the lake. Just standing on it seems to hurt more than walking. I mean pain is always there, but I have sort of gotten use to it. Come morning it feels okay again."

The next morning while Emma was preparing breakfast Rascal checked the thermometer on the porch. "20° this morning. I hope the lake doesn't freeze over for a couple of more weeks."

Then he filled both wood boxes and breakfast was ready.

There was ice in the mud puddles, but the lake was clear. There wasn't a wisp of wind and Rascal made good time to the head of the lake. He had two otter out of three otter sets along the brook. These were worth more than any other fur. In his two blind sets along the brook, he had a fisher and martin. This was starting out to be a good day.

The fox set on the bank had been tripped and then buried. This was strange that an animal after tripping the trap would bury it. The bait was still there so whatever it was wasn't after that. He reset and moved on. The next blind set was buried also. "What in hell is going on here?" He had never encountered this before. He reset and before moving on he replaced the .22 with the .45. Just in case. Every trap on that side of Ledge Swamp was buried in the same fashion. Even the two shallow otter sets, something had piled grass, mud and sticks on top of the traps. This might have been a beaver, but he didn't think so. He believed it to be the same animal that was burying everything else.

As he was wading through the shallows he saw a huge bear track in the mud. He momentarily froze. This s.o.b. was after him again. It had to be the same bear. Following his scent from trap to trap.

As he moved along he was more watchful and the .45 handgun held in both hands. He was making as little noise as possible, so he could hear if the bear came near. He was a long time getting around the swamp and back to the tracks and just like the other side these traps had all been buried also.

Rascal crossed the tracks towards Jack Brook. In those three traps he had a raccoon and two martins. He skinned what he had and headed back down the lake. Seven pieces of fur. He was sure it would have been closer to fifteen if that bear hadn't buried his traps.

He stopped to see Silvio before going home.

"Hello Rascal. Come in, Anita just took some cookies out of the oven and I just made a pot of coffee."

"Thank you, that would be good." Anita's cooking was

always good.

"You seem upset by something, Rascal."

"Silvio, when you were trapping did you ever have all your traps tripped and buried?"

"I caught another trapper stealing a red fox from one of my sets once, but nothing like what you're saying."

"I had set up along Jack Brook and around Ledge Swamp. Jack Brook produced seven pieces. But all, I mean all my sets around the swamp were tripped and buried. Even the watersets. Near there, I saw a fresh bear track."

"Isn't that where you said that bear that was chasing you and Elmo broke off and chased another bear?"

"Yeah."

"Seems to me it's the same bear. But it certainly is odd that he would follow your scent from trap to trap and only around the swamp and not along Jack Brook. I'm guessing the area around Ledge Swamp he is claiming as his territory. And I wonder if he remembered your scent, that's why he followed it to each of your sets around the swamp. If'n I were you, I think I'd give that bear the swamp and stay away from it. I don't know why, boy, but I'd say that he has it in for you. What did you do to him?"

"That's just it Silvio—nothing. Elmo and I didn't even see him until we were already on the handcar and ready to come back."

"There has to be something there. Maybe something you don't understand."

What Silvio had to say really didn't make him feel any better. Perhaps he'd use a little more caution from now on.

At the supper table that night he was telling Emma about the buried traps and how the bear must have been following his scent.

"Maybe the bear is afraid of you, Rascal. Sees you as a threat."

"But I have done nothing to that bear. I don't see how he could see me as a threat."

"Well maybe he saw you trapping all those beaver at mile

nine and understood what you were doing."

"Then that would mean he could think. Is that possible?"

"I don't know, Rascal, but something is going on with that bear. You be careful this fall, will you?"

"I'll be careful, Em."

Rascal tossed and turned all night. He was keeping Emma awake also. "Rascal, I can't get any sleep with you tossing and turning so."

"I don't know what's the matter. I'll go in the other room."

He sat up in the rocking chair for a while then he lay down on the sofa. Try as hard as he could, he could not stop thinking about that damn bear. He had decided that on his next tend up there he'd pull all the traps around Ledge Swamp and set up further upstream along Jack Brook.

Sometime after midnight he did fall asleep. But not for long. In his dream that bear had chased him up a tree and laughing at him with a human voice. He woke up drenched in sweat and he was too scared to even try going back to sleep.

When the sun came up Rascal was already up and stacking wood for both stoves. Emma got up shortly after. "My it's nice to wake up to a warm cabin. Did you sleep out here?"

He didn't want to worry her so he said, "After a while I got some sleep."

It was cold again this morning and Rascal wore a pair of gloves. He walked with Emma out to the road. "You be careful, Rascal."

"See you tonight."

His first trap was untouched and in the other two he had another red fox and another raccoon. In his first set in the cedar thicket he had a nice big lynx. It had been a few years since he had one. These were big money.

Across the top he picked up two more fisher and nothing more until he was at his last set where he picked up another raccoon.

He was home earlier than he thought and while the bodies

were still warm he skun them and put them on stretchers. He was glad now that before going in the army that winter he had made several stretchers, for something to do that winter, not knowing that sometime he'd be needing them.

He had supper ready when Emma opened the door, and much to her surprise.

"No bear?"

"Not today. Tomorrow I have to go back and pick up my traps around Ledge Swamp. And then I'll set further up Jack Brook."

He was so tired that he slept well until shortly after midnight, then the bear returned in his dream and again at the end of the dream the bear was standing on its back legs and laughing at him with a human voice. He bolted up in a sitting position and this awakened Emma.

"Your dream again?"

"Yes, I'll go lie down on the sofa so not to keep you awake."

* * *

Rascal didn't get much sleep for the rest of that night. But he felt more rested than the night before. And again the cabin was warm when Emma woke up with the smell of coffee and bacon.

"My, you should have these dreams more often. I enjoy waking up to a warm cabin and the smell of breakfast."

Today was not as cold and Emma rode in the canoe with Rascal to the wharf. "I'm glad to see you're taking your rifle too."

There was a little breeze, but not enough to slow him down.

After he had pulled his canoe ashore, shouldered his pack basket and with rifle—loaded, in hand, he stood there for a few moments as if trying to find the encouragement to start out. He had to will his legs to move. Again he had two otters in his first two sets and in the next otter set he actually had a mink. In the two ground blind sets he actually had another otter and another raccoon. At the last trap he stopped and skun those, so he would not have as much weight to carry as he picked up his traps.

After he had the hides rolled up and in his pack he hiked to the tracks and before crossing he just stood there, as if waiting for something. He could already see the fox set on the bank had been buried.

He stepped in between the rails and stopped again and looked around him before continuing on to the buried trap. He pulled it and put it in his pack and went on to the next and the next. And in all cases each one was buried except the two water sets. He pulled those two also.

As he rounded the end of the swamp he thought he heard something. He stopped and waited. Everything was quiet and he could not see anything. But there were two things that were bothering him. There were no birds and no squirrels. Squirrels were so numerous they were always scolding each other and anyone who hiked through the woods. This absence was creepy.

Eventually he continued on and stopping often to listen. Once he thought he had seen movement. But it was just a brief glimpse of something. But when he saw nothing he continued on. But at each trap set when he stopped he was positive that there was movement behind him. Whatever it was was stopping when he stopped. This continued all the way out to the tracks. As he was leaving the rail bed he heard something behind him and when he turned, the bear was on top of the bank watching him.

At first his heart seemed to stop and then it jumped up into his throat. He started to bring his rifle up to his shoulder and for some reason which he would never be able to understand, he lowered the rifle and stood looking at the bear who was staring back at him.

As much as this bear had tormented him, he did not understand why he was lowering his rifle. And oddly enough, he wasn't afraid. At least not as much as he had dreamed of being. The bear stood upon his hind legs. He stood really tall. The bear reached out with a front paw and made a sound that if not knowing where it was coming from, one might think it was laughter coming from deep in the woods.

For some reason that Rascal would never be able to explain he raised his arm, as if saluting the bear. The bear then got down on all four legs and wandered off. Rascal stood there watching until the bear was out of sight.

Rascal left and headed for Jack Brook. All while he was setting traps he kept thinking of the bear. And he could find no answer to explain what had happened. But there was one thing for sure, and that was he would not trespass again at Ledge Swamp, until winter.

He went a half mile up stream setting more traps. There were still three traps to check before he was back at his canoe. He had another otter and mink.

As he canoed back down the lake, he breathed a sigh of relief and he actually found himself relaxing.

He arrived home as Emma was walking in from the road. "Well how was your day, Rascal?"

"I'll tell you all about it after I have everything unloaded and cleaned up. In fact I think I'll put the fur on stretchers before I clean up. I'll be done by the time supper is ready. I didn't get that many pieces."

Emma was just putting supper on the table. As they ate Emma knew there was anxiety all around Rascal. Something out there today happened. And she knew enough to wait until he was ready to tell her.

When they had finished eating, Rascal said, "I could use a cup of coffee."

"It might keep you from going to sleep tonight."

"Not tonight." He waited until the coffee was ready. "I could really use a shot of whiskey in this." This really shocked Emma, but she didn't say anything.

He took a sip and then holding the cup between his hands, he told her the whole story. "That's a remarkable story, Rascal. If I didn't know you, I wouldn't have believed it."

"It happened just like I said."

"I believe you. And at the same time it is remarkable. What are your friends going to say?"

"I won't tell anyone, besides, you're right no one would believe it and I'd be made fun of."

* * *

Rascal checked his traps every day. One line or the other, and he was only getting a few pieces with each tend. Then one morning there was a think skim of ice on the lake and he knew it was time to pull his traps along Jack Brook.

This line was a good producer. He now had ten otter from this line and five mink and two more martin. On his other line he had picked up another bobcat, another fisher, three more ermine, and one more fox.

He had decided to pull both lines. He had done well and he wanted to leave some animals for seed.

When everything was dry and stretched he combed out the fur of each hide to make it look better and more valuable. He sorted each specie and for the season he had:

4 ermine
2 bobcats
5 fishers
52 raccoons
5 martin
4 foxes
10 otter
2 lynx
5 mink
17 summer beaver

He figured up what fur were selling for when he last trapped and decided he had at least $692.00 plus whatever the summer beaver would bring. That was almost as much as a mill worker would earn in a year. Plus he still had winter beaver trapping to come.

Emma was pleased when Rascal told her how much the fur were worth. "Can you get Friday off from work, so you can go with me to the fur buyer in Lac St. Jean? We would have to stay over Friday night and come back Saturday."

"I sure hope so. I have never been to Lac St. Jean. In the past I always had to look after Beckie and Jasper." Emma started crying then and Rascal hugged her trying to comfort her. She stopped crying as quick as she had started.

Rascal understood why.

* * *

Emma came home the next day and said, "Mr. Hitchcock said I could have Friday off, but I would have to come in on Sunday to catch up."

"I'll get all the furs bundled tomorrow so we can leave on the northbound the next day."

Emma was so excited about the trip to Lac St. Jean she could hardly contain herself. Even at work she was a chatterbox. At home she never stopped talking. "What shall I wear, Rascal? Are there any nice restaurants? What about a hotel?" She went on and on. And Rascal was chivalrous and he only grinned at Emma. He seldom had seen her so happy.

Thursday evening Emma laid out clean clothes for Rascal and herself. She knew Rascal would wear the same clothes the next day also, but she would take a change of clothes. They also took a tub bath. "I insist, Rascal, and let me trim your hair."

Emma was up early the next morning and she promptly roused Rascal. "Come on you, we have things to do today."

Rascal rolled out of bed and stood on a cold floor. "I'll be glad when we get enough snow to bank the cabin. These floors are so cold." He noticed she was writing something on paper. It looked like a list.

He built up the fire in both stoves. "You know the cabin will be cold when we get back."

"Can't be helped," she replied.

After an early breakfast they made sure all the containers were empty of water and the gravity fed faucet was open, just enough to keep the water from freezing. Emma carried a pack on her back and Rascal shouldered the bundle of furs.

He had to change shoulders twice on the way to the village . "Your leg giving you trouble?"

"The weight of the furs on that side made it ache. But I'll be okay."

They were a little early and they sat in the cafeteria drinking coffee when Elmo, Jeters and Silvio joined them.

"Haven't seen you around much, Rascal, since trapping. Thought maybe that bear had caught up with you." Rascal looked at Emma questioning if she had said anything. She shook her head no.

Silvio noticed the exchange and wondered what it was all about. "That's a nice bundle of fur, Rascal. I hear fur prices are better than last year."

"There are some out-of-state sports coming in next week to hunt deer. They'll be needing a guide probably, Rascal."

"Thanks, I'll check with them on Sunday." The train whistle just blew.

"Northbound at mile nine and half," Elmo said.

There were only a few passengers on board. "Would you like the window seat, Em?"

"Yes, that would be nice."

The train had to do a little switching to connect to the rail cars loaded with sawn lumber. The last car was connected and the engineer blew the whistle signaling it was leaving.

It was a cool day and the air was clear. "Point out Ledge Swamp, Rascal, and where you saw the bear."

It took a few minutes for the train to come up to speed, 25 mph. That was actually a lot considering it was on an uphill grade until mile twelve.

"There's mile eleven marker and that's Ledge Swamp."

"I'm disappointed. Can't really see much from here."

"No. The swamp actually sits behind this outcropping of ledge. That knoll right there is where the bear stood."

"Where were you?"

"I was on the other side of the tracks."

"If I didn't know you so well, Rascal, or watched as that bear chased you and Elmo up the tracks, I'd have to say that was some yarn."

"Just think how I feel, Em."

Chapter 5

The train ride to Lac St. Jean for Emma was exciting. She was seeing this wilderness country for the first time. "There's nothing out here, Rascal, but trees. It would be an awful place to be lost."

"That's right, Em. That's what makes this little corner of the world special. If a lost person was to go either to the north or south they would have a long hike before coming out any where. Not too many people come this far away from Whiskey Jack when they go hunting. Not even the locals."

Emma was quiet then, thinking about this wilderness and Rascal feeling so comfortable in it. The village at Whiskey Jack Lake was enough wilderness for her.

The train didn't even slow down when it crossed the border. There was nothing there except a concrete marker with a bronze plaque attached to it. Lac St. Jean was only a five minute ride from the crossing. The town was a little bigger than Beech Tree and for a Saturday morning it was a bustle of activity.

The few passengers who were already onboard also walked out of the car to the platform and were met by family or friends. "Where do we go from here?" Emma asked. The train was already pulling out from the station to switch to another set of tracks and uncouple the two cars with sawn lumber. Then the locomotive was directed to a turntable where four men pushed the engine around and in the opposite direction.

"We'll have to take a carriage across town." There was a carriage waiting outside the terminal building.

"Where you go, monsieur?"

"Marquis Furrier."

"Tres bien." Rascal loaded his fur and they climbed aboard.

Emma was enjoying the sights, but she could not understand any of the language. "Can you understand what people are saying, Rascal?"

"I only get a word here and there. Not enough to understand what they are talking about."

"Where did you learn French?"

"While I was in the hospital in France. I tried to learn some of the language."

At Marquis Furrier, Rascal paid the carriage driver and picked up his bundle and before Emma could open the door Monsieur Marquis opened it and said something in French. Emma asked, "Do you speak English?"

"Some. You come in. I look over you fur."

While Rascal and Marquis talked about furs and prices, Emma looked about the store. There was so many beautiful fur jackets and coats. All too expensive though.

"You take good care of fur, Mr. Rascal." Marquis began to laugh. "You have funny name. I like name." And he said it again. "R-a-s-c-a-l."

Marquis sorted them into species and ran his fingers through the fur of each pelt. "Nice fur, qui tres bien." Then with paper and pencil he began to do some figuring. When he was done he handed Rascal a list of prices for each species:

Ermine- 50 cents		the same as last year
Bobcat- $50		$20 more per fur
Fisher- $25		$5 more
Raccoon- $3		$1 more
Martin- $8		$3 more
Fox- $25		$10 more
Otter- $60		$20 more
Lynx- $250		$50 more
Beaver- Super large		$25
	Large	$20
	Small	$10

Marquis saw Rascal comparing his figures with his own. They were a little better across the board. "I give you $1811.00. Do you have the castor?"

"No, I used the castors for lure. That $1811.00 American money." Not a question and Marquis did not take it as a question.

"I can do that. Hate to, but I do that."

Marquis went into his office after the money. He was quite a while before he returned. He counted out the money and handed it to Rascal. "Thank you, Monsieur Marquis.

"Did you find anything you would like, Em?"

"Yes, the whole store. There is so many beautiful things here. But they are expensive."

"What would you like, Em?"

"I like this fur hat that pulls down over my ears. It would sure be nice on cold mornings walking to work. This one should fit you too."

He tried it on, "It does, I need a pair of boots also. How about you?"

"Can I get some fur-lined?"

"Sure, did you see a pair?"

"Yes over here," she was really excited.

"We both need long underwear," Emma said.

"Find a pair for me too."

Marquis was watching them shop and his eyes were like two cash registers.

They each got a pair of leather mittens.

If that is all, —come to $70.00."

Rascal gave him the money and asked, "Will you wrap those in a bundle please? Thank you, Monsieur Marquis."

From there they hailed down another carriage that took them to the St. Jean Hotel, downtown. There was even an elevator on the main floor. Neither Rascal nor Emma had ever used one and when it started to move Emma let out a shriek. Rascal grabbed the side railing. The hotel was five stories and they were on the fifth.

"Rascal! Come here."

"What is it, Em?"

"Look! Is this what I think it is? Our own bathroom. With a flush toilet and bathtub with running water. I've never heard of such a thing."

"The hospitals I was in had bathrooms and running water."

"I think I like this trip," Emma said and hugged Rascal.

"How much did you receive for your fur?"

"$1811.00"

"Holy-cow! I'd have to work three years to earn that much.

"I want to walk around and see the town and find some place where I can buy some cloth."

They walked around town first so they wouldn't have to carry packages with them.

They found a general mercantile store and Emma purchased bolts of cloth for making dresses, and shirts for Rascal, and curtains for the cabin. Rascal found some rugs and said, "I'm tired of stepping on a cold floor in the morning. How say you we buy a rug for each side of the bed?"

When they were through shopping, they and their packages almost filled the carriage.

Back at the hotel Emma said, "I'm getting hungry, Rascal. We were so busy walking around town we forgot to eat lunch."

There was a nice restaurant on the first floor of the hotel. "Have you ever eaten in a fancy restaurant like this, Rascal?"

"The only restaurant I have eaten in is in Beech Tree or the cafeteria. Whenever I came to Lac St. Jean before, I always returned the same day, however maybe late."

"What shall we have?"

"Anything you want, Em. Me, I'm going to have this seafood platter."

"Me too," she said excitedly.

The waiter took their order and Rascal said, "Would you bring us a bottle of white wine please."

"Rascal!"

"Now Em, there ain't nothing wrong with having wine with your supper. Heck the French in France have wine for breakfast instead of fruit juice. Even their kids drink wine. Hell, in the trenches, that's all we had to drink was wine. The water was usually so dirty you wouldn't wash your boots in it. We washed with wine, and when we were thirsty we drank wine. Have you ever had any, Em?"

"No."

"Then you should at least try some. It ain't like we're going to get drunk. It is just a good dinner beverage."

"All right, but only if you promise me you won't get drunk."

"I promise."

The waiter brought them a bottle of chardonnay. A very fine grape wine. He filled their dainty wine goblet and left the bottle and waited on new arrivals. Emma picked the goblet up. "Sip it, Em, don't drink it like water."

She took a sip and let the liquid slosh back and forth in her mouth before swallowing and took another sip. "I'm surprised this wine is actually good. No alcoholic taste at all." Rascal sipped his while thinking, Maybe she'll let me have wine at the cabin.

Before the waiter brought their meal Rascal had refilled each goblet. He was smiling as he watched Emma enjoy her drink. "What are you smiling about?"

"Oh, I'm just happy, that's all."

"I'm really enjoying this trip, Rascal. I'll have to come more often with you."

The waiter wheeled a cart over with their dishes, some with a candle flame under them to keep the food warm. The waiter served up dishes for each one and refilled their wine goblets. "Enjoy, mon ami."

"This all looks and smells so delicious." Haddock, shrimp, clams, scallops. Served on top of cooked seaweed. There was a side dish of rice and bread.

Rascal was hungry and didn't do much talking. Emma on the other hand kept up a rolling conversation in between bites.

"This is all so delicious," Emma said.

When they had finished eating they sipped wine. When Rascal poured the last of the bottle Emma said, "I would actually like another glass of wine."

"Well when we finish what we have if you still want more, I'll ask the waiter for another bottle."

"This is so good, Rascal, I can't taste the alcohol in it." Rascal knew she was beginning to feel the effects of the wine and questioned whether he should ask for another bottle.

"When their wine was gone, Emma said, "I feel like going for a walk before we go to bed."

Rascal was just as happy she didn't ask for another bottle of wine. Once outside, the air was cold and there was a slight breeze. "Maybe this wasn't such a good idea, Em."

"I'm cold already. Let's go up to our room."

Once in the privacy of their own room the effects of the wind were unwinding and dissolving all the frustrations and anger in Emma since the death of Beckie and Jasper. There had been very little emotion on her part whenever Rascal wanted to make love. She just took it without giving anything back to Rascal. Like she had no interest or need for sexual love.

Rascal had always been aware of this change with her since his return from the war. He always figured it was the effects of losing both Beckie and Jasper so close together. So he never complained. He simply remembered how she use to enjoy sex before he left.

She didn't even wait until Rascal had closed the blinds and turned the light off and she was already taking her clothes off and instead of folding them and putting them on the chair, she just let everything drop to the floor.

* * *

After an evening of fantastic love making Emma was now sound asleep in Rascal's arms. Before he drifted off to sleep he hoped when she awoke in the morning she would not have a hangover. She would never forgive him and he might once again have to sleep on the porch—in this cold weather.

Rascal awoke first. It was just beginning to get light outside. Emma was still sleeping. Somewhere in town a steam whistle blew and Emma woke up and looked at Rascal and smiled. "That was good last night."

"Yes, you are the best."

They packed up before going down for breakfast. "I'm thirsty this morning. Coffee or juice?" Rascal asked.

"Both. That fish last night must have made me dry."

Rascal drank a glass of water without saying anything so Emma would conclude that he also was thirsty.

"This coffee is certainly good—has a deep rich flavor and it smells so good," Rascal said.

As they were riding up the elevator to their floor, "I'm getting a headache. I wonder if this elevator rising so fast is causing it?" Emma said.

"Perhaps, or maybe you're coming down with a cold."

"Oh, I hope it is not a cold. I have to work tomorrow, remember."

"I'm sure it isn't anything." He was thinking to himself as they walked off the elevator, *If she ever finds out she has a hangover I'll be on the porch forever. But last night was worth a little risk.*

* * *

"Of the $1811.00 you started with how much is left? I think we splurged a little."

"Oh we still have $1500.00 left. Monday, why don't you put this in our account."

Rascal sat back with his head resting on the seat back. *Yes it had been a good weekend.* He wasn't feeling smug—only happy that Emma had let go, even if only for the weekend.

They arrived back in Whiskey Jack just as the sun was dropping below the horizon. "You know, Rascal, I really had a good time this weekend, but it's good to be back."

"We'll leave everything here and I'll go see if I can find a horse and wagon." As he was walking out of the station house he thought he had seen Jarvis disappearing towards the edge of town.

"What is he up to now?"

Chapter 6

The Hitchcock Farm had their own telegraph line to the mill office and on the other line, bypassed the village to Beech Tree, Jarvis had received a telegram from Earl Hitchcock at the farm, that some one was killing deer in the chopping and requested Jarvis' help.

Jarvis had planned to work around Beech Tree and close to home for a few days, but when he was given this telegram by special delivery, he decided he had better make new plans.

He put on warm clothes. A blanket in his pack along with some food and a thermos of coffee, flashlight and binoculars—said goodbye to his wife and boarded the train for Whiskey Jack.

He saw Rascal and Emma step onto the platform and he decided to get out of sight before Rascal or Emma noticed him.

The moon was just coming out and there would be enough light so he would not have to use his flashlight.

He walked parallel to the farm road, staying in the trees so in case someone might be out. When he reached the edge of the farm field he stopped. The telegram only said someone was killing deer, which he understood meant several. But the message did not say when or where. But the hunters were most likely workers. And that meant the deer were probably being shot in the choppings and not around the farm.

He had been on and around the farm many times in the past. All but two workers, those working in the woods had a dormitory style building where they ate and slept and the farm workers had their own quarters, and then there were two men who looked after the work horses and they had their quarters in the horse barn.

The illegal hunters had to be those two, since they were by themselves. Just then he heard a gunshot. But it didn't sound exactly like a rifle shot. He waited for another shot that never came. The second shot didn't come. "These guys are good."

He had a general idea where the shot had come from, a new set of choppings where the crews had all moved out. Staying in the shadows he worked his way around the edge of the field to the main road that went into the harvest area. It had taken him too much time to get where he wanted to be and he figured the culprits had already come back out with whatever they had killed.

He found a good place to wait and he pulled his wool blanket out of his pack and put it around his shoulders.

The lights were still on in the main farm house and both dormitory style buildings, but he couldn't tell about the horse stable. He stayed where he was until one by one the lights went out at the farm. And he still didn't know about the stables.

There was moonlight. Enough to walk in the choppings, but not enough to see what he needed to find. As much as he hated to wait for daylight, he knew there was no other alternative. At daylight, would be his best opportunity to search the choppings. For an hour after daylight the crews would all be busy eating breakfast and getting ready to go to work.

He did walk around enough to find where the crews were working and he followed another trail which brought him to a previous harvested area. The treetops were still fresh and green. If he was going to kill deer this is where he would look and not where the working crews might find something suspicious.

There was no more he could do now, so he found a good spot where he could hunker down, where he could still see the farm buildings, the road to the choppings and back away from the field enough so he couldn't be seen. He poured a cup of coffee and ate a sandwich and prepared to spend the night there.

Hours later as daylight was beginning to filter through the treetops he stood up, stretched and put his blanket back in the pack and shouldered it. There was now enough light to see what he couldn't have seen during the night. The first thing he saw was a drag trail which was not fresh; maybe four or five days old. But there were two sets of fresh men boot tracks coming and going. *Maybe the shot last night missed.*

It was quite obvious the two had used this path many times. This was going to be easier than he had first thought. He stopped walking and looked around him to make sure he wasn't being watched. The crews had done a nice job of cutting. There were still nice stands of younger softwood trees that would probably mature in ten or fifteen years. Just then he smiled and thought, *What a great life I have.*

Continuing on he could see gobs of deer hair that had pulled out of the deer as it was being dragged over small stumps.

The path left the main twitch trail and headed off to the right toward the newer choppings. After about seventy-five yards he came to a well-used deer trail. One that was obvious to any woods-wise person, that this trail was here before the forest was being lumbered. And the men's tracks disappeared also. Not wanting to make a lot of his own tracks, he stood there looking around for more signs of the two men.

He stayed to one side of the deer trail so he would not leave tracks. He found some broken branches which told him he was going in the right direction. But he then noticed broken branches on the other side of the deer trail also. He stopped and scratched his head.

As he was about to start following the deer trail again he saw something that he had been overlooking. Literally. Not more than three feet in front of him was a green fly line tied across the trail about two feet off the ground.

Before going any further he started looking the area over with a little more scrutiny. It was obvious the line had been tied across the trail for a reason. The line ran parallel to the deer trail through eyelets screwed in trees along the way. Then his heart stopped. Why hadn't he seen it before now? About eight feet behind the green line was a shotgun pointing down the trail and leveled about two feet off the ground. *A set gun.*

He side stepped the trail and line and now stood behind the gun. The hammer was cocked and the string was tied onto the trigger. Whatever came walking up the trail, deer, bear, moose or man, would be shot. He released the tension on the hammer and broke open the action. It was a .10 gauge parker shotgun loaded with .00 buckshot. That explained the broken branches.

The gun had obviously discharged the night before, but it didn't look as though anything had been hit. *Maybe a squirrel had hit the line or just enough wind to pull the line.*

Every time the shotgun was triggered, for whatever reason, the two would have to come out to see. That meant he would have to stay here and watch. Now he was wishing he had brought more food and a gallon of hot coffee. "And you wanted to be a game warden," he said aloud and then chuckled.

Even if the shotgun was tripped during the daylight the two probably wouldn't check until after darkness. He reset the trigger, being careful not to slip. Then he looked for a place to wait. *This is going to be like money in the bank.*

It wasn't long and he could hear the crews working. The yelling, hollering and cursing. The falling of tall spruce and pine trees. All these sounds were like music to his ears. Lumbering was a good life, except you were old by fifty.

He sat concealed in a thicket of small fir trees with his back against a tall straight cedar tree. All day he waited, occasionally dropping off to sleep for a quick catnap. He couldn't help it. He knew his face was dirty as was his uniform, he needed a shave and he could smell his own body odor. But he wouldn't trade his job for all the tea in China.

When the crews stopped for lunch everything was quiet. And instead of everyone going back to the farm for dinner, a wagon was brought out with hot food and coffee. Jarvis remained quiet, yet tense.

Since this area had already been lumbered he wasn't worried

that during noon break someone might be wandering around looking at what trees needed to be cut.

It was a long day sitting in one place without moving or stretching his legs and trying to stay awake and alert.

He was so hungry he'd eat a raw mushroom, but he didn't dare get up and look for one. There was nothing else to do but try to get some sleep. He was sure he'd wake if someone was about on foot or if a deer were to come along. The shot blast would wake him.

Again he managed to catnap most of the afternoon. At 4:30 or near to it, he heard the mill's steam whistle blow. He hoped this would signal the end of the day here also.

He could hear the crews leaving the woods now. They were tired and not as jubilant as in the morning. Eventually everything was quiet again. And now until dark which would be less than an hour, would be a typical time for the deer to move.

He looked in the direction of the set gun and saw a huge buck following the trail with its head held high. The deer would not see the fly line trip wire. Jarvis knew the two would come see even if the deer didn't die and he hated to waste a beautiful animal like this.

So he stood up and scared the deer off and when it was clear, he threw a dead branch on the trip line and the shotgun fired. He wondered how long it would be before the two men came down to check.

Then about the time it was completely dark he overheard two men talking and coming down the twitch road. It always happened when the excitement of waiting is about to burst; he had to pee. It never failed.

There was movement along the deer trail now and the men were no longer talking. He could see them plain now and it surprised him. They were both much older than he would have thought for doing something like this. Mid fifties, maybe. They both were tall, maybe six feet, and thin and wiry. Neither one had a gun, but they each held a knife in their hand.

"Dorcy, look at this. Another dead limb set off the trigger. We got to get us one more deer fore we go home and we ain't got but two shells, Dorcy."

"Alfie, we have us a lot of deer meat to go home now. I'm thinking we shouldn't press our luck too far," Dorcy said.

"You back out if you like; me, I want one more deer to can and go home," Alfie said.

Jarvis thought they both might be French, and that would be understandable being this close to the Quebec border.

"Alfie, I'll reset the gun, you try and knock down dead branches," Dorcy said.

"I not see so good, Dorcy. Maybe I got all limbs maybe not. You not cock that thing for me get out from front of it," Alfie said.

"Well, Alfie, you that scared, you come back here with me," Dorcy said.

Jarvis wanted to jump them before the gun was set. As soon as Alfie was standing beside Dorcy, Jarvis eased out of the thicket and walked down the deer trail. Their backs were towards him.

He was about ten feet behind them when he said, "That's an awful big gun, fellas."

Alfie who was resetting the shotgun screamed and hollered, "Jesus! Jesus! Where you come from?"

Dorcy looked like he wanted to fight, but when he saw Jarvis' set jaw muscles and his colt .45, he settled down.

"I am a game warden and you two are under arrest for using an illegal set gun. And more charges maybe coming after I look through the stables. Now, Alfie, you untie that shotgun, unload it and hand me that cartridge and the one in your pocket. Then lay the shotgun on the ground. Coil the fly line up."

"Okay, hand me the shotgun, Alfie. Now we walk out of here back to the farm. Are you two going to give me any trouble?"

No answer. "Alfie, are you going to give me any trouble?"

"No."

"Dorcy, how about you?"

"No."

"Good, because if you do I'll hurt you. Now move it. You two in front."

Much to Jarvis' surprise Alfie and Dorcy were not trying to delay the hike back to the farm. Instead they were walking right along.

"Where are you from?"

"Lac St. Jean," Dorcy said.

"I heard you say earlier you were going to take the meat home. So I understand you must have found a way to can it without Mr. Hitchcock finding out what you were doing. So how much do you have canned already to take home?"

"You find out for yourself," Alfie said.

That was the end of the pleasant conversation.

Jarvis marched them right up to the main house and when he saw one of the workers he said, "Hey you, would you tell Mr. Hitchcock that there is a game warden out here who needs to speak with him."

"Certainly sir," and the young fella ran into the house.

Mr. Hitchcock came out immediately and turned on an outside light. "Hello, Jarvis." Then he recognized Alfie and Dorcy. "What goes on, Jarvis?"

"Alfie and Dorcy are under arrest for illegally using a set gun to kill deer. And these two have been canning the meat and taking it home to Lac St. Jean. And at this moment there is a lot of it now in the stables. With your permission Mr. Hitchcock I would like to search it—without your permission I cannot search."

"Certainly, Jarvis."

Alfie and Dorcy were not looking too happy right about now. Mr. Hitchcock opened the stable doors and went directly to their quarters. A copper canner was on the floor behind the cook stove and in one bedroom were four wooden boxes containing sealed mason canning jars.

"How long have you two been doing this?" Mr. Hitchcock asked.

Alfie looked at the floor and said, "Long time. We have big family and deer help to feed them."

"What are your last names?" Jarvis asked.

"Alfie Gervais."

Jarvis looked at Dorcy and he said, "Dorcy Grispin."

"Well Mr. Gervais and Mr. Grispin the more serious law is the set gun. Do you two have any idea how dangerous that was. Anything walking along that trail, be it animal or man, would have been killed. I'm also charging you two with illegal possession of deer. And I'm confiscating the shotgun and the canned meat and I'm taking you both out of here to jail."

"Mr. Hitchcock, would it be asking too much if we sleep in the stables tonight and have someone take us by wagon to the station in the morning along with the canned meat. If you'd like I'll leave half of the deer meat here for you and I know some folks who can't afford to buy meat."

"Certainly, Jarvis."

"Now I want to lock these two in here, and Mr. Hitchcock, I haven't eaten since yesterday and I'd gladly pay you for a meal."

"Certainly, Jarvis, but you won't have to worry about paying for it. I appreciate what you did here. I had no idea this sort of thing was going on here."

Alfie and Dorcy were locked up in their own quarters (or what had been), and Jarvis followed Mr. Hitchcock into the house where Mrs. Hitchcock gave him a bowl of beef stew and a biscuit.

"How long have you been here Jarvis?" Mr. Hitchcock asked.

"I've been here for about thirty hours now."

"And you were out in the woods all this time?" Mrs. Hitchcock asked. She found it difficult to understand spending that much time alone in the cold and in the woods. And all to catch poachers. She walked off shaking her head.

"What will you do with them now, Jarvis?"

"If you'll supply a driver and wagon in the morning, I'll take them to the county jail in Beech Tree."

"Will they get any jail time?" Hitchcock asked.

"I wouldn't be surprised. Using a set gun is a serious offense. And if they can't pay the fine the judge will undoubtedly sentence them to several days in jail. I'm also going to charge them with illegal possession of deer meat.

"What will you do, Mr. Hitchcock?"

"I agree with you using that damn shotgun for a set gun and using .00 buckshot is serious and I won't stand for that kind of nonsense on the farm or in the woods. When and if they come back for their belongings I'll tell 'em they are fired.

Jarvis slept in the stable that night so he could keep an eye on the two. Even though they were locked in, he didn't trust them. So he slept on a bed of hay, waking often during the night.

Alfie and Dorcy made their own breakfast as they did every morning and Jarvis ate with Mr. Hitchcock and family.

"I have a driver for you, Jarvis. Whenever you're ready."

"I'd like to leave right away."

"Jarvis, there's one question I have to ask. When I first saw you with the two, your gun was holstered. Did you use it to make the arrest—I mean considering the seriousness of the offense. Say nothing that you were alone in the woods at night."

"I thought about it, Mr. Hitchcock, but I thought a drawn gun might aggravate the situation even more. When their back was turned toward me, I quietly walked up behind them. When I spoke, it sort of took the fight out of them. Them thinking they were alone."

"And people say lumbering is a dangerous job."

Butch Avery brought the wagon around and helped Jarvis load the canned meat. Jarvis also laid the shotgun in the wagon and put the green fly line in his pack. Then he took out two sets of handcuffs and went into their quarters and handcuffed them in front.

Alfie and Dorcy only had a cup of coffee for breakfast. They didn't feel too much like eating. And they weren't very talkative all the way to the station house. By now everyone was up and watched as the two climbed out of the wagon in handcuffs.

Rascal was just walking towards the cafeteria and met the three on the platform. "Good morning, Jarvis."

Jarvis only nodded his head. He was still tired. The southbound from Lac St. Jean was already at Whiskey Jack on a side track waiting for the northbound to clear.

Rascal sat with his friends and not paying too much attention to what was being said at his table. He saw the condition of Jarvis' clothes, his bearded stubble face, his unkempt uniform and the drawn lines in his face. He had two men in handcuffs. That could only mean they had committed not just a dastardly deed, but something more serious and Jarvis was not taking any unnecessary chances.

He would have liked to ask him what was going on, but that morning Jarvis looked all concern and seriousness.

Silvio asked, "I wonder what those two yahoos did—for Jarvis to have them in handcuffs?"

"Must have been pretty damn serious," Jeters said.

"Jarvis is looking like an old man this morning," Jeff Daniels said. "Maybe he should retire."

"That old man, Jeff, has more piss and vinegar in his system than any of us at this table. Don't ever underestimate that old man," Silvio said.

"I'd take Silvio's advice, Jeff," Rascal added. "At his age any man in this village would make a terrible mistake if he should think he could ever get the last of Jarvis Page."

Just then the train blew its whistle signaling it was approaching Whiskey Jack.

Jarvis kept Alfie and Dorcy on the platform and out of the way until all the passengers had stepped off the train and the platform. Jarvis noticed some of the passengers were sports looking to shoot a nice buck.

After the passengers had disembarked, the northbound continued on to Lac St. Jean and the southbound switched tracks and pulled up to the station house platform.

Rascal had left the cafeteria when the wagon driver, Butch, yelled to him, "Hey, Rascal, can you give me a hand with this stuff? I need to get back to the farm PDQ."

"Sure, where's it going?"

"Jarvis said to put it in the baggage car."

"This have anything to do with those two in handcuffs?"

"Sure does. There's jars of canned deer meat in these mason jars."

They loaded the crates in the car and Rascal went back for the rest of the stuff.

"If you can get it with one trip, Rascal, I'll leave. Thanks," Butch said.

Rascal didn't know if Jarvis wanted this in the baggage car or not, so he went on board the passenger car and asked, "Jarvis, where do you want this shotgun and pack and stuff?"

"You can put that stuff here in this seat."

It was obvious Jarvis wasn't in a talking mood so Rascal left. He had also seen the sport hunters get off the train and he went to talk with Elly Douglas at the hotel. "Hello, Rascal, what can I do for you this morning?"

"I was wondering if any of your guests will be needing a guide this week."

"In fact two from Boston have already asked and I took the liberty of telling them you probably would. You can go up and introduce yourself, second floor, room 202.

"Thanks Elly." Rascal climbed the stairs and knocked on the door. Ben Humphrey and Jack Merrill were all too eager to hire Rascal. "What do you get for wages, Rascal?"

"I get $50.00 a week per man. This includes a hot lunch that I bring with me. Now I want to make one thing clear, this is not a guaranteed hunt. I'll take you where I know there'll be deer."

"That sounds fine."

"That's $50.00 up front." Humphrey and Merrill didn't argue and they gave Rascal his fee.

"Okay, you'll probably eat breakfast in the cafeteria so I'll meet you there at 6:30 a.m. sharp."

"How will you guide both of us at the same time Rascal?" Merrill asked.

"In the morning I'll put one of you on stand and the other one will go on foot with me. Then after lunch you trade off. Have either of you been to Whiskey Jack before?"

"No."

"Have either of you ever hunted in the big woods before?"

"We have mostly hunted around farm land. This will be a new experience," Humphrey said.

"Then you'll want to follow my instructions exactly or you could get lost. There's a lot of woods around here. If nothing else, I'll see you at 6:30."

Rascal walked home and put together his pack for tomorrow. He made a large venison stew to take and enough for he and Emma for two days. He wrapped a loaf of bread and some sharp cheese, and a pot for tea. He put in a drag rope and a small lantern.

When Emma got home from work (early) he told her all about the two Jarvis had in handcuffs and the guiding job for the week.

"You'd better be careful, Rascal, or Jarvis will have you in handcuffs sometime."

With fall trapping behind him now he could concentrate more on his guiding. He would wait for the last week before getting his deer, so the warm air wouldn't spoil it. He had no doubts that most of the deer shot by sports spoil even before they got home.

Before going to sleep that night Emma said, "You know, Rascal, I really enjoyed the trip with you to Lac St. Jean. And you know, also, I liked the wine—it made me feel all good inside."

"Well, you'll have to go with me when I'm through beaver trapping."

* * *

Rascal was up before Emma and long before daylight. He put more wood in the heater stove and started a fire in the cook stove and put on a pot of coffee to boil. When Emma woke up the cabin was warm with the delicious aroma of perked coffee.

Rascal was making oatmeal with raisins and thick slices of bread warmed up on the stove top.

"There is enough stew for us tonight and to take with me tomorrow. Would you make a pot of beans to take with me on Wednesday?"

"I'll bake some more bread, too."

At exactly 6:30 that morning Rascal walked into the cafeteria and the two sports were ready to go. Rascal had his pack basket on and carrying his .38-55 rifle.

They walked across the mill yard to a woods trail that went up through a five year old cut. The end of the road stopped about a half mile from the current harvesting at the farm.

Rascal took out his compass and checked the direction of the road. "This road is in about a southwest direction. So remember that. To the south or our left is a wide brook that flows into Jack Brook below the village. You will pretty much be surrounded by roads, brooks and the farm, so if you do get turned around."

There was a slight incline and after a half mile the landscape leveled off and this was an uncut area. There was a wide swath of softwood and cedar trees and enclosed on both sides by hardwood.

In a low voice Rascal said, "I'll leave my pack here and we'll eat lunch here later. Who wants to sit this morning?"

Ben Humphrey said he would. "Jack, you stay here while I take Ben to a stand."

Once they left the road there was a clear game trail running through the softwood swath and parallel with the hardwood ridges. "This is what I wanted to find."

Rascal looked around and found a nice spot for Ben to sit under a spruce tree about thirty feet off the game trail. "You stay here under this spruce tree. I'll take Jack and head west and then hit this trail and maybe push a deer onto you. If you get one wait five minutes and then fire two rapid shots and I'll come right here. Do not leave this spot. Remember what I said about this being a big country."

Rascal went back for Jack and followed the line that the hardwood growth made, next to the wetter swath. They followed this line of trees for another half mile.

Rascal checked his compass again. "Okay, from here we still hunt through to the road we walked in on.

Rascal started out straight across the swath until he came to the same game trail. "I thought we'd find this again. You stay on this game trail and I'll be on your left. You'll be able to see me always. Don't get ahead of me. If you see something whistle. And I'll do the same. Remember, hunt your way along and not walk like you would down a sidewalk."

Rascal had hunted here once before. And although he didn't shoot anything he did see deer. There were no dry leaves to crackle under foot. The ground was carpeted with moss and spruce needles. This was a perfect place for deer. *Be good for trapping next year too,* Rascal was thinking.

They had only been on the hunt for a quarter of an hour and Rascal heard a deer blow, an alarm for other deer and hooves pounding on ground sounds. Jack whistled and motioned for Rascal to come over.

Jack was all excited. "I just saw two deer run off."

"Bucks or does?"

"Not sure. They were on this trail and I didn't see them until that one blew. When I looked up they were running off."

"Well now we know there are deer here." They resumed hunting and now Jack was watching more out ahead of him and not his feet.

Not long afterwards Rascal saw an eight point buck. The buck lifted his head and when it saw him, the buck ran to Rascal's right and across Jack's path, except Jack didn't see it. He never knew an eight point was so close until later.

That morning hunt went pretty good. Jack had seen two deer and Rascal, the eight point buck. Ben had heard something running but never saw what it was.

Rascal made a small fire in the middle of the road and put the kettle of stew on to warm up. He got water from a little trickle of water off to the side. "Is that water okay to drink?" Ben asked.

"Sure," and Rascal made tea.

When the venison stew was bubbling, Rascal removed three bowls and spoons from his pack and the bread. Instead of slicing the bread he tore off portions and gave them to Ben and Jack.

"This is good beef stew, Rascal," Jack said.

"It ain't beef. Venison." He better not say deer, that might require more explaining then he wanted. "The game warden gave me some moose meat that the train had hit."

"It sure is good."

"So is this bread," Ben added.

"Jack, not long after you saw those two deer, I saw an eight point buck that ran across the trail you were following. I'm surprised you didn't see it."

"I thought I heard something, but I didn't see anything."

"Well, we know there are deer in here," Rascal said.

While they ate lunch a slight breeze started to blow. It seemed to be following the low land between the two hardwood knolls. "That lunch was delicious, Rascal," Jack said. "Where will you have me stationed this afternoon?"

"Well, the wind is coming down this softwood valley and deer will be going into the breeze. We're going to do something a little different this afternoon. Jack, find a good spot around here where you can see up this road. That deer trail we were on crosses about one hundred feet from here. Ben and I will do the same as we did this morning, except on the other side here. If there are deer in here, and I think there will be, they'll go into the wind and probably cross this road, so be ready. The same thing goes if you kill or wound a deer. Don't go running off after a wounded deer though. Wait for Ben and me. We'll be back here before it is dark."

Rascal took Ben and followed the hardwood tree line about a half mile, like he had done with Jack. The deer trail was still running down the middle of the softwood vale. "Okay, Ben, you stay on this trail and I'll stay to your left. I'll keep you in sight at all times so don't worry about looking for me. Hunt slow and watch out ahead of you."

A thin layer of clouds were moving in the breeze. Rascal looked up at the clouds. This was his kind of hunting weather. He had never had too much success hunting when the sun was out bright. And this was beginning to give him the hunting fever. But he would wait for the cold weather at the end of the season.

On this side of the road Rascal was finding more deer trails and he found where a buck had rubbed its antlers on a cedar tree. He whistled and Ben stopped and looked. Rascal motioned for him to come over. "This rub was done probably while we were eating lunch. Look how he tore the ground up around the tree. He isn't far off now and he won't be able to scent us." Ben nodded his head and went back on the deer trail.

Even Rascal was getting excited now. He was wanting a meal of steak so much he could almost taste the gravy. There was something in the air. He stopped and sniffed again. It was unmistakable. It was the smell of a buck deer. The mixture of its scent glands on the inside of its knees and the smell of urine. When a buck is in rut, it'll paw at the ground and pee in it and lay down and rub his body in it for an extra lure for does. He wanted to tell Ben he could smell a buck that had to be close, but he didn't want any talking right now, no sounds or movement. Ben happened to look over at Rascal and he tried to signal Ben to slow down and pointed out front. Ben seemed to understand.

Ten minutes later Rascal saw the hind quarters and the rack about fifty feet ahead of him move to the right. He stopped so not to spook the buck. He saw Ben raise his rifle to his shoulder and it seemed to take forever before Ben fired. Rascal watched and saw him squeezing the trigger. The report was deafening even for a .30-30.

Ben had dropped his rifle to his side so Rascal assumed the deer had not run off. He looked at Rascal smiling. That was Rascal's cue. He walked over to Ben and there about a hundred feet down the trail lay the buck.

Rascal motioned for Ben to go forward. "Be ready to shoot if he should get up," he whispered.

Ben nodded his head.

But there was no need. Rascal could tell the deer was dead from thirty feet away. Ben rushed up and then checked out its antlers, "Six points, but look at that body."

"Where did you hit it, Ben?"

"In the throat."

"Nice shooting. I think we'd better drag it over to the hardwoods before we dress it."

"Why not right here, Rascal?"

"Too much smell of death will make the other deer in this piece real spooky. It isn't far."

But dragging a big buck without first field dressing—well, they both worked up a sweat. "That deer must weight three hundred pounds."

"Dressed, it'll go close to two hundred."

When they reached the definite line of hardwood trees and a gentle sloping of land they had to sit a spell and rest. "Have you ever dressed a deer before, Ben?"

"No. This is the first deer I have ever shot."

"Well, congratulations. It is a nice deer. We'd better get the innards out Ben. You hold the front legs so it'll lay on its back."

Ben watched with real fascination as Rascal went to work. Each cut he made was as neat as any surgeon's. "One thing you have to be careful of is not to cut the urinary track and plumbing. The urine can taint the meat. When I slit the belly hide I'll avoid the pecker. Then I'll cut it away from the sinewy flesh and pull the whole thing out intact."

Rascal was as good with his knife as any surgeon Ben thought. Every cut was clean. He cut away the sinewy tissue from the body and innards and then pulled everything out. There wasn't a drop of blood on his hands. But when he cut through the diaphragm blood gushed into the open cavity.

"Okay Ben, help me pick the deer up by the front legs so the blood will drain out. All that's left inside now is the heart, liver and lungs and we won't take those out until after we weigh the deer and hang it up."

Just then there was a rifle shot in Jack's direction. "That was Jack." They waited for the two signal shots that didn't come.

"Hum, he must have missed," Ben said.

Rascal was uncertain what to do. Had Jack wounded a deer and is now following it? Was it a clear miss? He would wait. He decided Jack was responsible enough not to go chasing after it. But, then he and Ben should get to Jack. Just in case.

"We should leave now Ben, in case Jack did wound it."

"Okay, let's go."

They were a little more than an hour dragging the deer out. They stopped a hundred feet from the road. "I'll go out and see what's going on."

There was nothing in the road and Jack was right where he should be. Rascal was a couple of hundred feet away and he didn't want to holler to him. Jack did see him and Rascal shrugged his shoulders and Jack gave a maybe sign. He stood up and started walking up the road. "Did you hit anything?" Rascal asked.

"I'm not sure; he kept running. I don't know if he fell over once he was off the road or not."

"Was the buck's trail up or down?" Rascal asked.

"Up I think."

"If it was up, you didn't hit it. If it was down you hit the buck."

"I'm sure it was up," Jack said.

"Where did he cross?"

"It looked like he crossed right by the deer trail."

"Was he in a hurry?"

"No, in fact when I fired he was standing in the middle of the road."

"Okay, I'll follow his tracks to see if he is bleeding. You go down and help Ben drag his deer up where we had lunch. He's only a hundred feet off the road."

Rascal didn't find anything that looked as if the deer had fallen and there was no blood. He followed his tracks for a quarter of a mile before he stopped and went back.

"I didn't find any blood at all. I think it was a clean miss. There isn't much daylight now, so we'll head back." Rascal put his rifle in his pack and carried Ben's and Jack's rifle." If one of you get tired I'll spell you."

"How big was the deer, Jack?" Ben asked.

"It was a big deer with a lot of points. I don't know how many," Jack said.

With the cloud cover, it didn't take long for darkness.

A bobcat yowled off to the left. "What was that?" Jack asked. He seemed a little nervous.

"Bobcat. He won't bother us." But they both picked up the pace and Rascal didn't have to drag at all.

They weighed the deer at the tagging station, at Douglas' store and it weighed 195 pounds.

"That's a nice deer, Jack. You should be proud, being your first deer and all."

They then hung it on a game pole near the hotel, and Rascal went home.

He thought he would be more tired than he was; after all, he had been at it for fifteen hours. He had already formed an opinion of Jack and Ben.

"Ben seems to be a good hunter, but Jack seems a little nervous. He shot at a standing broadside big buck at a hundred feet and missed. Actually I think he was sleeping when the buck came into the road."

"Well, you have five more days with him," Emma said.

"You know, guiding is more work than I remember."

"You getting soft?" Emma asked jokingly.

"Go to sleep, Em."

* * *

At breakfast the next morning, Ben asked, "Is there any animal I can hunt? I mean I have the rest of the week."

"Only bear and most of them probably have hibernated for the winter already. You can go out and sit, maybe a bear might still be out. There isn't any point of you tagging along with me on a stand."

"Well, maybe I'll come along and after lunch I'll come back."

Rascal and Jack started hunting in the same place, "Ben, no fires until noon. The smell of smoke now will alert the deer."

"Not a problem. I'll just hang out here."

There was no breeze yet and Rascal took Jack to the same spot as the day before. "Okay Jack, we know the deer are using this trail so stay alert. Same as yesterday."

The air was colder and in some places the frost on top of the moss was crunchy. But by 10am the sun was out bright and the frost had melted.

At exactly noon Rascal and Jack stepped onto the road. Ben had just started a fire and had gotten water for tea. He was enjoying this wilderness adventure. And like he said, after lunch he walked back to the hotel.

Every day for the remainder of that week Rascal and Jack saw deer, some were small. But they both had seen two huge bucks with massive antlers. Jack had fired at one of those large deer, and one other on another day and had not hit either one.

In frustration on Saturday morning before they were in the woods, Rascal tried out Jack's rifle. At twenty-five yards it was an almost bullseye shot. "There's nothing wrong with your sights, Jack, I think you may be looking at the deer and pointing your rifle and not taking aim. It's a common occurrence."

Ben had stopped going on the morning hunt with them. He spent his time walking around the village and one day he walked out to the farm.

"Rascal, there are so many nice deer here. And I don't want to go home empty handed. I'll pay you $50.00 if you shoot me a buck."

"Are you sure, Jack?"

"Yes. I'm that desperate."

"Okay, you stay on the road, just in case I kick one out."

Rascal checked the air and no breeze yet. Every other morning he and Jack had hunted the right side first. This morning he would hunt left. And like before he walked the line between the softwoods and the hardwoods. Except this morning he went a little further. And in so doing, he found where the deer trail left the softwood vale and went through the hardwoods. Probably to the choppings at the farm. He would remember this if he has a chance to guide more sports. As much as he wanted to sit and watch the deer trail as it crossed into the hardwoods, he still had a hunter on the road. So he started hunting along the trail back towards the road, slowly. He had the ability to cruise through the woods as quiet as any deer. And he was always looking around him for something moving or a horizontal line. In the woods most everything was vertical.

He hadn't been on the trail long when he came to a fresh pile of deer droppings. These were so fresh, when he picked up a few they were still warm to the touch. He stood still and sniffed the air. He could smell deer, but the scent was too faint to be close. But there is no breeze, so the deer could still be close.

He was taking a few steps at a time, now and then stopping to listen and look around. He thought he had seen movement up ahead. But it had stopped or it was gone.

He took a few more steps and then he saw it. A doe had lifted her head up high and was sniffing the air. Perhaps she smells a buck. Either way, she was not aware of Rascal. She moved on, staying on the trail. He gave her some distance. Thinking a buck would pick up her scent and come in behind her.

He heard a low buck grunt off to the right. The doe stayed where she was and lifted her head again. She knew a buck was close. She was playing hard to get and started moving forward and switching her tail and fanning her scent for the buck.

Rascal waited where he was. Waiting for the buck to make his move. Just as he thought he might have stayed too long waiting for the buck to show, he saw movement at about his one o'clock. At first all he could see were antlers. They were huge and the buck stopped. Sniffing the air. There was a cedar tree beside him and Rascal slowly brought his rifle up and steadied it against the tree. He sighted in just behind the head and squeezed the trigger. The buck went down hard and fast and he knew it was dead.

Now he had to go get Jack. Jack heard the shot and only the one shot. He was almost as excited as Rascal was.

Rascal walked right along the deer trail, not wasting any time. Jack was standing on the road watching down the trail when he saw Rascal coming.

"Well, well did you kill me a buck?"

"Yeah, he's down. Now I'll take that $50.00 before you forget."

Jack gave it to him gladly.

When they were back where the buck lay, "Holy cow, Rascal, I have never seen such a big deer and look at all those points. How many?"

"Fourteen," Rascal answered. And like Ben's deer they dragged it off the deer trail to the edge of the hardwoods before dressing it.

By the time they were back on the road Jack said, "This buck drags harder than Ben's."

"Yeah, he's more than two hundred."

"You think so?"

"Well, you've been dragging him for a half hour, what do you say?"

147

They dragged him down where they made a fire and had lunch of baked beans. "You want something good to go with those beans, Jack?"

"What do you suggest?"

"We take the heart out and roast it over the fire."

"I have never eaten heart before. What the hell, let's do it."

Rascal removed the heart from the chest cavity and washed it off in the water and then he sliced it. "Get us two small branches or saplings we can use to roast the meat." While he was doing that Rascal put the pot of beans on the fire to warm up.

As Jack was finishing his beans and heart and mopping up the juice with his last biscuit he said, "I would never have thought heart, deer heart, would taste so good. You are an ingenious person, Rascal."

"It comes with living in the wilderness."

"I think you are fortunate, Rascal, to live where you so honestly enjoy it, but I don't know if I would ever be content to live out here permanently."

"I've been to the city, Jack, and I was never comfortable."

"I guess I can understand that. Hey listen, Rascal. Do me a favor and not say anything about me not shooting this deer."

"You can count on it Jack. It is against the law to shoot someone else's deer and get paid for it. So you can be guaranteed I'll not say anything."

They were at the Douglas store about 4 p.m. The deer weighed 230 pounds. "What a beautiful deer," Ben said.

"We're leaving on the morning train, Rascal," Jack said, "and here's an extra $25.00 for a tip."

Ben gave him a tip of $25.00 also.

"Thank you and have a nice trip back."

"We both want to thank you, Rascal. This has been a splendid hunting trip."

Rascal gave his tip money, $50.00 to Emma to deposit in their account and kept the $50.00 for shooting Jack's deer. He didn't want to tell her what he had done.

* * *

The next afternoon came in cloudy and with it the cold dark clouds, moving in from the west. "It's gonna snow tonight boys," Silvio said as he and the others sipped coffee.

"Where did you hear that, Silvio?" Jeters asked.

"I didn't. Just look at the sky—those dark clouds gathering. Besides, me feet tells me it'll storm."

"What's your feet got to do with it?"

"Me feet gets to aching something terrible just before a storm. Mark my words."

Rascal was about to leave when two obvious sports stepped into the cafeteria. One of them announced, "We're looking for someone named Rascal Ambrose."

Rascal stood and said, "That'll be me."

"We're looking to hire a guide and Elly Douglas at the hotel said you are the best and the only guide in this quaint little village."

"I guide and I get $50.00 a week each, and paid up front."

"You're hired and here's $100.00. My name is Howard Baker and this is my friend Antonio Romeo."

"Hello, Howard and Tony; I'm Rascal Ambrose."

"It isn't Tony. I dislike being called Tony. It's Antonio." Rascal nodded his head.

"You fellas will probably have breakfast here in the morning. I'll be here at 6:30 a.m. sharp. I'll bring lunch with me. We may get some snow tonight so dress accordingly."

Rascal went home and Emma asked, "I thought you were coming right back?"

"I was, but I ran into two New Yorkers who want me to guide them this week."

"Are you going to?" Rascal laid the $100.00 on the table.

"I'll take the same stew and beans and biscuits as last week."

It did snow during the night. Two inches. It would be excellent for tracking deer. There was more wind than Rascal would have liked, but he'd make do and maybe he could use it to his benefit.

When Rascal met up with Howard and Antonio they both were dressed in new and expensive outerwear. It was clear to everyone they were sports.

Rascal went out the same road as the week before and hunted both sides as he had the week before. There were deer tracks in the fresh snow everywhere, once they were in the woods. This was looking real encouraging to Rascal. It soon became evident to Rascal that these two had little interest in hunting. When they talked, deer would be able to hear them for a great distance and even though there was snow on the ground they were anything but quiet.

As they were eating lunch, Howard said, "I'll be honest with you, Rascal, neither Antonio or I have much interest in killing a deer. So what would you charge to kill one for each of us?"

"$50.00 and paid up front." Howard and Antonio both handed Rascal a fifty dollar bill.

"So, am I to understand you would rather go back to the hotel?"

"Yeah. You shoot us a deer and we'll come out to claim it and help drag it back."

"Okay, you're free to leave, but don't go broadcasting that I'm hunting for you. The game warden may get word of it and then all three of us will be in court."

Howard and Antonio left—and Rascal, after putting out the fire. Then he started following the deer trail to the right. The snow had all melted now. He wanted to see where it went more than shooting a deer. He wasn't long before he had traveled beyond the point where he had started hunting back towards the road. The deer trail seemed to be skirting the hardwood knoll. And there were no trails here going into the hardwoods.

He wasn't long before he crossed the farm road and the deer trail kept going. It was not going in the direction of Ledge Swamp. There were still a lot of deer signs but he stopped and headed back. He was as close to Ledge Swamp as he wanted to be. Until he crossed the farm road, he kept looking behind him.

No more than fifty feet off the farm road was a six point buck with his nose to the ground walking towards him. Rascal whistled and the deer lifted his head and Rascal shot it in the throat. The deer fell to the ground and after a couple of death kicks it lay still.

There was still some daylight left, and Rascal had an idea. He put boughs on top of the deer to conceal it and he hiked back to the village. He went as fast as his leg would let him. There was still some daylight left.

He found the two sports in the cafeteria and he joined them. "Didn't expect to see you back so soon," Antonio said.

"I have a deer down. One of you or both come with me and we'll drag it in." They still had their hunting clothes on and they left. Rascal had to remind them to bring their rifle.

"Why are we taking this road Rascal? This morning we were on a different one," Howard asked.

"I hiked through to this one. The deer is just off the road."

It was the beginning of twilight when they were at the deer. "Okay, who wants this one?"

"I'll take it," Antonio said.

"Okay, fire your rifle into the ground." Antonio did and then the two held the deer while Rascal field dressed it.

When he had finished there wasn't enough daylight left to hike through the woods to his pack on the other road. "You two drag and I'll carry the rifles." Rascal hoped there wouldn't be any arguing. And to his surprise they each grabbed one side of the antlers, and dragged it without stopping to Douglas' store.

"I'll leave you now and I'll go back after my pack. Howard, to make it look better, I'd prefer if you went out with me in the morning. Then you can come back after lunch if you prefer."

"Sure. You're going into the woods in the dark, Rascal?"

Rascal didn't answer; instead he said "I'll see you at 6:30 a.m."

That night while eating supper Rascal said, "I'm beginning to think that six weeks of hunting is too much."

"Yeah, but look at the money you're making. You surely couldn't make the same in the woods or the mill."

"I know, but when you guide, you have to expect you're going to work at least twelve hours a day. And that's if everything goes good."

Emma didn't comment. She thought Rascal was pretty lucky to make the kind of money he was. *Maybe he's just tired.*

* * *

Rascal met Howard at 6:30 sharp the next morning. The temperature had dropped to 20^0 during the night.

"This sure is noisy walking this morning," Howard said.

"It'll be quieter in the woods."

Rascal stopped and took his pack off further away from the deer crossing. "It's colder this morning and you'll get cold without a fire, so go ahead and make one. It'll keep you busy and you make some tea."

"If I shoot something I'll come out and get you, otherwise don't go wandering around or leave."

As he was walking away, he was thinking how different Howard was from Antonio. He didn't care for Antonio.

He stopped to check the tracks at the crossing and they were all going to the left. So he went left and again along the hardwood tree line. But further this time. He figured to go about a quarter of a mile further. This distance would be a good hunt and still time to make it back to the road by noon.

Just as he was stopping a bear blew and took off running up through the hardwoods. Rascal's forehead was beaded with sweat. He thought sure that most bear would be hibernated by now.

When he found the deer trail he checked to see if there were as many tracks using the trail here. He could only be sure of one set of tracks. Then the others have gone elsewhere or maybe have bedded down.

Here the walking was still quiet. The moss covered ground did not freeze during the night. Up ahead as far as he could see there was a deer that had turned off the trail and headed for the hardwoods. He didn't see the head and he wasn't sure if it was a buck or a doe until he saw a smaller deer following. He waited so not to spook it. A buck might be following her scent. He waited and waited. Then after two hours he heard antlers rattling some low bushes. His heart started beating faster and he could feel the adrenaline surging through his veins and he started shaking. But something was wrong. There was too much noise and then he saw it. A huge set of moose antlers only showing above the low vegetation.

Not wanting a confrontation with the bull he stepped way off to the right and waited for the bull to pass. Then he proceeded following the deer trail. He was surprised to see the bull. He had some time to make up. Although he was moving somewhat faster, he was still aware of his surroundings and in particular the deer trail.

Twenty minutes beyond the bull, two does had been bedded down next to the trail and they ran off. If there were does here he was sure there would be bucks not too far behind them. He found a spot with good visual clarity about two hundred feet ahead. He stepped off the trail just enough so he wouldn't be profiled, and he began to wait.

And then when he least expected it he could see a buck with his nose to the ground smelling the does' scent. He was sure it was an eight-point buck. He raised his rifle slowly to his shoulder and then whistled. The buck stopped and lifted its head and Rascal fired. The buck fell and by the time he had walked up to it, the deer was still.

He dragged the buck about twenty feet off the trail and then headed out to get Howard. When Howard saw him step into the road he raised his teacup and waved for Rascal to come over.

"I'm assuming that shot was yours. We might as well have a bite to eat before we go to work. I thought you'd be here shortly, so I warmed up the stew and biscuits."

While they ate, Rascal told Howard about the bear he saw. "This one is about the same size as Antonio's but an eight point."

When they had finished eating, Rascal put everything in his pack and put the fire out. There was no need now to keep quiet so on the way to the dead deer Howard talked constantly. Rascal didn't mind now.

"Rascal, I watched you clean Antonio's deer, I'd like to do this one."

"Sure," and Rascal handed him his knife.

It wasn't quite as clean a job as Rascal would have done, but he didn't have Rascal's experience either. When he had finished, he was blood from his finger tips to his shoulders. He stood up and looked at himself and began laughing. So did Rascal.

"I may not have shot this deer, Rascal, but I feel just as excited as if I had."

"Howard, let this be the last time you say you didn't shoot it.

"Okay. One thing, you'd better fire your rifle and then put the empty shell in your pocket."

* * *

Not being in any particular hurry they stopped often to catch their breath. "You know, Rascal, this hunting is a lot like work. When we get back, you'll have to have a drink with us."

When they arrived at the Douglas store Jarvis was inside checking to see who had tagged a deer. He watched as Rascal and Howard dragged his deer across the mill yard to the store. Jarvis went outside to see the deer.

"That's a nice buck, Rascal, yours?"

"Not hardly, Mr. Warden. That there is my deer. Aint he a beauty?"

Jarvis looked at Howard and all the blood on his arms and

decided maybe he had shot his own deer. He was just suspicious because he was with Rascal.

"How did those two from the farm make out, Jarvis?" Rascal asked.

"Because of the set gun the judge fined them a $100.00 each and five days in jail and dismissed the possession case—said the five days in jail was enough for both charges.

"Where did you shoot this, Howard?" Jarvis asked.

"About a half mile out that road," and he pointed, "and a half to three quarters mile on the left in a cedar vale next to a hardwood knoll."

"You haven't tagged up, Rascal." Statement, not a question.

"No, not yet. I'll wait for the last week, so it'll be cold enough so the meat won't spoil."

Howard signed the tag slip and weighed in. "The same. 195 pounds."

They hung it on the game pole and then went inside and had a drink. "The first drink and toast—to Rascal Ambrose. You are one hell of a guide. I'm so happy, here's a tip." And Howard gave him another $50.00 bill. Antonio didn't.

That night at the supper table, Rascal gave Emma another $50.00 to put in the account. "How much did you make this week, Rascal?"

"$250.00. I kept $50.00."

"What are you going to do for the rest of the week?"

"Oh, maybe I'll get some firewood. There's some good biscuit wood on the flateau behind the cabin and I'll see if I can rent a horse."

"I thought you had enough wood already?"

"Probably do, but I'd feel more comfortable with a little extra."

* * *

The next morning Rascal had coffee and donuts with his friends before seeing if he could rent a work horse for the day.

"You aren't guiding today, boy?" Silvio asked.

"No, they both tagged out already and they're leaving this morning."

"On the front page of the newspaper is an article about Women's Suffrage and Prohibition. It's looking like both are going to pass Congress next year. Ain't that something; it'll be against the law to have a drink once that becomes law. There's something terribly wrong with this country, if you ask me," Silvio said.

"What you going to do for the rest of the week, Rascal?"

"Stay home and get drunk," he replied straight faced.

"That'll be the day," Jeters said. He stopped grinning when Rascal looked at him.

Silvio thought Rascal was serious until he said, "I'm going to go over to the stables and see if I can rent me a work horse. I know where there is some nice biscuit wood beside the road behind my house."

"Ooh, those tall dry trees sure do make a hot fire," Silvio said.

The morning coffee hour broke up and the southbound train was leaving. With Howard and his friend Antonio. As he was walking over to the stables he began wondering where Jarvis was. Had he gone back to Beech Tree or was he still around Whiskey Jack?

"Good morning, Owen."

"Morning to ya, Rascal."

"Owen, could I rent a work horse with harness today?"

"Sure can $1.50 a day. You gonna be needing a whiffle tree with the harness, Rascal?"

"Yes, and a light chain."

"What you gonna be doing, Rascal? You don't bring the chain back, I'll have to charge you for it."

"I found some biscuit wood behind the cabin on the flateau."

"Um, I sure would like me a plate of those biscuit your Mrs. bake. Best biscuits in town." Owen's wife had died four years ago. A heart attack the doctors said. Owen was seventy at the time and the doctor told him if he didn't stop working and start resting more he'd have a heart attack also. That was four years ago. "I'll see that Emma bakes you a pan of biscuits, Owen."

The cold air was just right for working. Though he still was working up a sweat and he soon had to remove his jacket. The trees were dry and light and the horse could twitch two at a time back to the cabin.

At noon he gave the horse some water and grain and after lunch he sharpened his axe. Dry wood dulled the axe quicker than the green wood. On top of the knoll there was still some snow in the shadier spots and there were deer tracks in them all. One particular huge track. This would be an exciting buck to chase after, but a smaller one would be better eating. Rascal had never considered himself a sport hunter. He hunted for meat, for food. And to him there was a difference.

By day's end he figured he had a good cord of biscuit wood. He returned the horse and chain and waited to walk home with Emma.

She was surprised when he walked into her office and more surprised when he said, "I thought I'd wait and walk home with you."

As they were eating supper, "I think I can have this wood all chunked up and piled up this weekend."

"The entire village is going to get together this year for Thanksgiving dinner at the cafeteria. If needed, the connecting doors to the school room will be opened so we'll have extra room. Mr. Hitchcock said the dinner will be provided by the company if the women folks will bake pies and rolls and biscuits."

"That sounds good and specking of biscuits, I promised Owen Haskel that you would bake him a pan of biscuits. He said your biscuits are the best in town."

"Surely, I'll do that this weekend."

By noon Saturday Rascal had all of the wood sawed into stove length pieces and piled. It was a back breaking job leaning over with a bucksaw all day. But he was happy to have the wood. Especially when the temperatures dropped really low.

"I'm going to do some baking and clean the cabin. I don't want you in the way, so why don't you go have coffee and donuts with your friends. The biscuits will be ready by noon."

The lake was making ice every night. As Rascal lay in his bed each night he could hear the ice snapping and groaning as it froze and expanded.

Much to everyone's surprise Owen had come to the cafeteria this morning and joined Rascal and the others. Jarvis was on the morning train and he joined the group for coffee and a donut. Elly brought over another pot of coffee and another plate of hot donuts. "You boys forming a club or something?"

Silvio was always quick witted and he said, "Yeah, Elly, we were thinking about naming this here cafeteria The Poachers Club." Everyone laughed, even Jarvis.

"Are you guiding again this week, Rascal?" Jarvis asked.

"I don't know. No one has asked for me yet."

"You had pretty good luck those last two weeks. Four hunters, four nice bucks. Where have you been hunting?"

"Now, Jarvis, that would be just like telling you where my special fish hole is. Like I said before, I'd sooner give you my wife." Everyone laughed and some spit up their coffee. Even Jarvis was laughing. Owen was listening and watching all this good natured bantering and he was figuring that Jarvis Page wasn't that bad of a fellow. Least-wise he was not like some folks seem to think.

As the group was breaking up a very distinguished looking man and his wife walked into the cafeteria. He was about the same height as Rascal. Silver hair, well dressed and it was difficult to say how old he was. The woman with him was also smartly dressed and probably his wife. He spotted the game warden's uniform and asked. "Sir, is there a Mr. Ambrose here?"

"Yes, this is Rascal Ambrose right here. Looks like you have another client, Rascal," Jarvis said.

"Did I hear this officer correctly when he called you Rascal?"

"Yes."

"How odd. How did you come by such a name?"

"My grandmother gave it to me," and then he had to tell the whole story.

The others in the group had all left. "Would you like to sit down. What is your name?" Rascal asked.

"Oh, my apologies—oh, Rascal. My name is Alfred Cummings, and my wife is Beverly."

"How do you do ma am."

"We're from Clearville, Pennslvania. That's southern Pennsylania.

"I would like to hire you as my guide for the week. Mrs. Douglas at the hotel tells me you are the best and the only one available in town."

"I can guide, Mr. Cummings, and the fee is $50.00 up front. I'll bring lunch with me each day and we'll start a fire and have hot food and tea."

"That all sounds reasonable enough. Now I'll get right to the point, Rascal. We own a dairy farm in Clearville and I have shot many hundreds of deer on my own land. But nothing compared to the big bucks in Maine. So, I am not looking for any average deer. I am wanting an especially large deer. The more points the better. If you get me one with more than twelve points I'll give you another $100.00."

"That's very generous, Mr. Cummings."

"Knock off the *Mister*, Rascal. We'll be spending days together so call me by my first name ,Alfred, or better yet, Al.

"There are two more points. One, my legs or rather my knees are not what they use to be twenty years ago, so I'll require conveyance to wherever we hunt and I'll pay extra for that."

"That won't be a problem, Al. I'll speak to Owen Haskel. He was one of the men at the table when you came in. He runs the company stable."

"And the most important point, Rascal, I don't have to shoot it." He said in a whisper. "As I said earlier I have shot hundreds of deer. I now want a large set of antlers to mount. But I will certainly go out with you every day."

"What do you have for a rifle, Al?"

"I have a model 1894 .38-55 octagon barrel."

"Good rifle.

"I have to be leaving now, Al. I'll be here at 6:30 sharp tomorrow morning."

"Let's say 7:00 o'clock, young Rascal. You know the more I say your name the better I like it. Probably suits you well also."

"Yes sir, that's what my grandmother said."

Rascal left and went home to tell Emma about the Cummings, but he didn't tell her about the deal he had made with Al. With Jarvis around, he was already playing a dangerous game and he didn't want anyone to know.

"The biscuits are ready for Owen. Keep them wrapped in this towel to keep them warm. I just took 'em out of the oven."

"I hope you made a batch for us too."

"Of course I did. Now go before they get cold."

The bundle of biscuits were still warm as Rascal stepped inside of the stable. "Hello again, Rascal. What have you there?"

"Emma's biscuits I promised."

"Oh boy, I thought you might have forgotten. Come, sit down. I just put coffee on the stove. They're best when warm." He opened a tub of butter and put it on the table. Owen waited until the coffee was brewed before he set the biscuits on the table.

"Um, are these delicious boy. Sure wish I knew her secret."

"I'll see you get it. Owen, I'd like to rent a horse and small wagon this week. Starting tomorrow morning." Rascal told Owen about Al.

"I know just what you want. It ain't no wagon. You don't need no wagon for just two people. I have a buggy here that'll do just fine. Big enough, too, for couple of deer."

"Okay, can you have it ready for me at 6:30 tomorrow morning?"

"Sure thing. Horse and buggy—how's $2.00 a day?" Rascal nodded his head. "You can pay at the end of your use."

When Rascal was back home he took his axe and went down to the lake to test the ice. He hit the ice once and almost lost the axe. There was only maybe a half inch. He was shocked. He thought he might be able to walk on it.

* * *

Morning the next day came and at 6:30 a.m. Rascal opened the door to the stables. "Got time for coffee?"

"Sure thing. One cup though."

Rascal led the horse by the halter across the mill yard and tied it up. Al was just finishing his coffee. When he saw Rascal he got up and joined him. "Let's go, Rascal."

Rascal's back pack was behind the seat. The horse's hooves made quite a clatter crossing the wooden planks on the dam. "This road on the left, Al, goes to my cabin."

"Before the week's end I'd like to see it."

"Certainly."

"I'm really surprised, Rascal, that there aren't any roads into the village. Only a railroad."

"Well, the village is a company town and I suppose it is less expensive to send their sawn lumber out by rail than building ten miles of road. The only question people in Whiskey Jack have is what will happen when there is no more timber to harvest."

"They'll have to leave. There isn't any employment here. What would you and Emma do?"

"We have talked about that and as long as the C&A runs through here, we stay. I can make a good living by trapping."

Rascal stopped on top of the flateau and back away from the trap line trail he had used. He tied the horse and said, "If your rifle isn't loaded you'd better do it now."

Rascal built a smokeless fire and showed Al what wood is best. "Dry softwood limbs. Keep the fire small. It should be enough to keep you warm." Then he pulled a wool blanket from his pack and said, "If you get cold wrap this around your shoulders. There is clean water over there" and he pointed. "I'm going to hunt along a game trail that I trapped on earlier. I'll be back at noon for lunch. And of course you'll know what to do if your buck comes out and stands in the road. Oh, and one more thing: don't go wandering around, Al."

There were fresh deer tracks traveling in both directions. He then looked on the other side of the road and the deer were crossing. He checked the wind. It was still.

He headed along his old trap line route and the deer were following it. Only a few steps at a time and then stop look and listen, and of course sniff the air. By mid-morning he had hunted to the point where his trap line had turned down hill toward the head of the lake. He leaned back against a rock, listening.

There were red squirrels and blue jays screaming alarms. He didn't know if the alarms were because of him or something else in the area. He waited. Eventually he saw him. Just a glimpse at first to the north. Whatever it was, it was not a deer, moose or bear. He remained as still as he possibly could. Not even blinking until he had to. There was more movement toward the southeast. Rascal was more than curious now. It was circling him—to attack, whatever it was, or to get around him?

Rascal had patience. He stood there for an hour before he saw it cross the trap line trail. Because of its size there was no doubt it had to be a lynx. And a big one. The lynx left the area quickly and Rascal started back. There was a doe and lamb traveling along the same trail ahead of him and once in a while he would see a white flag flicker. And surprising, he followed them to the road and Al saw them cross about five minutes before he saw Rascal.

"Tea hot?" he asked jokingly.

"It is and the stew and biscuits. The smell of the stew was making me so hungry I was almost determined to eat before you got back."

As they ate a hot lunch Rascal told Al about the lynx. "I have never seen a lynx. Bobcat yes."

"They look very much alike. The lynx stands a little taller and is a little bigger."

"What are your intentions for this afternoon?"

"All the deer that are using the trap line trail I was following are crossing the road. So I'll hunt on the other side. There is a slight breeze now and it'll be in my face and deer will be traveling into it also.

Before leaving the road, Rascal checked his compass. . .how the road ran and what direction he was now going. The forest cover on this side was much like he had been in all morning. But there were two things different here. A buck had been rutting here and scraping trees with his antlers. This was encouraging.

He found where the deer were going across the snow in the shade and he found several spots where a doe had peed. He rubbed some of the yellow snow on his clothing to mask his scent and so the bucks would smell the estrus in the pee and think a doe was in the area.

He soon came to another area where the trees had been rubbed hard and the ground pawed at. This was looking more and more promising. In a way he wished Al could see this. There were several deer trails coming into this shady spot so Rascal backed off behind a thicket of low cedar trees.

The gentle breeze had turned to a 5mph wind, which Rascal thought might improve his chances. Because of the doe pee on his clothes now, he doubted if any buck would pay too much attention to his scent.

And a few minutes later he was proven right as a six point buck came strutting down the deer trail from the road behind Rascal. He went on by Rascal never slowing down. There was probably a doe in heat just out of sight.

For some reason the six point started running with head down and his hooves hitting the ground so hard the sound was like a drum. The deer ran out of sight and then there was a clash, grunts and moss and dirt flying in the air. The six point had apparently found another buck with the same desires on the does. They were just out of sight. The clash of antlers and grunts lasted for several minutes. Then the six point came running back with a gash in his neck. The victor followed for a short distance and then he too was gone. Neither one of them was what Al was wanting.

Rascal moved on also. Every once in a while he could see the rump of the eight point victor. There were two does traveling with him. He was hoping a bigger buck would come along and try to steal the does. So he kept following until it was time for him to head back to the road.

It was dark by the time he was back at the buggy with Al. They put the fire out and put the pack back in the buggy and headed for home. On the way Rascal told him all about the two bucks fighting. "I wished I could have seen that. It sounds like we are in the right place."

Al began sniffing the air and asked, "What is that smell?"

"Doe pee. When does come in heat there is estrus in the pee that drives the bucks crazy. I found some and put it on my clothes to mask my own scent."

"Did it work?"

"Yes. That six-point went by me and never paid any attention to me. And when the fight was over, the eight-point paid no attention."

"I have never heard of such a thing, but it is understandable why it would work."

"I almost shot that six-point when he crossed the road. He was a magnificent stag, but I'm looking for a larger set of antlers."

"Will we come back here tomorrow?"

"Yes, we know there are several deer here. It's just a matter of waiting for the trophy buck. If after two more days we don't see anything I have another spot where I know there are deer."

* * *

At the supper table that night Emma asked, "Ooo, what is that awful smell?"

"Doe pee with estrus."

"And you have it on you? How?"

"I found where a doe had peed and I spread it on my clothes to mask my scent and lure a buck."

Emma started laughing, "You'd better be careful a buck doesn't try to mount you."

The next day was almost a repeat. Rascal saw the six point with the gash on its neck, an eight point and several does. But nothing big. "I know I said we would give this two days, but I think we should try the other road behind the mill."

"Anything you say. You're the guide."

Al was enjoying himself and he liked Rascal's company.

That night in bed Emma snuggled up close to Rascal; she wrapped her arms around him and said, "If you lose any more weight, Rascal, you'll be nothing but a sack of bones. You need to start eating more," she kissed him and then rolled over on top of him.

He wrapped his arms around her and kissed her with real passion. "Em, I'd like to invite the Cummings for supper some night."

"I think that would be a very good idea. When are they leaving?"

"Not until Sunday morning."

"Good that'll give you time to go to Beech Tree and get a couple of bottles of that wine we liked. That would go good with supper."

This surprised the heck out of Rascal. Emma was asking him to buy two bottles of wine. But he didn't act surprised. He didn't want to ruin the moment.

165

* * *

The next morning at the same fireplace setting, Rascal tied off the horse and unloaded his pack. "I'm going to hunt to the left. There is a big buck that travels this softwood and cedar vale. There's a good chance you might see what you want crossing this road. If one comes out whistle and I'll guarantee he'll stop and look at you. If I hear you shoot I'll come right out. Keep the fire low and smokeless. I'll be back at noon."

In the last five days there had been many more deer crossing back and forth on the road and Rascal had a good feeling about the day.

A hundred feet in from the road a pine martin came running up to him. It screamed a blood curdling scream and ran off towards the hardwoods. It climbed a tree and started screeching. Rascal picked up his pace so to get away from that noisy bugger.

There was no breeze yet and most of the tracks seemed to be only milling around. Probably during the night. Occasionally he'd see a white flag flicker but not the deer, and supposed it was only does or lambs.

Then there was something coming from the right through the noisy hardwood leaves. It sounded like a deer. Rascal waited and then he thought he would try something. He leaned his rifle against a tree, cupped his hands around his mouth and grunted, only once. The noise of something walking through the leaves stopped. And after a couple of minutes Rascal grunted again and then picked his rifle up. Whatever it was, was now running at him. He could hear the hooves thundering as they hit ground.

Rascal was excited too and he had to pee. But that would have to wait. The deer came onto the trail about twenty feet in front of Rascal. It wasn't the trophy Al was wanting, but if this had been the last week of hunting he would have shot it. It was a big bodied ten point. When the buck spotted Rascal it lowered its head and charged. There was a big cedar tree to his right and he jumped behind that. The buck was so intent on Rascal, when it swerved to his left his antlers caught a three inch cedar tree and the buck hit the tree head-on knocking him off his feet.

Enraged, the buck got to his feet and charged again, and again he hit the same tree dead-on, knocking him off his feet. Knowing when he was beaten he stood and ran off up the trail towards the road. Rascal had to wipe the sweat from his face and now he peed. Never in all his life would he imagine a buck would react like that. He suddenly realized he was shaking a bit.

As he kept hunting along the trail, he kept seeing flashes of tails and rumps disappearing to one side or the other. But he was assuming they were only does or smaller bucks. He wished he had the time to follow the trail even further, but it was now late morning and he needed to get back.

He didn't rush back, but he didn't stop to look around unless he saw movement. As he knew he was getting close to the road; he kept seeing familiar signs. A buck had been laying down in the trail and had suddenly gotten to its feet and ran towards the road. Rascal didn't think the buck ran because of him. Maybe there was another buck coming into this buck's territory.

Then he heard the familiar sound of grunting and antlers clashing together. He ran up close enough so he could see the two bucks were on the road. And one of them had an enormous rack of antlers.

Al had heard both deer running towards the road and had enough hunting experience to understand that two bucks were about to engage in battle. And this was the most exciting thing that was about to happen than anything he had ever seen. The two bucks met head on in the center of the road. Both deer going down on their knees. Dirt was being kicked up into the air and both bucks were grunting and straining. But the best thing, although both bucks had huge bodies, the one that had come in from the right had a more impressive rack. And this was the buck he wanted. He brought his rifle to his shoulder trying to get a good shot, but the two bucks were moving too much for a good shot.

When both bucks stood, the larger one was almost broad side and Al fired and the buck dropped. The other one stood there looking at the one lying dead and wondered what had happened. Then he heard Rascal coming in from behind him. Thinking it was another challenger he raced down the deer trail to meet his new opponent. Rascal was now only thirty feet away and he decided to take his shot in the throat of the charging buck. The buck came to a full stop ten feet in front of Rascal.

Al knew Rascal had shot the other buck. He hollered, "Yahoo!" as loud as he could. Then he walked down to inspect his deer. Rascal came onto the road just as Al reached his buck. "I'm assuming you got yours also."

"I didn't have a choice, when he heard me coming, he must have figured me to be another buck ready to challenge him. He came charging at me and after I fired he practically fell at my feet. He's a nice ten point.

"And I guess you have your trophy buck, Al. Have you counted the points yet?"

"No, let's do."

"I get fifteen points, Al. He sure has a heavy beam. Let's get him dressed off and then we'll do mine."

Al was still too excited to do much other than hold the buck on his back. He marveled at Rascals expert ability to dress a deer without getting covered with blood.

When Al shot, Jarvis had just come out from the cafeteria. He decided to walk out. And then there was another shot. "Same rifle." He figured Rascal had just shot two deer. One for his client. The old man. So he walked out to have a look see. He was standing near the horse and buggy as Rascal was leaving the road. One deer was laying on the road. Al had laid his rifle on the buggy and now Jarvis picked it up and ejected an empty .38-55 shell, but this was an octagon barrel. Not Rascal's rifle. As he walked by he couldn't help but notice how extraordinary large the body and antlers were. He could hear the two talking and he walked in to them.

"Another nice deer. This one has a large body too."

"Ah, Al, this is Jarvis Page, local game warden."

Jarvis helped Rascal drag his deer to the road and couldn't help but notice he didn't have any blood on his hands. *How in hell can he do that?* He was thinking.

"I put the pot of beans on to warm up. I hope I haven't ruined them."

"They'll be okay. Al, do you want your heart?"

"No, you can have it."

"I was thinking about roasting it to eat with beans and biscuits. Can you stay for lunch, Jarvis?"

"I can't refuse an offer like that."

Rascal reached up into the chest cavity and pulled the heart out. "I'll go rinse this off. Jarvis, can you find us some roasting sticks?"

Al had no idea what Rascal was talking about. But it soon became clear.

Al said, "This is a marvelous way to end my hunt. Good company and roasting deer heart over an open fire and from the deer I shot. Yes sir, this whole trip has been worth it."

Rascal told them over sipping tea about how earlier his deer had charged him and chased him behind a cedar tree and how he had hit a smaller tree head on and knocked himself to the ground. "Not just once, but he did it twice."

And Al had to tell them his story about the two bucks running at each other and coming toward in the middle of the road.

"We should be leaving, Al, that hide will come off a lot easier if the body is still warm. Jarvis, will you help me load these two?"

"Sure."

Jarvis rode back to the village with them and he hung around to see what each buck would weigh.

Al's deer weighed 255 pounds. Rascal's was 230 pounds. "I thought your deer, Al, was heavier than Rascal's."

Rascal hung Al's back up by its hind legs and began skinning. Once he had the four legs skun he simply pulled the hide down and over the head. He cut the neck off at the shoulders. "There I'll find a wooden box for this, then you should leave it outside to freeze."

He knew the mill carpenter sometimes had wooden boxes and he went off to talk with Gerry. "Sure, Rascal. Come see what I have."

"Do you have a top for this one?"

"Sure do."

"How much?"

"A dollar."

Rascal gave him the dollar and took back the box and folded the hide, head and antlers into the box. "Perfect fit."

"Are you going to take the meat back with you, Al?"

"No. You can have that if you want it."

"I know two older people who could really use it."

"That would be fine. Do you need any help?"

"Sure do, I'll go get a meat saw from Ole Man Douglas."

While Al held onto the deer, Rascal sawed it down the middle. He returned the saw and he and Al loaded it onto the buggy and went first to the stables. "Owen, this is Al Cummings, Al, Owen Haskel."

"Mr. Haskel, would you like half a deer?"

"Would I, would I! Hell yes!"

Owen and Rascal hung it up in the stable.

Silvio and Anita were just as excited.

"This has been quite a day, Rascal. I'm almost sorry to be leaving on Sunday."

"Oh, that reminds me, my wife Emma and I would like you and your wife Beverly for supper Saturday night."

"We would be delighted.

"This has been quite a day, Rascal, and I can't remember when I have had a better day. I can't say this enough, but thank you, Rascal. And I know I said I would give you a $100.00 for shooting me a buck such as I did. You treated me like an active hunter and put me where I would have my chance. You have earned it, Rascal, and I'm glad to give you this." Al gave Rascal a $100.00 bill.

"Thank you. I will see you again before Saturday. Good night, Al." Rascal took his deer home and hung it up.

* * *

As Rascal was telling Emma about the day and telling her about his buck chasing him behind the tree and then knocking himself down, she was laughing and laughing. Finally she was able to say, "I guess it was a good thing he didn't catch you bending over." She laughed some more until her eyes were red.

"I'll go to Beech Tree tomorrow for the wine, so make a list for me if you want anything else."

"Have you decided what you would like to eat Saturday evening?" Emma asked.

"How about a variety. We could have a few frog legs, some beaver, canned moose, biscuits, of course and how about a small squash and some fiddleheads?"

"That actually will be pretty easy to prepare."

He walked to the village with Emma in the morning and had coffee and donuts with his friends while he waited for the southbound train.

Silvio wasn't there this morning; he was busy taking care of the deer meat. Rascal, Jeff and Jeters talked until the southbound pulled in. "See you guys."

"Where you going?"

"Emma needs a few things in Beech Tree."

There were a few passengers but the train had to couple four car loads of lumber. The Hitchcock mill was doing a fantastic business.

As the train passed the beaver flowage at mile nine, the beaver had not rebuilt the dam. But at mile 8 ½ and again at mile seven there were beaver flowages that were not yet troublesome to the railroad bed. But he would be down to trap as soon as the season and ice allowed.

Emma's list was short, besides the wine which he had decided to get three bottles and not two. She wanted another case of Mason jars, another copper canner and some pretty smelling bath soaps. He could put everything inside the copper canner and tie the cover on secure.

He went to the general store first. It was closest. He found everything except the bath soaps. "For that, Mr. Ambrose, you should try Muriel's at the corner of this street."

"Could I leave the jars and canner here until I come back?"

"Sure thing. I'll just set them in back."

Muriel's was a ladies store and Rascal felt odd going in. "Hello, can I help you? We don't get many men in here."

"I'm looking for some sweet smelling bath soaps for my wife. At the general store I was told you would have something."

"Surely, they are over here. Do you know what your wife was wanting?"

"She didn't say."

"Well here is a package of several different kinds of different scents."

"I think that would be fine."

"Would there be anything else?"

"I can't think of anything."

He put the soaps in the canner and asked Mr. Felps for a piece of rope to tie the canner top secure. Then he carried it back to the train station and asked the station master, "Is it alright if I leave this here until the northbound to Whiskey Jack leaves?"

"Certainly, just set it against the wall. No one will bother it."

It was noon so he found a restaurant not too far away. He ordered a thick beef steak with baked potato and gravy and peas and carrots.

As he waited for his meal he kept thinking about the deer hanging in the cold storage cellar and how it had almost done him in. That was quite an incident having a huge buck trying to have at you like that. Then he thought about Al Cummings and how happy he was for having shot his own trophy buck, and not having to pay him to do it for him. He will certainly have stories to tell when he gets home in Clearville, Pennsylvania.

When his meal came he forgot about everything else. The beef steak was so good.

There were few passengers on the return trip and the conductor let Rascal carry his heavy canner on board the passenger car.

At the Whiskey Jack station, the southbound from Lac St. Jean was coupling four freight cars and as Rascal was getting off he noticed Jarvis with two prisoners in handcuffs and he began wondering what they had been arrested for. More illegal hunting at the farm? They both looked like they had been punched in the face several times.

He picked the canner up and started for home in the dark. He had to stop several times to rest.

"I see you were able to get everything, even my soap." She opened the package and exclaimed, "How lovely this smells."

The next day Rascal pulled the hide off his deer while being careful not to get too much hair on the meat. He would let it hang until Sunday before he would take care of the meat. There was a lot of fat on the rump and around the neck. This usually meant a cold winter ahead when deer had this amount of fat. *Let it come,* he thought. *We're well stocked with food and wood.*

Saturday morning after breakfast Emma shooed Rascal outside. "I need to clean the cabin and I don't want you under foot. This afternoon after I have finished I want you to get what you want to eat from cold storage and then you are going to take a bath. And hang your jacket with deer pee on it in the shed. I'll not have the cabin smelling like a doe in heat."

Rascal checked the deer hanging in cold storage. A crust was forming on the outside of the meat. This was good. It would help to seal in the flavor. He filled the wood boxes before going to the cafeteria for coffee and donuts and good conversation.

"Silvio, you know everything that goes on here in Whiskey Jack. When I stepped onto the station platform yesterday, Jarvis had two men in handcuffs that looked like they had been punched in the face several times each. What happened?"

"All I know, two friends from downstate somewhere were drinking in their room in the hotel and things got out of hand and they started punching each other. Jarvis was here having coffee and was called to break 'em up. I'm guessing he had to arrest them. I don't know what they were fighting over. Probably a girl, though."

From the cafeteria he went to see Owen at the stable to rent a horse and buggy. "I'll bring them back later tonight. Will you still be up, Owen?"

"If my light is on, I'll be up. If not just leave the buggy outside and take the harness off and put the horse inside."

After lunch Rascal went out to the cold storage and brought in what he wanted to eat tonight. Frog legs, beaver and canned moose meat, a squash and fiddleheads. "I'll only have to bake the biscuits and cook the squash. Everything else all I'll have to do is warm it up."

Rascal took his bath and Emma used the scrub brush on his back. When he had dried off and dressed he dumped the water and Emma filled it with hot water and some jasmine soap. She leaned back soaking in the hot water and enjoying the scent of jasmine.

At 6 p.m. Rascal drove the horse and buggy down to pick up the Cummings. Al helped his wife into the buggy and then he climbed in and Rascal said, "Emma and I are so happy you two could come to supper tonight."

"We are delighted. I cannot wait to meet your wife, Rascal," Beverly said.

When Rascal pulled into his dooryard at the cabin Emma came out to greet them. "Al and Beverly Cummings, my wife Emma."

"So pleased to finally meet both of you."

"It is our pleasure, Emma," Beverly said. They went inside out of the cold.

"When you told me you and your wife lived in a cabin this is just how I pictured it."

"It is so warm and comfortable," Beverly said.

Emma already had the hot food on the table. "Be seated please. Everything is all ready. Rascal, would you pour the wine?"

"And wine, too, plus this fabulous food?"

"Em's idea."

"It all smells so delicious—but what is it?" Al asked.

"Well, we have frog legs, beaver, canned moose meat, squash, fiddleheads and biscuits," Emma said. "Help yourself."

To be polite, Al and Beverly took a little of everything.

"I must admit, Beverly and I have never eaten any of this— but biscuits."

Al was trying a bite of everything and seeming to enjoy it. Beverly's reactions were a little slower coming. Al started laughing, so much so, he was having trouble breathing. Finally he was able to compose himself. "In all my life I have never eaten such strange and unusual food and enjoyed it so much. Is this what you two eat all the time?"

"Well, we have a lot of canned brook trout and when I get to taking care of the deer we'll can much of that also."

"My friends at home will never believe me when I tell them that I ate beaver and frog legs or moose. That beaver was so sweat. It is the tastiest meat I have ever eaten. And I have never heard of fiddleheads, what are they?"

"Fiddlehead is a type of fern." Again Al broke out laughing and this time so did Beverly.

Rascal refilled everyone's glass with more wine and he opened a second bottle.

"Would you believe me if I told you that my first taste of wine was only a few weeks ago with Rascal in Lac St. Jean, Quebec. I never believed it could be so good," Emma said.

"This is fine wine, Emma," Beverly said.

When everyone had finished eating Al pushed back from the table and patted his bulging belly and said, "I don't know when I have eaten so much. Emma, you are a marvelous host. In fact you are as nice of a host as your husband is a guide. I may be wrong, but I don't think I am. You were counting on me all along of shooting my own deer. You worked each hunt so expertly, I'm sure I'm correct."

Emma looked confused, "Isn't that what he was suppose to do?"

Al then told her about the agreement he had made with Rascal on Sunday.

Beverly helped Emma clean up after supper and Rascal and Al sat in what he considered the living room. Al wanted to know all about heating the cabin with only wood and how much wood it takes, ". . .and how do you get to the village once there's snow on the ground?"

"The road behind the cabin is a twitch road for the horse crews in winter. The timber crews cut lumber out back where we hunted for two days. Then we keep a path packed down with snowshoes out to the road. Then we walk."

"Your life here in Whiskey Jack is so simple and beautiful. It's like a wilderness paradise. And do you work, Rascal? Besides guiding?"

"I trap and I make three times what I would working in the woods, in the mill or for the C & A Railroad. Plus, I now receive a monthly disability from the Army."

"What happened?"

"I was in the trenches in France and I was wounded twice. The second time took a piece of bone from my right leg."

"That explains your limp."

As they were saying goodnight, Al said, "I envy you two with your life here in Whiskey Jack. Good night."

Chapter 7

Sunday morning after breakfast Rascal walked down to the cafeteria to wait for the morning train in hopes some hunters would get off and would be needing a guide.

This morning only Silvio and Rascal met for coffee and donuts. Silvio was still concerned about the Women's Suffrage Movement and more so about Prohibition. That was almost a certainty to pass congress, where as women's right to vote looked at present to be about half-and-half.

The train pulled in and only two hunters got off. They were only a little older than Rascal and spoke with a slight accent.

They went to the hotel desk and asked for a room and, "Madam are there any hunting guides in this quaint little stopover?"

"The only guide in Whiskey Jack is in the cafeteria. His name is Rascal Ambrose."

They both laughed at the name Rascal. They went back into the cafeteria and said, "We're looking for someone named Rascal." And they both started laughing again.

Silvio looked at Rascal and said, "Go get 'em boy."

Rascal stood up and walked over and stood in front of the two and said, "If you two would stop your laughing, I'd introduce myself to you." Rascal could smell whiskey on their breath.

"You this Rascal guy?"

"Yes my name is Rascal. And I've decided not to guide for you. That is not until you sober up and talk decent." Rascal left and went home.

Silvio laughed and laughed. "How'd you two flatlanders like that?" And he laughed some more.

"Are you guiding anyone this week?" Em asked.

"I talked with two from Massachusetts, but they had been drinking and I found them insulting."

"Oh. They were drinking, huh?"

"Yeah." He went outside to work around the cabin.

Wanting something to do he cut off the tenderloins from his deer and took them inside. Then he quartered the deer and left the quarters hanging. Tomorrow while Emma was at work he would take care of the meat and can it. All except for one hind quarter which he would leave hanging and cut steaks from it when he and Emma wanted venison steak. As cold as it was becoming the meat would remain good for a long time inside the cold storage cellar.

He used a bristle brush to remove the hair and dirt from the meat.

"Have you seen the sky, Em? Dark storm clouds have blown in. Wouldn't surprise me none if we get a few inches tonight."

"Oh I hope not. I wish the snow would hold off until after Thanksgiving."

The next morning there was three inches. "It could have been worse, I suppose," Emma said as she laced up her new boots.

"I'll walk with you to work. After coffee at the cafeteria I'll come back and finish taking care of the deer meat. You look like an Eskimo all bundled up, Em."

"As long as I'm warm."

* * *

"Those two young flatlanders lit out of here pretty early this morning—looking to cut a fresh track. It'll be my guess they come back with nothing but track soup," Silvio remarked.

"I'm surprised they were able to get up so early—I mean they had been doing a lot of drinking yesterday."

Rascal only had one cup of coffee and left. He had a day's work ahead of him.

He brought in the two forward shoulders first and stripped the meat off and cut the meat into smaller pieces. There was very little that went to waste. Then he went and brought in one hindquarter and the best cuts of steak, he saved. The rest went into mason jars. Then he took his knife and a bowl and went out and stripped away every piece of meat left on the ribcage, neck and back bone. There was enough meat to fill the bowl.

As the canner was boiling Rascal suddenly thought of a good practical joke to pull on those two young sports. He'd wait until long after dark and take the head and cape from his deer and take it out where the two were hunting. The same place he and Al had shot their deer.

He took the canner off the stove just before Emma got home and the Mason jars were on the counter. When he told Emma what he intended to do with the head and cape, all she said was, "Boys and their games."

Rascal waited until about 8 o'clock. He couldn't wait any longer. The air had been getting warmer all day and he knew by morning the snow would probably be gone. So he wasn't worried about leaving tracks. He hoped no one would see him crossing the mill yard.

About halfway to the softwood vale he found what he wanted. At the end of a straight stretch, the road turned a slight corner to the right and directly off the corner he wedged the deer head in a crotch between two trees and propped the head up so it would be looking down the road. There was a small fir tree in front which helped to make it good, like a natural setting.

Early in the morning he figured this would look pretty good. He walked back a ways and looked at it in the moonlight. It looked good.

He was back home before midnight.

"Are you done playing now?" Emma asked.

Apparently these two sports were not much of early risers. They were just walking across the mill yard as Rascal and Emma were walking across the dam. She went to her office and as much as he wanted to trail along behind the two and watch, he went to the cafeteria. He sat on the deck outside waiting for Silvio.

Silvio came along soon and asked, "What are you doing sitting out here?" Then there was a rifle shot in the direction of the deer head. Then another and another and two more.

"I wonder if that deer is still running or is full of holes," Silvio said.

* * *

Bill and Jim had had too much to drink the evening before and now Tuesday morning in the hazy morning light, they saw a huge buck standing on the edge of the road about two hundred feet away. "Look at that, Jim." Bill said as Jim was already lifting his rifle to his shoulder. He fired and the deer stood there. Bill fired and the head rocked back and forth a little. Jim fired again and missed completely. Bill on his knees now fired and the deer head rocked again. He fired and Jim fired and the head fell from the crotch. They ran up expecting to find a nice deer and there was only a head and hide.

"Some joke," Bill said.

"Better not let on that we fell for it, Bill," Jim said.

"What does it matter? They heard the shots."

"Hum, five shots."

"They were pretty rapid too," Silvio added.

Rascal didn't let anything slip that he knew more about those five shots than he was letting on, but Silvio looked at him questioningly. He suspected Rascal was up to something.

When the two came in at lunch time Rascal, of course, had already gone back to his cabin. As Bill and Jim ate lunch they kept looking around them to see if anyone had any of particular interest with them. They had decided not to say anything . They had a suspect, but there was no way to prove it.

The next morning, Wednesday, they didn't go directly to the woods. They hung around the cafeteria until they saw Rascal come in. Bill motioned for him to come to their table.

"Sit down, Rascal." Nobody laughing about his name now. "We aren't having much of any luck seeing deer. Monday morning with the snow on the ground there were tracks everywhere. But we just aren't having any luck. We see deer but we just can't get a shot at one. Jim and I have been talking it over and we really don't want to go home without anything. What if you were to shoot a couple of deer and we pay you?"

"Okay, that's $100.00 each, up front." They handed it to him without question. "Now, we do this my way. I'll be here at 6:30 a.m. sharp. You be outside on the deck. You go into the woods with me. To make it look good. I'll bring lunch we can warm up at noon. As far as anyone who sees us, I'm only guiding you."

"What if you fail to get us a deer," Jim asked.

"I'll give you your money back."

That evening while eating supper Rascal told Emma about the deal he had made with the two. "Do you trust them, Rascal?"

"I hope I can."

"Yeah, or you'll be in front of the judge again."

* * *

The next morning at 6:30 sharp, Bill and Jim were waiting for Rascal on the deck. Rascal had his backpack on. Without much talk they left and headed out along the same road. Rascal noticed the deer head was no longer there and walked on by without any indication that he knew that anything had been there.

When he was at the same fire pit, he said, "You two build a small fire. Use dry limbs on trees so it won't smoke. I'll be back at noon."

Today he went to the right side. There wasn't any wind yet and he was hoping the deer would still be filtering down to the fresh choppings from the Ledge Swamp area. There was a lot of sign indicating that a few deer had gone through during the night. Today he was going to try something different. Instead of

181

walking along on the deer trail he stepped about ten feet off to the side. Just enough so he could still see up along the trail, in most spots. He wasn't too worried about shooting a buck with a large spread of antlers. Six or eight point would probably be fine.

An hour later a doe with twin lambs came along. The doe was a lot more alert than the bucks. She knew something wasn't right and stopped. Rascal could see she was sniffing the air and then she caught his scent and turned to look at him and then the three ran off in different directions.

He waited to see if a buck would be following and a half hour later his hunch paid off. A six point with his nose to the ground not paying any attention at all to Rascal's scent. Rascal shot him and as he was dressing it another six point came along with his nose to the ground also.

Rascal had his two deer and his agreement with Bill and Jim was done.

When both deer were cleaned he walked back to the road and Bill and Jim were laying close to the fire, asleep. He woke them and said, "I have shot a deer for each of you. As soon as we eat we'll go up and drag'em out."

As they were eating stew and biscuits, Bill said, "That didn't take long."

"It depends if you know what to look for when you're hunting. Both of you get your hands bloody so it'll look more natural."

When they had finished eating Rascal took them out to claim their deer. "They look just alike," Jim said.

"They could be twins."

Neither deer was a two hundred pound animal and the drag back to the village didn't take long.

"Well fellas thank you and you're on your own. When will you be leaving?"

"We decided to go as soon as he had our deer, so tomorrow morning."

"Well, have a good trip back." Rascal walked home and had the cabin warm and supper ready when Emma was home from work.

"I didn't expect to see you home this early."

"They got their deer, both of them, by noon. They're leaving tomorrow morning."

"Next week is Thanksgiving and I need to make three batches of biscuits and I'm going to need more flour."

"I'll get some at Douglas' store today."

As Rascal was having coffee and donuts with Silvio, Jeters and Jeff, Rascal saw Jarvis. He walked over to say hello. "Good morning, Jarvis. My, you look like you have had a rough few days."

"I had some things to look at near the border. I'm going home for some well earned sleep."

"See you later, Jarvis."

Rascal went back with his friends.

When the southbound arrived Jarvis found a seat in the back where maybe he'd be able to sleep a little on the way to Beech Tree.

Bill and Jim loaded their deer in the freight car and then found a seat that was close to Jarvis. Bill and Jim had been drinking whiskey since the night before, celebrating taking home nice stags. And they were still being loud.

Jarvis pulled a blanket out of his pack and pulled it up over his head trying to shut out the intruders. There were only a few other passengers in that car. Somehow Jarvis managed to fall asleep again. But when the train lurched forward as it began to depart he woke up again.

Bill and Jim were even louder now. And Jarvis was using all of his restraint to ignore them. But he could not go back to sleep.

He gave up finally of going back to sleep. He leaned over in his seat with his blanket still pulled up over his head.

"I've never seen such a backwoods place in my life," Bill said.

"Yeah, they're living a hundred years behind times. And I'm glad we brought our booze. You can't get a mug of beer in that hole."

"Can you imagine having a name like that Rascal guy? What an idiot," Bill said.

"And that guy called Jeters, what kind of name is that," Jim said.

"And the name of the town, Whiskey Jack, and there isn't a drop of booze in the whole damned town," Bill said.

"And I know damn well that it was that idiot Rascal who set up that deer head for us to shoot at. He must have thought we were pretty stupid."

"Well, Jim, we were weren't we. How many times did we shot at it before we knew something wasn't right."

The mention of Rascal's name got Jarvis' attention. Now he was interested in listening to anything they had to say.

"What about the old guy they called Silvio, he looked like some old codger. And the way he kept looking at us."

Jarvis was smiling, this was getting interesting. As long as he pretended to be asleep the two probably would keep talking.

"You know, Bill, there ain't no law of any kind there. I wonder if that place is some kind of a hole in the wall."

"Maybe John Law is on the take and stays away on purpose."

"Ah, they're just afraid to go in there, probably," Bill said.

Jarvis was having a difficult time to keep from laughing.

"You know though, Bill, that Rascal guy, he sure can hunt. He was what maybe two hours and he had a six point buck for each of us."

"I'll give him credit as a great hunter, but the S.O.B charged us $100.00 each for a six point."

"Well Jim, it's better than going home empty handed and having to explain to our wives why we didn't get anything."

"I suppose."

This was getting better and better, so now he had Rascal for selling deer—two deer. And if he wanted he could have those two idiots for buying deer. But he had an idea that would work out better.

He let them continue talking, the whiskey making them feel brave. But how much of what Jarvis had heard was in fact just the whiskey talking? He would have to make a decision soon.

The engineer blew the locomotive whistle signaling the train was approaching Beech Tree. Jarvis needed these two in possession of the two deer before he could have an illegal act. When he left the car he kept the blanket around his shoulders to hide his game warden insignia. They were so unsteady with the effects of the whiskey they probably would not have recognized his badge or insignia.

Jarvis' biggest worry was, would this freight car stay coupled all the way to Portland or would the contents be shifted to a different car. The southbound from Beech Tree was always a bigger locomotive because of the additional cars and loads. He would have to have them in possession before he could do anything.

Then as luck would have it the conductor told Bill and Jim their deer would have to be transferred to a different car as this one had a two day delay. So Jarvis followed the two to the freight car where he watched them drag their deer from the freight car onto the platform.

Jarvis waited until the two men were alone before he approached them. He removed his blanket and put it in his pack and walked over. "Good morning, Bill and Jim."

This man in uniform knowing their names was unsettling, to say the least.

Bill said, "What can we do for you, officer?"

"Nice looking deer. Did you shoot these in Whiskey Jack?"

They both looked at Jarvis. He had four days of whiskers. His clothes were dirty and smelled of smoke. And it didn't look as though he had washed for days.

"Yeah, that's right."

"Oh, excuse me. I didn't introduce myself. Jarvis Page,

Game Warden." He saw Bill and Jim swallow hard and look at each other.

"What did you use for a rifle?"

"We both had .30-30s," Jim said.

"Then I should be able to dig out a spent .30 caliber slug from each deer."

"That's right," Bill said.

"But what if I were to dig out a .38-55 slug from each deer? What would you say then?"

"What are you getting at mister?" Bill asked.

"Well, first let's see if I can find a .38-55 slug. You see both deer were shot in the neck and there is no exit wound. So the bullet will still be in there." Bill and Jim didn't say anything.

Jarvis cut the hide back exposing the fleshy part of the neck. The entrance wound was obvious. He put his finger in the hide and said, "There's the bullet." He cut the neck and peeled the tissue back and there was the bullet lodged in the spine. Jarvis held the bullet up and said, "Yep, just what I thought. It's a .38-55. Now for the other deer."

The second deer he had to dig a little deeper to find the bullet. But it too was a .38-55. "Now tell me the story, boys."

Neither Bill or Jim wanted to say anything.

"Boys there is only one person in Whiskey Jack who hunts with a .38-55. And he is a very good shot. You know what I think? I think you paid him to shoot these for you."

Sill no comment. "How much did it cost you, to buy a deer?"

"You seem to know all about it. You tell us," Bill said defiantly.

"A $100.00 each. Now if you two don't want to go to jail— oh yeah, because of the weekend there won't be any court session until Monday. That means you'll have to stay in jail, let's see this Thursday—four days. Are you ready to spend four days in jail and then have to face the judge? "It's your choice. You decide."

"What do you want?" Jim asked.

"I want the entire story."

Bill and Jim started talking and once they started it was difficult for Jarvis to get a word in edgewise. So he let 'em talk. Finally he had the whole story.

"This is what I am going to do, boys. I'm confiscating both deer and you're free to go home. But I want your names and addresses first." Jarvis handed them a small notepad he kept in his shirt pocket.

"What's this for? We have told you everything," Bill said.

"Just in case your stories don't check out."

"You know, Bill," Jim said. "I don't feel so bad now. We don't have to go to jail or court. We did lose our deer, but I think it'll be Rascal who will be in trouble."

"Yeah, and after what he did I don't feel a bit sorry," Bill said.

"What did Rascal do to you?"

They told Jarvis all about the deer head and hide. "We thought we really had something at first. Every time we fired that head would rock back. We shot five times before it fell to the ground. And even then we thought it was a real deer until we walked up". Jarvis couldn't help it, he burst out laughing.

"Okay, boys, you're free to go."

Jarvis hired a taxi to take him and the two deer home.

Chapter 8

Jarvis went home and slept for eighteen hours before getting out of bed. He had been away from home for four days.

There wasn't any urgency to settle things with Rascal, so Jarvis spent the weekend at home with his family.

Come Monday morning, being well rested, a clean uniform and breakfast with hot coffee he boarded the northbound train for Whiskey Jack. He expected to find Rascal at the cafeteria. And of course he had his pack along with him.

Jarvis sat at a corner table and waited for Rascal. His other friends were already there. Jarvis got up and poured himself another cup of coffee and filled another cup and set it on his table. Silvio and Jeters were wondering what was going to happen now. It was obvious he was waiting for someone.

"Do you suppose he's waiting for Rascal?" Jeters asked in a low voice.

"I don't know, but we are about to find out. Here's Rascal now."

When Rascal started to walk over to the table where Silvio and Jeters were sitting Jarvis motioned for him to come over. "Sit down, Rascal. I even poured you a cup of coffee."

"That was a pretty good joke you pulled on those two guys from Massachusetts." Jarvis sipped his coffee.

Rascal knew Jarvis knew. But how? He didn't say anything. He sipped his coffee too.

Jeters and Silvio sat watching them.

"Those six point bucks are going to taste awful good this winter." He sipped at his coffee again. Still Rascal did not answer. He knew Jarvis was toying with him.

"$100.00 each, Rascal, for a six point buck? Didn't you think that was kinda high?"

"$50.00 for the deer, $50.00 for guiding, each."

"I can't let this go you know, Rascal."

"You going to take me to jail?"

"Nah, this is only a misdemeanor. I can't arrest unless the crime happens in my presence. No, I'll give you an invitation to court a week from this Wednesday."

"Judge going to give me any jail time?"

"For selling deer? Nah. But bring plenty of money. You pressed your luck too far this time, Rascal."

"What gave me away?"

"Bill and Jim. They were drinking before boarding the train and they kept drinking all the way to Beech Tree. They started talking. Not to me. Talking between the two of them. I was in the seat behind them."

"Are they going to be in court too?"

"No. I took their deer, and they gave me the whole story. I let 'em go. It was the seller—you—that I wanted."

"I should have known better. I didn't like those two the first time I met them."

"Tell me about this buck head."

Rascal told him the whole story. How he had waited until after 8 o'clock and was able to get across the mill yard without anyone seeing him. "I only wish I could have been there."

"But why Rascal?"

"Well, I guess coming from outside and having all the luxuries and money in life and treating people here like they were spit—well, I just wanted to put them in their place."

"Then why did you agree to guide and shoot their deer for a fee?"

"When I told them how much, I really didn't think they would go for it. When they agreed, I said, 'What the heck, I could use the extra money.' Besides, there wasn't anyone else wanting a guide. And part of it might have been because I didn't like the way they first treated me and I saw a way to take some of their money and ego."

"That's a pretty good story. And I believe you, Rascal, but it won't cut any ice with Judge Hulcurt.

"Oh. . . " Jarvis reached into his pocket then held his palm out. "I dug these slugs out of their deer. After court I'll give 'em to you."

"You know, Jarvis, when I saw you get on the train that morning, I had a real bad feeling."

The northbound had signaled it was about to leave and Jarvis stood up. "That's my call."

"Where you going now, Jarvis?"

"My work near the border isn't over yet."

Silvio, Jeters and now Jeff watched as Jarvis stood up to leave. They couldn't wait to hear what Rascal had to say.

Rascal sat down with his friends. His coffee was cold, so he poured another cup. "Well?" Silvio asked.

"Apparently those two from Massachusetts got liquored up and talking too much when Jarvis was in the next seat behind them. He heard the whole story and how much I charged them."

"Charged them for what, Rascal? Guiding?" Jeters asked.

"I shot them their deer and charged them for it."

"When do you have to be in court?" Silvio asked.

"A week from Wednesday."

"Well, hunting is over in five days. You coming to the Thanksgiving celebration?" Silvio asked.

"I'll be here."

Rascal went home and brooded about being caught. He should have been more careful—and stayed away from those two. But the possibility of earning another $200.00 clouded his common sense.

He had a lot of nervous energy so he went for a walk out back along the road. It was odd, there was no snow on the ground. Usually at this time in November there'd be a foot or more.

On top of the flateau there were two huge bull moose ready

to start sparring. They were so intent on each other they never noticed Rascal. Knowing how temperamental bulls can be and the damage they can cause, he stood behind a rock maple tree. They locked horns and they both went down on their knees and they started going around and around. Dirt was flying ten feet into the air.

They went around and around for several minutes. It wasn't an aggressive fight. Neither one was doing damage to the other. It was more like a contest of which bull was stronger.

Finally, as suddenly as it had started it was over. They both stood and after a few moments of staring at each other they both walked off, unhurt, in separate directions.

Rascal returned to the cabin and had supper ready when Emma arrived home from work. As they were eating, Rascal said, "Remember those two men from Massachusetts that I sold deer to?"

"Yes."

"Well they were liquored up when they boarded the train and of all places to sit, they chose a seat in front of Jarvis. And in their liquored state they started talking too much and before reaching Beech Tree Jarvis had the whole story. He has the two deer and I have to be in court again a week from Wednesday."

"Will you have to go to jail?"

"Jarvis said he didn't think so. He did say, though, that if he had been present when the two gave me the money, he would have taken me to jail then."

"So all of this came to light, to Jarvis' attention, because those two were liquored up. Drinking whiskey. Can you see the reprisal in this, Rascal? Because those two were drinking."

"Yeah, but Em, I wasn't drinking. If they had offered me a drink I would have said no, because I didn't like them."

"Then why did you sell them two deer?"

"Because I put a big price tag on them and they agreed to pay."

"Well, jail time or not, at least you'll be here for Thanksgiving."

The village was busy preparing for the Thanksgiving celebration. Everyone was anxious. It was always a good time. And this would be Rascal's first Thanksgiving since returning home. And he was as excited about the celebration as Emma.

The evening before, Emma put Rascal to work helping her mix together the flour and ingredients while she rolled out the dough and cut with her biscuit cutter. "I think we are going to need more stove wood, Rascal." By midnight Emma figured they had enough biscuits for everyone.

Rascal rented a horse and buggy from Owen. There were too many biscuits to carry and there were some icy spots on the road.

They left early. Emma needed to put her biscuits in the oven warmer, so people would have hot biscuits to eat.

There was a steady stream of food being brought in and tables to set up to self-serve.

The delicious aroma of all the food is now extending out into the village and mill yard. Which was beginning to draw people. Even Rudy Hitchcock was drawn to the cafeteria a little early because of the delicious smells.

No one was allowed to start self-serving until every villager was there. Soon all conversation stopped as everyone was busy eating. People went back for seconds and thirds. There was enough food.

When the meal was over the children helped the women folk clean up and take care of the food. And like all celebrations at Whiskey Jack Lake the more unfortunate and needy were given the leftovers. And they as always accepted the gift without any embarrassment. While the kitchen was being picked up and cleaned, the men gathered in another room and Rudy Hitchcock had two jugs of hard cider.

Once the meal was over, Rascal had to endure a lot of ribbing about being caught by Jarvis for selling deer. Eventually though, the topic of their conversation turned to Women's Suffrage and Prohibition.

"It is going to happen, men. Congress is going to enact the Volstead Act soon after the new year. Personally I think Prohibition will cause more problems than it'll solve. Here in Whiskey Jack Lake we do not see the ill effects of drinking. But in the large cities, as I understand, abuse of liquor has been a terrible plague."

Silvio said to Rascal, "Maybe, Rascal, before Prohibition becomes law we should purchase ingredients to make our own beer."

"Is it difficult to make beer? I have never seen it made."

"It isn't difficult, only time consuming. When you go to court, before leaving Beech Tree buy several cans of malt. I'll get the hops and sugar."

"I'll have to give you the cans of malt, Silvio. If Em finds it, there'll be hell to pay. Believe me."

After the hard cider was gone the women joined the men for conversation. When Emma saw the two empty jugs of hard cider, she gave Rascal a stern took. Rascal tried to ignore her look, but she was surely making him feel uncomfortable. He knew he would pay for his drinking once they were home.

It had been a joyous day for everyone and now it was time to go home. Emma never said a word all the way home. But once inside the cabin she said, "I saw all you men drinking again. You're not welcome in my bed tonight. I will not share my bed with a drunk." With that she closed the bedroom door and went to bed. Rascal was left standing. "Hell, yes, I was drinking, but I ain't drunk."

There was a cold wind blowing in from the north and Rascal filled both wood boxes and then lay down on the couch. Because of the hard cider he was feeling good and he really didn't care if he couldn't sleep in his own bed or not. Someday he'd find a way to even the score.

During the night as Rascal slept, bitter cold blew in from the northwest. He had to get up twice during the night to feed the wood heater. The wind was whistling around the cabin. This would finish freezing the ground and the lake groaned all night as ice was making and expanding.

As the sun was beginning to break against the darkness the wind suddenly stopped and it began to snow—heavily. When Emma woke up it was so cold in her bedroom she came out into the kitchen to dress. Rascal's drinking hard cider all but forgotten.

"You'll need to dress warm this morning, Em, when you walk to work. It's frigid cold this morning.

"The lake made ice all night so I think I'll take my traps and go up to the head of the lake and set for beaver before I have to use snowshoes or there is too much ice to cut through. There are two houses up there with feed beds."

"You be careful, Rascal."

Instead of hiking up Rascal decided to take the train. The engineer would stop anywhere along the tracks to let passengers get off or board. This gave him a few minutes to socialize with friends before going up.

Rascal shouldered his pack basket and walked with Emma to the village. "This looks like it's going to be a bad storm, Rascal. You be careful trapping."

Rascal talked with the station master, Greg, "Greg, any problems if I get dropped off at mile 11 this morning?"

"Just let the conductor know."

"Thanks, Greg."

His friends were not in the cafeteria, so Rascal had coffee and went back to the station house to wait for the northbound to leave.

When the train pulled in there were two passengers who stepped off. They looked like businessmen. "The weather bureau is predicting this storm to last for forty-eight hours. Two feet or more."

"Thank you," Greg replied.

When the northbound left it was still snowing heavily. Rascal was thinking he could have picked a better day to trap.

"Rascal, we're coming up to mile 11 now."

"Thank you, Kippy."

Rascal still carried his colt handgun. Just in case. *But that ole bear should be asleep now. But then again, he ain't no normal bear, either.*

Rascal wanted to set up on the swamp where he had seen the new works when he was fall trapping. The swamp there had only three inches of ice. He set two baited bank sets in two shallow beaver runs and one baited pole set near the feed bed. It would be much easier and more profitable to set on the dams like he had done for the nuisance beaver, but they were nuisances and it would be illegal to set on the dam now. When the ice gets thicker he might have a change of heart.

When that new colony was set he beat-footed for Jack Brook. There was a new house at the mouth of the brook and another in the cove to the left. He set two traps at each house. Then he started hiking down the lake staying close to shore.

There was a little more ice in the two colonies at the head of the lake. Inspite of the cold and snow, he was glad he had come out today. Tomorrow or even after the snow storm there would be more snow to wade through, he would have been more tired. As he was on his way down the lake, his bad leg was beginning to cause him to limp more pronounced.

He was cold and tired and he went straight home, not stopping at the cafeteria.

When Emma came in from the storm she was covered with snow and looked like an eskimo. "Are you going out tomorrow?" she asked Rascal.

"No, I heard it's suppose to storm tomorrow also. Even if it doesn't I'll wait until the wind has blown the snow off the lake."

The snow storm blew out mid-afternoon the next day. It was Saturday and Emma was thankful she didn't have to trudge through the snow to work. Rascal shoveled snow around the cabin to bank it against the cold and wind. The floors inside were noticeably warmer.

He snowshoed the path to the road behind the house and a team of horses were working back and forth the length of the road to settle the snow so it would harden in the cold air. Rascal didn't get to town at all.

When the snow storm quit there were two feet of new snow. Albeit dry and it would soon settle or be blown away.

The wind blew strong all Saturday night and by morning the lake had been blown clean. "I'll go up with the train in the morning and check the traps I have out now." It was so cold during the night, making thick ice on the lake and in the usual places pressure ridges had started to form.

Rascal decided to wait for Monday to check his traps. On Sunday there is no northbound train from Whiskey Jack and he would have had to walk the tracks to Ledge Swamp.

Monday morning was not as frigid and there was no wind. But it was still a cold walk to work for Emma. "I guess I'll never get use to this cold, Rascal."

"You getting soft, Em?"

As cold as it was, this was the weather that those working in the woods liked best. The wet areas and mud had frozen and the horses had an easier time twitching out their loads. The men—most of them still worked in their shirt sleeves, some sweating profusely.

Even though there had been two feet of snow, it was dry and light and Rascal didn't think he would be needing his snowshoes. He got off the train at Ledge Swamp and the snow was up to his knees.

He was cutting quite a trail through the snow, but it didn't tire him too much. With the new snow it was a little difficult to see where he had set up. But eventually he found his sticks and shoveled the snow off the ice. There was big air bubbles under the ice and in the trap hole. This usually meant beaver.

In the two shallow bank sets he had a super large beaver in each and nothing had touched the baited pole set. He reset those two traps and rubbed snow in the fur and put them in his pack.

He was glad he had cut such a deep trail. It made walking back easier.

At the head of the lake he started a fire first and skun one beaver and cut off a hind leg to roast. Then he skun the other beaver and checked the two traps at each of the two colonies. He had two more super large beaver. He skun those while the beaver leg was roasting.

Four super large beaver was a good day's work. But the work wasn't over yet. He still had to stretch and nail 'em to drying boards. When the meat was done, he ate his fill. He shouldered his pack and started down the lake.

He was back early and had all four hides on drying boards before Emma was home from work. "How'd it go today?"

"Four nice beaver and on the way back I worked up a sweat and then I got chilled to the bone."

"Are you going out tomorrow?"

"Don't think so. I have court on Wednesday and I don't want something to happen and make me late or not able to go."

He worried all day on Tuesday, how much Judge Hulcurt would fine him. His friends in the cafeteria were teasing him about getting caught. "Gee, Rascal, as chummy as you and Jarvis have become, I'm surprised he didn't let you go," Silvio taunted.

"Any idea how much it'll cost you?" Jeters asked.

"Jarvis said it all depends on how the judge is feeling."

"Ah he won't give ya more'n a week in jail, Rascal," Jeters said and then laughed. Silvio laughed too. Jeff didn't know what to think and he wasn't about to make fun of him.

Rascal was down at the station house early and the conductor announced, "The southbound train will be a few minutes late. The crews are still coupling the freight cars."

This didn't make Rascal any happier. Although it wouldn't be his fault for being late he remembered what Jarvis had said.

The only passengers this morning beside him was four business-looking men. Finally the passenger car was jolted as the freight cars were coupled. The engineer blew the whistle and the train lurched forward.

Rascal was figuring on coming down to the two other beaver colonies as soon as he had the adults from the head of the lake. With the new snow there wasn't much to see.

The engineer was trying to make up for the delay at Whiskey Jack, but even so Rascal was twenty minutes late. Jarvis was in the hall waiting for him. "Judge Hulcurt has already called your case, Rascal."

"The southbound was twenty minutes late leaving this morning. There was nothing I could do."

Rascal followed Jarvis into the courtroom and sat down. Hulcurt waited until he had heard each of the other cases before calling Rascal to the front of the court.

"You'd better have a good explanation for being late, Mr. Ambrose."

"I do, Your Honor."

"Well what is it?"

"The southbound train from Whiskey Jack was delayed because the crews had to couple four additional cars to the train. I came straight from the station."

"Fair enough. The charge against you, Mr. Ambrose, is selling deer. That is two deer. You guilty or not, Mr. Ambrose?"

"Guilty, Your Honor."

"Are you going to offer up any excuses or reasons why?"

"No, Your Honor.

"What do you do to earn a living, Mr. Ambrose?"

"I collect total disability from the Army and I trap and guide a little to help out."

"Why is a young man like yourself on disability?"

"I was wounded twice in the trenches in France."

"Yeah, that was a dirty war. I lost my only son in the trenches. So you figured to earn a little extra money by selling two deer to two out of state sports." Statement not a question.

"That's not quite correct, your Honor."

"Then perhaps you had better explain to the court."

"Well, more than anything I did it so those two would feel a little humility."

"Explain."

"When they arrived in Whiskey Jack on Sunday they were already liquored up and making fun of the village and everything there and my name, Rascal. They wanted me to guide for them. I told them I didn't like their attitudes and I turned them down. Then a couple of days later they saw me at the cafeteria and said they were not having much luck shooting a deer. They were seeing deer and shooting at them and missing. They asked me if I could shoot one for each of them. I told them I would, but it was going to cost them a $100.00 each. I figured $50.00 for the deer and $50.00 for guiding them. One of my stipulations was they had to go out in the woods with me."

"Warden Jarvis, how did you happen onto the two sports?"

"I was on the train with them to Beech Tree. I was sitting in the seat behind them. They were both liquored up and still drinking and they started talking too much."

"How did you know that it wasn't just talk?"

"They each were using a .30-30 and I dug .38-55 slugs from both of their deer. They gave me almost the same story that Rascal just told the court. Rascal is the only resident in Whiskey Jack that uses a .38-55."

"Um, this has certainly been an interesting case. I can not condone what you did, Mr. Ambrose, and although I may understand why you did, I can neither condone that. I do believe you to be a honest man though, but I have no choice but to find you guilty. You say you charged each of them $50.00 for selling them their deer and the other $50.00 you say was for guiding. Since, as you say you didn't sell the deer for money but more to teach them some humility then you should have no objections if I fine you $50.00 for each deer." Hulcurt hit the bench with his gavel and said, "Case closed."

"Oh, Warden Jarvis, what happened to the two deer?"

"I have them at my house, Your Honor."

Jarvis walked with Rascal to the clerk's office and after Rascal paid his fine Jarvis said, "How about lunch."

Once outside the courthouse, Jarvis said, "Jesus, Rascal, when you told the judge you didn't exactly sell the deer for money, I thought you'd dug your own grave. Hulcurt was in a good mood today I guess.

"What did you bring your pack basket for?"

"I need to pick up some things before going back."

After having lunch with Jarvis, Rascal went to the general store and bought four cans of malt and then two two-gallon jugs of whiskey. The malt he would have to keep at Silvio's and he doubted Silvio would mind storing the whiskey. Besides, he still had one full bottle hidden in the woodshed.

Chapter 9

"Why did you take your pack basket with you to court?" Emma asked.

Rascal was not about to lie to Emma so he told her the truth. Most of it at least. "In lieu of Prohibition becoming law soon, Silvio asked me to pick up some whiskey for him."

"Does he really drink that much?"

"Not really; he and his wife Anita usually have a nightcap every evening. He says it helps his circulation, and it's a good cold medicine."

Emma didn't respond to that.

Rascal filled his pack basket with traps and boarded the southbound and got off below mile nine. He was a while finding the beaver runs under two feet of snow, but he did find them and he set two bank sets and two baited pole sets.

The second flowage was not far and he set two bank sets there. When he next tended at the head of the lake and Ledge Swamp he had two more super large beaver and three large or two year olds. One more tend and he would pull his sets there. These were not nuisance beaver and he wanted to leave some seed.

Two days later he tended at mile seven and the other close flowage and had one super large in the first flowage and two large beaver in the next one.

He wondered if some two year olds had ventured out on their own. The next tend would tell. Usually he caught the older beaver first.

At the head of the lake and Ledge Swamp he pulled all of his sets. He had three more two year olds. He knew there were more beaver but he didn't want to take them all. Two more tends at mile seven and he had two super large beaver and one small. He pulled his sets there also.

In three short weeks he had trapped eighteen beaver. Besides, the snow was getting deep and he had to use snowshoes. He took particular care of the beaver hides. He wanted top dollar for these. A trip he and Emma wouldn't make until April. With deep snow many trappers would be hamstrung and if the number of available hides were low, the price should go up. If he waited any longer to sell the warmer weather would ruin them.

"Mr. Hitchcock is providing a Christmas dinner for everyone this year and with a bonus for all employees. He said their business has been so good the company can well afford it," Emma said.

Christmas this year was on Sunday and much to everyone's surprise the Reverend Phillips from Beech Tree was there and held church services before Christmas dinner. Emma looked around and smiled. Everyone from Whiskey Jack was there. As much as some would grumble, the services, she knew, would be good for them.

The temperature dropped again soon after Christmas and the pressure ridges making during the night could be felt in people's homes like earthquakes.

In spite of the extreme cold people gathered at the cafeteria on New Year's Eve. This was more of an adult party and kids stayed home as did some of the older residents. There was no meal but most people brought snacks. Silvio volunteered to make a punch which he managed to slip in a little whiskey. Just to spice it up. He didn't let on that he had spiked the punch. Everyone thought it was very good, even Emma.

Rascal, after one taste, suspected Silvio had added a little whiskey and he watched as everyone enjoyed it.

A husband and wife team, the Newburgs, were both fiddle players and Mrs. Newburg was a pretty good singer. They played music and Mrs. Newburg sang, when she knew the words, and people danced. Rascal and Emma were good dancers and many of the men, especially the older men, wanted their turn with Emma. Rascal didn't mind. He was glad to see Emma having a good time.

He smiled whenever she looked his way and he refilled her punch glass.

At midnight they all sang Auld Lang Syne and then people left to go home. Many of them feeling the effects of the spiked punch.

Emma slipped on the snow and fell once and then Rascal put his arm around her waist to steady her the rest of the way home. In spite of the cold, Emma laughed and giggled all the way home.

The cabin was still warm when they stepped in from the cold. "I'll stoke the heater with wood before getting ready for bed."

Emma was standing beside the wood heater and took all of her clothes off and said, "I'm ready for bed now."

Rascal picked her up in his arms and carried her into the bedroom and laid her on the bed. The room was cold and Emma scurried under the covers. Rascal turned the lights out and joined her. She rolled over and laid her head on his chest and was instantly asleep.

Come morning the temperature was not as cold. Rascal was up early and put more wood in the heater and started a fire in the kitchen stove and then he made some coffee and waited for Emma to get up.

Once the coffee was perking and the smell filled the air Emma wasn't long getting up. She came out and stood by the wood heater. "Oh, that feels good," she said.

"Em—don't you think you ought to put on some clothes."

"Um—guess I forgot I took all my clothes off last night. The heat sure does feel good though."

While Emma pulled her clothes on, Rascal fixed her a steaming cup of coffee.

"Here, this will wake you up."

She took a sip and said, "This is good, Rascal. I must be coming down with a cold or something. I have a headache this morning."

"Do you want a cold press for your head?"

"No, it isn't that bad. But I'm glad I don't have to go into work today."

Rascal knew what was causing Emma's headache, but he surely wasn't going to tell her she was suffering from a hangover. He'd never hear the end of it.

* * *

The new year came in with heavy snow and wind. The ice on the lake was now three feet thick and making more ice every night. Rascal was glad he had pulled all of his beaver traps. He had originally wanted to trap more into the season, but the weather had stopped him.

Needing to keep busy, Rascal would go around the village helping people shovel their pathways and bank their houses. After one extreme storm he even volunteered to help dig out the railroad tracks. Without the railroad, the mill town could not exist.

With the deep snow and more and more orders coming in, Hitchcock and company had to do something about getting the logs to the mill faster. Where the crews were lumbering behind Rascal's cabin and on top of the flateau was not a problem. It was a down hill twitch and a short twitch at that to the mill. But the problem was getting the saw logs from the farm to the mill faster. So two weeks into the new year the C&A railroad delivered a Lombard steam log hauler. When the northbound train pulled onto a siding where there had been made a ramp, the log hauler was already belching smoke and steam and ready to be driven off the railcar. Those not already working turned out to watch as the steam-belching monster churned its way off the ramp and across the mill yard.

"So this contraption is suppose to replace the horse, huh," Silvio said. "I'll believe it when I see it."

"It's being used already, Silvio, in other parts of the state," Rascal said.

There were ten empty log sleds in the yard and they were connected to the log hauler and it disappeared out of sight towards the farm at 4.5 miles per hour.

Just before dark the log hauler returned from the farm hauling ten loaded sleds with eight hundred board feet of lumber per sled.

On the morning of the eighteenth, Rascal joined his friends for coffee. "I guess I was wrong about that log hauler. That was some impressive train it was hauling yesterday. Maybe it will replace the horse, that is on long hauls like this," Silvio said.

Then on another note, "Did you boys see the paper yet?"

"What about the paper, Silvio?" Jeters asked.

"Congress passed the Volstead Act at midnight last night. From this day on it will be illegal to manufacture, sell or drink alcoholic beverages of any alcohol content greater than half of a percent. Prohibition, boys, is here."

"This is a sorry day indeed." Jeff said, "Does that include beer?"

"Sure it does, beer has more alcohol than half of a percent. So does hard cider."

"Do you need warm weather to make beer, Silvio?" Rascal asked.

"Yes, unless you work it in your living space in your cabin. You need warm air for the brew to work."

"So, we should wait for spring before we try to make some beer?"

"Yes."

"Have you ever made wine, Silvio?" Jeff asked.

"Now, there you go boy. Yes, and it's stronger than wine you buy in a store too. I prefer rhubarb mix with raspberries. That's a fine tasting wine. Now if we take the cured wine and boil it in a still we could have us some jim-dandy brandy. It'd have a hellva kick to it too."

"All this is illegal ain't it?" Rascal asked.

"Yeah but—we'd be doing it for ourselves, not to sell. Ain't that different?" Jeters asked.

"It isn't bootlegging, but it's still illegal manufacture of alcohol," Silvio said. "But if we don't sell any, who's to know?"

"Okay, so when it warms up in the spring we can make beer. Then when the rhubarb is ripe, which Anita just happens to have a large patch between the garden and the woods. She only ever uses a little. A pie maybe and rhubarb sauce that she cans.

"Rascal, you must know where we can pick raspberries?"

"Yeah, on the flateau behind my house," Rascal said.

"Okay, we four keep this to ourselves. No one else needs to know," Silvio said.

"Who's going to be enforcing these Prohibition laws?" Jeters asked.

"Probably the county sheriffs," Silvio said.

When the coffee group broke up Rascal wandered over to the mill yard to look at the log hauler. The empty sleds from yesterday were being coupled to the log hauler. When all were coupled the operator signaled clear and no faster than a walk the log hauler train started its long journey to the farm. Rascal found this new machine fascinating.

That evening as he and Emma were eating supper he told her all about the log hauler and what he watched it doing. "That one log hauler will haul as many logs in one trip as horse teams could haul all day. I could almost walk as fast as it moves, but the power that machine puts out is unbelievable. The operator said he could haul twenty or more loaded sleds. Only the mill yard is too small to handle that many all at once.

Rascal was so fascinated with the new log hauler, one day he asked the operator if he could ride with him out to the farm. One man steered the machine from the front end and another fed fuel into the boiler and operated the valves. Even though it was a cold day it was comfortably warm standing next to the hot fire box of the boiler.

March came in like a lamb and the haul road to the farm had softened so much they had to stop using the log hauler. The mill yard was almost full now. Not wanting to leave the logs at the farm they brought the excess down and were piled down on the ice.

One morning while they were having coffee and donuts, Rascal said, "That steam log hauler has surely proven its usefulness. It is quite a machine."

"Yeah but," Silvio added, "it ain't no good unless there's snow and ice. Those lags wouldn't last a day running through mud and on gravel."

"But look how much work it has saved already this winter," Jeff said.

Silvio was from the old school and couldn't see any benefit in anything that would soon put men out of a job.

The end of March came back, not like a lion but more like a Siberian nightmare. Winds so strong it was too dangerous for the crews to work in the woods. And it was a difficult job to generate enough heat to produce steam for the log hauler, so it was backed into the barn at the farm. For five days without a break the wind blew and the temperature stayed below zero even in the day time. With the warm air the snows began. Light and fluffy at first, then as the air became wetter the snow was heavy.

Even the C&A trains found it difficult to stay on schedule.

But like everything else, the cold, wind and snowstorms passed and the roads, mill yard and twitch trails were a ribbon of mud.

One night at the supper table Rascal asked, "Em, I'd like to take my beaver to Marquis Furrier in Lac St. Jean. Any chance you could get Friday off?"

"I'll check. It shouldn't be any problem. But like last time, I might have to work on Sunday to make up."

Rascal spent the next days preparing the pelts for the furrier.

He washed the fur side only and as the fur was drying he would brush it and untangle any knots. The flesh sides were now white and all eighteen pieces were looking exceptional.

"Mr. Hitchcock said I didn't have to come in on Sunday. Maybe we could stay two nights?" she pleaded. "You know this has been an awful winter."

"Sure we can."

The next day, Thursday, Rascal bundled his pelts, bathed and laid out clean clothes to take.

As they were walking on the side of the muddy road to the station house Emma said, "I have always hated this time of year here. Everything is so muddy. At least in the winter everything is covered with a white blanket of snow."

"You're talking like you want to leave Whiskey Jack, Em."

"No, not really. It was just a God-awful cold winter. Come on, I'm looking forward to this weekend."

Emma joined the boys club this morning for coffee, donuts and conversation. The northbound soon rolled to a stop and it would be a few minutes before the switching was finished.

Jeters acted a little nervous. He always did around Emma, since Rascal had cornered him last summer and made him tell the truth about getting drunk at the head of the lake. And Silvio was one who always was pushing things, "...to test the water," he would say.

"Rascal, would you pick me up a bottle of whiskey. Can't get anything out of Beech Tree any more."

"I'll see what I can do, Silvio." Emma threw a disgusted look towards Silvio, but he pretended not to notice.

The engineer blew the whistle and Rascal and Emma boarded the train and sat down. Again Emma wanted the window seat so she could see the countryside.

Even though warmer weather had returned, she noticed just how much snow there still was in the woods and there were still snow banks along the tracks.

In Lac St. Jean, Rascal hired a Model T Ford taxi to take

them to Marquis Furrier.

"Ah, Monsieur Rascal and your beautiful wife. Ah, you have beaver for me. Maybe these ones will have the long guard hair, no? Put them on the table and we will look them over." Marquis looked each pelt over closely, running his fingers through the fur and looking for holes. "These more better than what you brought in before. These I like me. Good for you Rascal, price much better too. I give you $40.00 each super large, $25.00 large, $10.00 small one. That $570.00. You take?"

"No. I'll take $600.00."

"You throw in d'castors. I give you de $600.00."

"I don't have the castors. I use them for fall trapping. $600.00."

"You hard man, Rascal. I give to you $600.00—without d'castors."

Without the bundle of fur to carry, Rascal picked up his pack—he didn't have a grip—and the two of them walked to the hotel. It wasn't too far.

They were able to get the same room as they had on the last trip. "I want to walk around some, Rascal. It's such a beautiful day."

"That sounds good. You be the guide. I'll go wherever you want."

First, they walked the full length of main street in both directions. Window shopping mostly. They did find a sidewalk café and ate a sandwich with their coffee. From there, while Emma was in a ladies dress shop, Rascal went next door where liquors were sold. He bought a bottle of whiskey for Silvio and a bottle of applejack brandy, made from hard cider, for himself.

When Rascal went back to the dress shop, Emma was trying on a dress. "I purchased one, Rascal, that's fashionable in Boston and New York and now I want another, more country dress. I hope you don't mind."

"Not at all."

"What do you have?"

"A bottle of whiskey for Silvio. I promised, and a bottle of applejack for me. It is also a good cold medicine." Emma didn't say no. In fact she didn't say anything at all.

When Emma had her two dresses Rascal hired the same taxi driver to give them a tour of the city. Rascal could see Emma was really enjoying herself on this trip. More so than last fall.

When the tour of the city was over they went to their room. "Now I want a hot bath," and she had brought some of her flowery smelling soap.

"Rascal, do you think you could build us a bathroom inside the house, with running water and a flush toilet? I'm so tired of having to go out to the outhouse every time. Especially in the winter."

"I could do that I suppose. I could use one of the empty bedrooms, and get enough piping from the mill maybe."

"And I'll go to Beech Tree and pick out a toilet and tub."

Emma soaked in the tub until the water had no more heat. Rascal was in and out and Emma still hadn't dressed.

"You'd better get dressed, Em. You'll look pretty funny going down for supper like that. Although you'd certainly have everyone's attention."

"It's taking a long time to dry my hair."

"That's okay, Em. I like looking at you with no clothes on. I don't have much of a chance anymore."

"Well, enjoy it while you can."

When her hair was finally dry and brushed out and wearing her new Boston and New York fashionable dress, "My word Em—you look so beautiful."

"Are you ready to eat?" she asked.

She walked beside Rascal with her arm linked with his and as they walked into the dining area everyone stopped to look. "You are the center of attraction, Em. Everyone is looking at you. Give 'em a smile."

She did and they all smiled back. "I don't know why, Rascal, but I feel like a queen just entering a ballroom."

"Well Em—then you are a queen," and he squeezed her hand gently.

They were escorted to the best table in the dining room.

"Rascal, order us a bottle of that good wine before we order our meal."

The wine came and Emma sipped hers and said, "This is so much better than what we had last time."

"What are you going to have, Rascal?"

"I liked the fish platter we had last time, but you know, we don't get to eat much good beef. I think I'll have the prime rib roast. What about you Em?"

"I was going to have the fish platter again, but I think I'd like the rib roast also."

While they waited for their meal they sipped wine and talked and laughed. "Oh, Rascal, I'm having so much fun."

He was surprised that Emma had not said anything to him about buying the whiskey and brandy. He knew she had not forgotten about it.

It was a good thing they were both hungry because the prime rib roast alone was one plate and then the potato and vegetable on another plate. "I don't know if I can eat all this."

Before their meal was half gone Rascal ordered another bottle of wine.

It took a little doing, but they each finally finished their meal. The waiter cleared the table, all except for the wine and glasses.

"This is a nice restaurant, Rascal. We should plan on coming up here twice every year. I wonder if anyone would mind if we took the rest of this wine and the wine glasses back to our room?"

"I don't think there'll be any problem."

They stood up and stepped away from the table and Rascal had to steady Emma for just a moment. They left the dining room with their arms around each other, and up the elevator to the fifth floor to their room.

Emma filled their glasses with the last of the wine. Rascal turned the light switch off and with his arm around Emma he guided her to the big window. They sipped their wine and Emma said, "From here look at all the city lights. It's so beautiful, Rascal. It makes me feel like we live in a backwoods village." She sipped her wine.

"Em, we do live in a little backwoods village. And I wouldn't want to live anywhere else. I like our log cabin, Em, and I like living in Whiskey Jack."

"I do too, Rascal, that isn't what I was trying to say." She finished her wine and set the glass down. Rascal had already finished his.

When Rascal switched the light back on Emma had taken all of her clothes off and was folding her new dress. Rascal was so taken with her sheer beauty, he stood there watching her.

"Well, you country bumpkin are you going to take your clothes off or not?" She giggled and picked the wine bottle up. Yes, it was empty.

* * *

Later as Em laid exhausted in his arms, Rascal was smiling. And then he started thinking about Emma, her attitude toward liquor and drinking, especially his drinking, her reactions to wine and the only time her love making was like it use to be before he went off to war, was after she had a little wine and then not realizing it was the wine that was offering her this mellow arousal in her sexual appetite.

Then he started thinking, wondering, if the death of their two children so close together wasn't the cause of her pious attitudes and toward drinking and her lack of sexual desires. The death of Beckie and Jasper to handle alone while he was in France had to be terrible, and without a doubt much more difficult for a mother to cope with. If she was ever to discover that the wine she likes that puts her into a seductive mood was actually an alcoholic beverage there would be hell to pay. So on these occasions he would have to limit her consumption.

She awoke the next day again with a slight headache. "I have another small headache, Rascal. I hope I'm not coming down with anything."

"The last time you had a headache had you bathed with any of your sweet smelling soap?"

"Yes, I did."

"Maybe they are causing some sort of reaction with you. Next time try a different one." He didn't know how much longer he could keep her from learning the headaches were caused by the wine, a hangover.

* * *

"You know Rascal, my headache is gone now. Maybe it is something in the hotel room. Next time we ask for a different room."

The cabin was cold when they arrived home. Now with both woodstoves going it wasn't long before Emma had to open the kitchen door for some cooler air. "The hotel is nice, Em, and the food in the dining room is very good, but I still like our cabin better."

"I do also, Rascal. Only it is good, for me, to get out of Whiskey Jack once in a while.

"When do you think you can start on our indoor bathroom?"

"I can start the inside work any time. But I'll have to wait for the ground to unthaw first before I can dig a pit."

"I'll have to make a wooden tank, sort of, to hold the solid waste until it breaks down and dissolves. The water will drain into the soil but I'll need to make a list of things I'll need. Maybe I can get some at Douglas' store and some at the mill. Maybe Douglas might have some catalogs for you to look at for the flush and tub."

"Do we have enough money, Rascal, to do the whole bathroom?"

"We should be okay. And here's what's left of the fur money."

After lunch Emma couldn't wait. "I want to go see Douglas now."

Rascal put his bottle of brandy in the cold storage. "I'll go down with you Em, I need to give Silvio this bottle of whiskey."

"Okay, don't you go drinking whiskey with him."

"You go look at Douglas' catalogs and I'll go give this to Silvio."

Everything was still muddy so Rascal had to pick his way to Silvio's. Silvio was sitting on the front steps. "Rascal."

"Silvio, here's your whiskey."

"How much Rascal?"

"$2.00."

Silvio paid him and asked, "Was the fur prices good?"

"Yes, but I thought they'd be better considering the deep snow this winter."

"Maybe you should have waited another month."

"I can't stay Silvio, Em is expecting me at Douglas' store."

Emma had already found what she wanted before Rascal was there. The piping Rascal knew he would be able to buy at the mill's machine shop, but he needed drain piping and fittings. Those he was able to order from Mr. Douglas. "It may take a few days for this Rascal. It'll have to come out of Portland, the same with the tub and flush."

"That'll be okay. I have a lot of work to do before I'll need it."

Monday morning after coffee at the cafeteria, Rascal went to see Howard Williams at the machine shop. Rascal had to rent a horse and wagon to get everything up to his cabin. Besides the piping he also had to borrow a pipe threader and stand. Rascal didn't know it would involve all this when he said he could do it.

The days went by and every day, after coffee and donuts at the cafeteria he would spend each day cutting, threading and running pipes for both hot and cold water to the new bathroom. He was methodical and rechecked each measurement.

He kept all the piping inside the cabin so the pipes would not freeze in the cold weathe.

When the water pipes were all in place and the tub, the flush and drain were not in yet, Rascal began digging a hole. And as it turned out, a big hole. Big enough to build a log sided box with a cover on the top, all from cedar.

When the tub and flush finally came in on the train, it was all Rascal and Emma could do to lift it off the wagon and carry it into the cabin.

"What is this made of? It's so heavy."

"Cast iron."

He was two more days connecting the tub and flush to hot and cold water pipes. He checked and rechecked to make sure he had everything done right before he would open the valves. The tank in the flush filled and there was both hot and cold water in the tub. Now all he had to do was back fill the tank and level off the ground. When Emma was home from work she was ecstatic. So much so there were tears in her eyes.

In between planting the garden and coffee with his friends, Rascal found time to go fishing at his secret spot. At the head of the lake, at the mouth of Jack Brook. He caught only twenty-five and gave half of them to Silvio and Anita. Then he would spend the rest of the day in the garden.

He took the fencing down around the garden and used it for pea fencing. Now that he was trapping again he could keep the raccoons out.

One day after the garden was planted and while having coffee with his friends, Silvio said, "The rhubarb is ready."

"What are we going to use to ferment the rhubarb in?" Jeters asked.

"I have a large crock especially made for fermentation. I'll need more sugar, Rascal."

"Okay, when we leave here I'll pick some up at Douglas' store."

"Mr. Douglas I need a twenty pound sack of sugar," Rascal said.

"Why so much Rascal?"

"We're all out at home and Em is going to do some canning."

Silvio had the rhubarb stalks cut and in his workshop. He and Rascal worked together to cut the stalks in small pieces. "Okay, now we add warm water. Anita has been warming some in the house."

"Why warm water, Silvio?"

"The natural yeast in the rhubarb will start working sooner. We'll have to add some too, but not much."

With the sugar, only fifteen pounds for now, and water were stirred sufficiently Silvio covered the top with cheese cloth to keep the flies out.

"How are the raspberries looking Rascal?"

"There is a lot of them up behind the cabin on the flateau. When will we add those?"

"Not until we start distilling the rhubarb wine. There is very little sugar in raspberries. We add them a day before we start distilling for flavor."

"How do you know all this, Silvio, about making beer, wine and brandy?"

"Before Anita and I moved to Whiskey Jack we use to make several gallons each year. The recipes were handed down from my father and his father."

"Did you sell any?"

"No, it was all used within the family or families. We never made it to sell. And I remember all the recipes."

Two days later before going home Emma stopped at Douglas' store for a few items. "Two more pounds of sugar Emma. You must be doing a lot of canning. I mean Rascal bought twenty pounds a few days ago."

"Oh, yeah, Mr. Douglas, I am." She was speechless now. Wondering why Rascal would buy twenty pounds of sugar. There was only one reason. He and Silvio and the others were making liquor. She decided not to say anything just now.

At the supper table that day she was unusually quiet, still

thinking about what she suspected Rascal and his friends were doing.

Emma was bathing each evening, now that she could soak in her own tub. And there was no going out to the outhouse in the middle of the night any more. She wanted to be happy, and if not for what Rascal was doing with all that sugar, she would be.

One morning while having coffee and donuts Rascal asked, "Silvio, would you like to go fishing today?" Jeters and Jeff had to sleep before going into work.

"Yes, but we need to check the wine first. Are you taking lunch?"

"Nah, if we catch anything before noon we'll build a fire and have roasted trout. We can pick us some fiddleheads too."

Rascal grabbed a bucket for fiddleheads and a gunny sack for brook trout. Silvio was waiting on shore when Rascal canoed over. As they were canoeing up the lake, "How is the wine doing?"

"Good, it's still fermenting."

"When do we bottle some and start distilling?"

"As soon as the fermentation stops. When gas bubbles stop coming to the top—fermentation has stopped."

Nothing more was said until they were at the mouth of Jack Brook. This wasn't Silvio's first trip to the head of the lake and he knew enough to wait in silence before casting a fly. When they both saw a trout break the surface, they knew it was time. Silvio laid a grasshopper fly where the trout had broken the surface and the trout took the fly and dived for the bottom.

He played it for a long time, tiring it out before bringing it in. "Do you have a net, Rascal?"

"Nope. Silvio if you can't land that brookie without a net you don't deserve to keep it."

"Seems to me I said the same thing to you once."

"You did."

Silvio brought the trout in gently and reached down and picked it up by the gills. "Two pounds at least," Silvio said.

Rascal soon brought one in about the same size. Before long they had several and pulled ashore to give the water a break and clean those. "You start a fire Rascal and I'll clean these."

They put the two trout on a stick to roast and sat back. "While you watch these, Silvio, I'm going to pick fiddleheads up along the brook."

Many of the fiddleheads had gone by, but there were plenty to pick. Rascal ate a couple raw. It didn't take long to fill his bucket. "Dinner cooked yet, Silvio?"

"Just been waiting for you."

They ate fresh cooked brook trout and raw fiddleheads. "We have quite a mess of trout now, Silvio, let's head back. Besides, I have fiddleheads to clean before Emma gets home."

When they left the protection of the cove there was quite a wind blowing. There were a few white caps. Luckily the wind was blowing down the lake. But still they stayed close to shore.

"Silvio, all right if I leave my canoe pulled up? The lake is too rough for me to canoe across."

"Sure thing."

Rascal gave half of the trout and fiddleheads to Silvio and Anita and walked home with the gunny sack over his shoulder and carrying the bucket of fiddleheads.

It took longer cleaning the fiddleheads than it did picking them. He finished just as Emma walked in. "I've been cleaning fiddleheads and haven't started supper yet. I have fresh brook trout also."

Emma walked over and kissed him. (No whiskey breath she noticed.)

Every day there were deer tracks in the garden but it didn't appear the deer were doing anything but walking through. The vegetable plants were all above ground. So Rascal wasn't too concerned, yet. There were no skunk tracks, or raccoon. And no bear problems in the village.

The station master, Greg, said one day. "Rascal, beaver are back at mile nine. If you can take care of it tomorrow I'll let you have Elmo Leaf and a handcar."

"Okay, have Elmo and a handcar ready to go as soon as the southbound clears the station."

From the station house Rascal had coffee with his friends. "Rascal, are the raspberries ready to pick?" Silvio asked.

"In about a week."

"Good, that'll be good. The rhubarb is almost finished fermenting. If they're ripe before then, pick 'em."

From the cafeteria Rascal followed the road to the flateau and the raspberries were almost ready to pick. He ate a few that were sweet and juicy. But too few to pick.

* * *

The next morning Elmo had coffee with the group and noticed Rascal was wearing a handgun. "You expecting that bear again Rascal? You're making me nervous."

"Just in case, Elmo. I've never understood why he chased us two miles to Ledge Swamp". He almost told his friends about his encounter with the same bear while he was trapping. But decided against it.

The southbound train whistle blew and Rascal and Elmo left the cafeteria and put the handcar on the rails and started down to mile nine. It was a quick trip and both Rascal and Elmo were watching for the bear.

"I thought we removed all of the beaver last year, Rascal," Elmo said.

"Well, I think we did. These are probably new beaver. A pair of two year olds or adults who had used up the area where they were and had to look for another area with a good flow of water and food.

"Look Rascal, there's one now bringing wood down to the dam," Elmo said.

"Step back Elmo, if we scare it, it might be a while before it comes back. Let's sit on the bank. The beaver won't be able to see us there."

While the beaver was securing his piece of wood in the dam Rascal prepared the trap. From where they were they could hear the beaver working on the dam. "There he goes, Rascal."

"Okay, help me dig out a channel, Elmo." The two working together had a channel in only a few minutes and Rascal set his trap. While he was setting that one Elmo was digging out another channel about six feet away. When Rascal had the second trap set they pulled back away from the dam and Rascal began looking for a trail the beaver were using from the water to land. They were just in time to see a large beaver dragging a popple top to the flowage. "Once he is out of sight we'll set another trap here."

"These buggers are sure hard workers."

"They have to keep chewing wood, Elmo, because their chisel teeth never stop growing. If he wasn't always chewing on wood the teeth would grow and pierce his jaws."

The beaver now out of sight Rascal worked quickly to set that trap just below the water surface in the beaver's trail. Just as he was finishing there came a loud crashing sound behind them. Both Rascal and Elmo jumped. "I hope that wasn't that damned bear, Rascal!"

"Sounded like a tree coming down to me. We'd better clear from here and look for another trail to the water."

They circled the flowage and only found a coffer dam where Rascal set another trap. From there they hiked back to the tracks to check the dam traps and they had a really large beaver. "Start a fire, Elmo, back away from the flowage, while I skin this and cut off the hind legs to roast."

As he was finishing that beaver, Rascal heard the second trap snap close and then a splash in the water as the beaver dove in. Not thinking about what he was doing Rascal rushed right down to the dam and instead of letting the beaver drown before pulling it in, he grabbed the chain and began pulling. At first there was no resistance and as he was starting to straighten up, the beaver on the other end had a different idea and he began to fight. The water was boiling, mixed with mud from the bottom and Rascal was pulled off his perch on the dam and took a nose dive into the boiling water.

Rascal should of let go of the chain, but he didn't and now that beaver with his last act in his life began pulling Rascal under water and up the flowage. Elmo heard the first splash when the beaver went into the water and he saw Rascal take a nose dive and he could see him being pulled upstream under water. Elmo began laughing and trying to holler at Rascal at the same time to let go of the chain. He was still laughing when Rascal's head broke the surface. Elmo was still laughing his fool head off.

"What did ya have to do, Rascal? Go swimming after it?" He was still laughing.

Rascal didn't think it was all that funny. He still had the chain in his hand and the beaver had stopped fighting. It took a while to get into shallow enough water where he could stand up and better drag the beaver behind him. By now Elmo had come down to the shore. He had stopped laughing.

When Rascal was able to drag the beaver out of the water, "Well look at that beaver, Rascal, I never knew beaver could get that big. That tail must be eight inches wide."

"Here, give me a hand carrying this Elmo." Rascal grabbed the front legs and Elmo the back legs.

"This fella must weigh sixty pounds Rascal."

"It's the biggest beaver I have ever seen, too. You aren't burning our lunch are you?"

Rascal finished skinning and fleshing the first beaver and rolled the hide up. He had the second beaver almost skun when Elmo said, "Beaver is cooked."

Rascal finished skinning and rolled the hide up and began eating roasted beaver leg. "My guess is, Elmo, there are only the two beaver here. We'll hold up a while and see if any more come to the traps."

Elmo was constantly looking around everywhere. "What are you looking for, Elmo?"

"That bear. That's what. He had the devil in him last year and

I don't want to meet up with him again."

They waited almost to dark before pulling the other traps. There were no more beaver. The afternoon southbound had already gone through so they knew the tracks would be free of trains.

Rascal gambled that those were the only beaver there and he and Elmo returned to Whiskey Jack. When he walked into the kitchen Emma asked, "What have you been doing, Rascal? You're all covered with mud and you smell."

When he told her the entire story, she broke out laughing just as Elmo had done. "I wish I had been there.

"What is it with you, Rascal, and that beaver flowage and animals?"

"I don't know."

* * *

The following week Rascal checked the raspberries again and they were ready to pick. He went back to the cabin and found a bucket and went back to the flateau. He could smell the sweet scent of the raspberries in the air. He picked all afternoon and filled his bucket. About two gallons. These would have been delicious to eat with pancakes or shortcake, but these berries were to be mixed with the rhubarb wine to flavor it while distilling it to brandy. As plentiful as they were he would come back again and pick some for he and Emma. He put the berries in cold storage.

He was home before Emma, so he started to fix supper. Warmed up biscuits, trout and last year's green beans cooked with a piece of salt pork.

The next morning he took the raspberries with him to the cafeteria. "I picked these yesterday, Silvio. I hope it'll be enough."

Silvio lifted the bucket and said, "This should be good. I'll take this home, Rascal, and if you would get some cheese cloth at Douglas store. You'd better get a case of Mason jars too. Anita won't let us use any of hers."

"Jeters, just so it doesn't look conspicuous you get a case of Mason jars too. It might raise Douglas' eyebrows if Rascal goes in and buys two cases," Silvio said.

"You go in first, Jeters, then I'll wait some before I go in."

Rascal wanted to give Jeters plenty of time and he didn't want it to look to obvious. So he went back to the cabin and just behind the garden was a doe with a spotted lamb. He threw a rock at the doe and she ran off blowing and waving her tail about. He walked up and down the garden and didn't see any fresh deer tracks. He pulled a few weeds, got some money and hiked down to Douglas' store.

"A case of Mason jars please, Mr. Douglas."

He set a new case on the counter and said, "I wonder what the attraction is? This is the second case of Mason jars I've sold this morning."

Rascal paid him without commenting about the sales. "Thank you, Mr. Douglas." Rascal closed the door feeling rather sheepish. Maybe because he knew what he was doing was wrong. But he never felt like this when he poached brook trout or a deer. *Why not then? What was the difference?* Emma was the difference. He knew if Emma knew what he was doing there'd be hell to pay.

Silvio, Jeters and Jeff had squeezed almost all of the rhubarb mash through the cheese cloth when Rascal arrived. "I thought you'd put the raspberries in the mash with the rhubarb Silvio."

"The mash would soak up too much of the flavor. This way we'll get a better yield."

Once all of the mash had been squeezed through the cheese cloth Silvio set everything aside and said, "Now boys we need to mash up these berries before we add them. Wash your hands good. Jeff go in the house and tell Anita we'll be needing four of her largest mixing bowls?"

Silvio poured the berries in each bowl and began mashing them with his hands. With all four helping it didn't take long.

Then he poured the mashed berries and juice with the new rhubarb wine. Silvio stirred the liquid a bit and then took a dipper full and tasted it and passed the dipper to the other three. He smacked his lips and said, "Mighty fine."

"Holy cow, Silvio, that's already stronger than any wine I have ever had. And it sure does taste good."

Jeters and Jeff said about the same thing.

"Now what do we do, Silvio?" Jeters asked.

"We let this set for two days then we fire up the still."

Silvio already had a still. In parts and pieces, that is, and he had managed to get it together.

"How long will it take to distill all of this?" Jeff asked.

"It's a slow process, maybe thirty hours."

"This sure is a lot of work just to have some liquor to drink," Jeff said.

"Trust me, it'll be worth it," Silvio said.

* * *

After work Emma stopped at the Douglas store before going home. "Well hello Emma what can I do for you?"

"I need a case of Mason jars, Mr. Douglas."

"You need another case already Emma? Rascal bought a case this morning."

Many things were going through Emma's mind. And first and fore most was Rascal and his friends. Could they be making an alcoholic beverage? " I'll take another case just in case, Mr. Douglas."

"Was there anything else Emma?"

"Ahh—there was but I can't think of it now."

On her way home she kept thinking why Rascal would buy a case of Mason jars? He had no idea she had needed more. She was sure he was up to something with Silvio. For now she decided not to say anything about the Mason jars or her suspicions.

When she walked through the door the first thing he saw

was the box of Mason jars and he swallowed real hard. Emma saw the expression on his face change and she said, "I picked up more canning jars. We have so much canned meat still, I'll need more for the vegetables."

All through supper Rascal was unusually quiet, while Emma was chattering away. She knew she had Rascal in a corner and she wasn't going to let on that she knew he was up to some no-good. Not just yet.

* * *

Instead of having coffee with his friends, Rascal hiked back up to the flateau and picked another bucket of raspberries. It took a little longer this time. The good picking was gone. Besides, a mother bear and cubs had been there ahead of him.

All the time while picking berries he kept thinking about Emma and her bringing home a case of Mason jars. Surely Mr. Douglas had told her he had also bought a case of jars. But she had not said anything about it. *Why? What is she up to?* This was worse than being thrown out of his own bed or spending a night in jail.

He put the berries in cold storage and then walked out back to look at the garden. There were fresh deer tracks again. But nothing had been touched, probably waiting until things were ripe.

He picked a few radishes and pulled a few weeds. The garden was doing good. The lettuce would be ready soon as would the peas. Emma particularly liked fresh lettuce. She would take a lettuce sandwich to work. As soon as it could be picked.

He stayed away from the cafeteria and his friends for two days. He was troubled why Emma had not said anything about the Mason jars he had bought. That was not like her. *Unless—unless she was planning something. But what? A lecture on the viles of alcohol. Or was she scheming to get me in church again to listen to a sermon on how bad alcohol is to the spirit, body and mind?*

Not knowing was worse than *knowing* what she was planning. "Or am I being paranoid?" He said aloud to himself.

* * *

Jarvis stepped off the morning train as Rascal was pulling away from the public wharf. He met Emma on her way to work. "Good morning, Emma."

"Good morning, Jarvis."

Jarvis watched until Rascal was out of sight around the point. His first instinct was to hike up the tracks and then down to the lake and watch to see what he was up to. But he was there in Whiskey Jack to walk around the cuttings at the farm.

* * *

It was a warm sunny day and Rascal was glad to be by himself. There was only a gentle breeze. Just enough to keep the deer flies and mosquitoes at bay. He caught a few frogs first and then he moved over so he could cast his fly in the mouth of Jack Brook. He waited several minutes after disturbing the water. His first cast brought in a two pound brook trout. "This one will be dinner." It had an orange belly and blue down its back. He caught several more nice trout. But not as big, and he went ashore and built a fire and put the two pound trout on a spit to roast and he cleaned the other trout and put them with some grass in the gunnery sack.

As he waited for the fish to cook he made some hot tea. He laid back looking at the blue sky. He took a short catnap while he waited for the fish to finish cooking. He poured another cup of tea and checked the fish. The skin was beginning to peel away. A sure indication that it was cooked. The meat was unusually sweet and good and he ate every bit. He even picked away at the head.

He laid back again and he really could have gone to sleep.

His belly was full of good food and it was a hot, lazy day. But he needed to catch more frogs and a few more trout. He had to force himself to get up and put the fire out and go back to frogging.

He pushed off in his canoe and quietly guided it to another spot among the lily pads. There were frog heads peaking above the water everywhere.

As he dangled the fly in front of the frogs, he was once again having a difficult time staying awake. He decided to catch only a few more and then he'd catch a few more brook trout. He unhooked one frog and extended his fly rod out and dangling the fly in front of another frog. His head was dropping and his eyes were hazy and hard to keep open.

Then he fell asleep and fell out of the canoe, almost completely turning it over. When he hit the water, he woke up and suddenly realized what had happened. He immediately righted the canoe. It was still half full of water. Everything stayed in the canoe except his fly rod. That was now in the black muck. He could see the fly line still floating on top of the water and he grabbed it and was able to pull his rod to him. He put it in the canoe and then started trying to pull it ashore so he could turn it over and empty the water. But there was very little to brace his feet on while pulling the canoe and it took him a long time to get it ashore.

* * *

At the same time that Rascal was eating brook trout for dinner, Emma had decided what she was going to do about Rascal and his friends making liquor. She wrote a short letter to a friend who lived in Beech Tree, Nancy Libby. Asking her to forward the enclosed letter to Sheriff Lee Burlock. She explained why she had to stay anonymous.

Then she had to write a letter explaining to Sheriff Burlock of the illegal manufacturing of liquor in Whiskey Jack.

Dear Sheriff Burlock

For reasons I cannot explain I must remain anonymous.

There are four men in Whiskey Jack who are manufacturing liquor.

Silvio Antony, Rascal Ambrose, Asbau Jeters and Jeff Daniels. It is occurring behind Silvio's cabin in a shed. I have noticed since yesterday smoke coming from the shed where I believe it is being cooked.

To lend credence my husband, I'm not saying his name, is involved.

Signed, Anonymous

She put both letters in an envelope and addressed it to her friend and posted it at the C&A station house. Sheriff Burock might receive it in the afternoon or tomorrow. She hoped she was doing the right thing.

* * *

Everything that was in Rascal's pack was now soaking wet. Even his matches. He really didn't want to canoe all the way back, soaked to the bone and smelling like an outhouse. He was covered with the black muck. It took some doing to pull the canoe on shore enough so he could turn it over and empty the water. But after a while he managed to push it back in the water and climb in.

As he began paddling, he could hear the southbound as it went by Ledge Swamp. Although he was soaking wet he wasn't cold. Only he smelled awful. So he paddled with urgency.

* * *

Jarvis was walking towards the station house when he saw Rascal pull his canoe ashore at Silvio's cabin and then Rascal picked up a gunny sack. The southbound came through then blocking out Rascal. Jarvis was tired and he needed to get home. He hoped Rascal was only brining the Antonys some brook trout and not a little deer.

He shrugged his shoulders and found an empty seat.

"Silvio!" Rascal hollered.

Silvio came out and immediately started laughing. "Boy, are you a sight. What, did you fall out of your canoe?" He laughed so loud Anita came out to see what was happening. And she began to laugh also.

"I have some brook trout for you, if you want them."

"If you don't mind, Rascal, I'll take the trout, but you need to go home and clean up." He took the sack of fish.

"Rascal, we'll start the still tomorrow. I'll see you for coffee and donuts first, though."

The mill's steam whistle blew and Emma's work day was over. Rascal canoed down the cove near the cafeteria. Emma was walking across the dam. She hollered, "I'll walk!"

When he pulled his canoe ashore in front of his cabin he waded out into the water and submerged. Trying to wash off some of the smelly mud. Emma saw him clothes and all go in the water and wondered what that was all about.

When she got to the cabin, Rascal's clothes were piled up outside. She picked them up to look at them and instantly understood. She wondered what he had been doing this time.

Rascal took his clothes off outside and went inside and jumped in the tub. When Emma walked in and closed the door she was laughing. "What happened to you?"

"I was covered in that black, stinky mud."

"How did that happen?"

"I fell out of the canoe while frogging."

"Were you drinking?" real serious like.

"No, I wasn't drinking. I fell asleep and fell out of the canoe."

Emma broke right out laughing. She laughed so hard she had to sit down on the toilet.

Rascal couldn't see the humor in it and he remained straight faced and serious.

Finally she composed herself and asked, "You want me to believe that you fell asleep and fell out of our canoe?" she was laughing again. "Coming from anyone else but you, Rascal, I'd say you'd been drinking and that was a tall tale. But after the experiences you had last year with that bear, —well I guess I can believe it," She was still laughing when she left Rascal alone in the bathroom. Rascal's feelings were hurt.

* * *

The next morning at the cafeteria Rascal had made up his mind not to say anything about the day before. They wouldn't understand and would only laugh. He only hoped Silvio wouldn't mention it. "Well, you boys ready to start the still?"

They followed Silvio to his shed behind the cabin. All four walked together over to his cabin. Emma had gone to the file cabinet with some papers and looking out the office window, she saw all of them heading towards Silvio's cabin. She knew what they were doing and she now had no regrets about her letter to Sheriff Burlock.

Years ago Silvio had made a fire box with bricks. The top was just right to hold a large copper canner. Stovepipe from the back vented the smoke outside.

"Help me lift this canner on top of the hearth." It fit perfectly. "Jeff, the top is over there in the corner."

"Jeters we'll need that copper spiral tubing." With the top on the canner and secured, the copper spiral cooler threaded on the top. "Now we're ready to heat."

The open end of the spiral copper tubing cooler stretched out and down so that the distilled liquor would run into a Mason jar. "It'll take some time to bring this to a boil. As the alcohol evaporates and runs through the copper spiral it will cool and condense and only liquid will come out the open end into the jar. Now boys, if you get the fire too hot and it boils to fast you might cause steam vapor to come out the tube. If you do just back off on the fire some."

"How long will this take, Silvio?" Jeters asked.

"Well, it'll take about two hours each day to start to boil and we probably shouldn't let it boil or add to the fire after four in the afternoon. If I start the fire each morning before I go to the cafeteria, we might get two or three quart jars a day. You need to understand this is a slow process."

* * *

As Emma stood in the window and watched as the four men walked to Silvio's, Nancy Libby was delivering her letter to Sheriff Burlock. He read it and asked, "Do you know who this is from, Mrs. Libby?"

"I'd rather not say Sheriff. I do not want to be brought into this, okay."

"That's okay. I was just curious that's all. Thank you."

Sheriff Burlock had never been to Whiskey Jack. There was never any need—until now. He didn't know the people nor was he even acquainted with the names in the letter. But he knew someone that had had a lot of dealings in the past in Whiskey Jack. And he left his office and walked over to his house and knocked on the door.

Jarvis' wife Rita answered the door. "Good morning, Rita, is Jarvis home?"

"Yes, come in, Sheriff."

"Good morning, Jarvis, is there somewhere we can talk in private?"

"Sure come into my office." Jarvis closed the door and asked, "What's up, Lee?"

Lee gave Jarvis the letter. "I received this only this morning. And I can't say how, Jarvis."

Jarvis read the letter and put two and two together and

figured he knew who the anonymous writer was. "I know all these names."

"Do you think it is worth looking into? I don't know the village nor anyone there. You'd have a better understanding."

"Well, all four would be capable. The ring leader is probably Silvio. He is the oldest and the most time on his hands. How big of an operation is it, Lee?"

"I don't know. The information I have is that it is ongoing. I would like to take the train up there tomorrow morning. I could sure use your help, Jarvis, since you know these people and the village."

"Sure. No problem. One suggestion though, Lee."

"What's that?"

"That we don't take the train into Whiskey Jack. Everybody there knows everybody else and their business. If you show up and you have never been there before, within five minutes everyone will know—suspect why you are there."

"Then what do we do?"

"We ride in the freight car so no one knows we are onboard and I'll ask the conductor to let us off at mile nine and a half. We'd have a half mile walk to the village."

"Okay, you get us there and I'll take it from there."

"If you find they are operating a still, what will you do? Arrest them or only summons them?"

"I received a bulletin on how to handle it. If they are only consuming an alcoholic beverage then I am to summons, unless there are other circumstances involved. If they are manufacturing liquor, running a still, then I am to arrest them."

"That makes it pretty clear," Jarvis said.

"What time does the train arrive in Whiskey Jack?"

"Usually between 7:30 and 8 o'clock. When it does arrive the four are usually having coffee and donuts in the cafeteria. I sometimes join them."

"I'll meet you in the morning then at the station house."

* * *

The next morning Rascal walked with Emma across the dam and kissed her goodbye. "See you tonight."

As she sat alone at her desk, she was thinking she should feel guilty for what was to happen to her husband that day and the three other men, but she didn't. Losing her two young children with the fever while Rascal was off fighting changed her, and she wanted to live a pious life and she wanted the same for Rascal. She had convinced herself that a little hard medicine might be good for his soul.

Rascal joined his friends at the corner table in the cafeteria for coffee and fresh donuts. "I started the fire at sunrise this morning. We distilled two quarts yesterday. I stayed with it until after supper. By noon we should have another two quarts. It was already boiling before I left to come here."

"Well, how is it, Silvio?" Jeters asked.

"Excellent, it has just a bit of raspberry flavor. It's something you'll want to sip and not drink," Silvio said.

* * *

Sheriff Burlock and Jarvis boarded the freight car without anyone seeing them and Jarvis asked the conductor, "Jim, would you stop the train for us at mile nine and a half, so we can jump off?"

"Sure thing, Mr. Page. Can I ask why?"

"Better if you don't know anything."

"Okay, Sir."

The train slowed at mile nine and a half and Burlock and Jarvis jumped off. The train then picked up speed and continued on. They walked the rails for a ways and then Jarvis turned left and up through the woods. "Where are we going, Jarvis?"

"You can't expect to walk into the village, across the mill yard and to the upper end of the village without people noticing, can you? We'll walk around the town and come in behind Silvio's place without anyone noticing."

"Are we following some kind of a trail, Jarvis?"

"Well, I've used it so much through years I guess I sort of beat down a path."

"Do you always work like this?"

"People usually don't see me until I want to be seen. It doesn't always work out that way, but that's how I work."

They were on a knoll overlooking the village when Jarvis said, "There, Lee, do you see those four men walking to the left?"

"Yes."

"Those are the men you are after." They stood there and watched as the four men went to the shed behind the cabin.

"There's smoke coming out from the shed. That's where they're cooking."

They continued through the woods until they were directly behind Silvio's cabin. "Your show from here, Lee. I'll assist. They won't give you any trouble, I can assure you that much."

There was no windows in the shed and Jarvis and Lee didn't have to sneak up. The door was closed but not latched. Lee opened it just like he would any door. Silvio, Rascal, Jeters and Jeff all turned to look and their mouths dropped open. Rascal was the first to speak. "Hello, Jarvis."

Jarvis didn't say anything, he just smiled. Rascal was thinking, *I had a feeling something was going to happen.*

"Are you Silvio?" Lee asked.

"Yeah. And you?"

Sheriff Lee Burlock said, "I don't suppose you're doing laundry in that canner."

Silvio began laughing. Then he started coughing and he took a sip of the new brandy and he had his voice back. "Right now I wish we were."

"How much have you guys distilled?"

"Almost four quarts."

"Who are you selling it to?"

"Selling! What the hell are you talking about? Have you ever made any kind of liquor? Probably not. Well, let me tell you Sheriff, there's too, too much work involved here to ever think about selling. This here was for us."

"Then you know the Volstead Act became law and making the manufacture of any alcoholic beverage illegal."

"Even for your own use? How can that be, Sheriff? Are you sure of that?" Silvio asked.

"Even for your own use, Silvio."

"So what happens now?"

"We destroy your still and arrest all four of you and take you to jail."

"Jarvis, if you would give me a hand, we'll take this contraption outside and break it up." Jarvis took one end and Lee the other and they carried it outside and took the top off and emptied it and took an axe and beat the hell out of it. Silvio was almost in tears. "You know, Sheriff, that has been in my family for fifty years."

"I'll take one quart of this for evidence and dump the rest."

"Sheriff, if you're going to arrest us for manufacturing alcohol, how do you know we weren't simply making some animal lure for trapping this fall."

Jarvis thought that was a good point.

"Why not take a taste, before you do something you might regret," Silvio said.

Lee thought Silvio was trying to trap him somehow until Jarvis picked up a jar and took a sip. "That is good, raspberry and what else?"

"Rhubarb."

"A good combination. Try it, Lee," and Jarvis gave the jar to him.

"That is good. One hell of a kick to it."

Rascal said, "Can we each have a sip too?"

"One only," Lee said.

"Sheriff, can I go tell my wife Anita what is going on so she doesn't worry?"

"Go ahead."

"Sheriff, when we get to the station house I'd like to take a minute and withdraw enough money for the fine," Rascal said.

"That won't be a problem."

The southbound whistle just blew. "Lee, I should leave and ask the station master to delay the train until we are ready to leave," Jarvis said.

"Okay."

Jarvis ran over to the station house, "Where's the station master?" Jarvis asked.

"He just—here he is now."

"What can I do for you, Jarvis?" Greg asked.

"Would you delay departure for a few minutes? Sheriff Burlock has four prisoners that need to go to Beech Tree."

"I can hold it ten minutes, no longer," Greg answered.

"That'll be long enough."

Sheriff Burlock and the other four men were not long behind Jarvis. "Rascal, I'll go with you to withdraw some money. We have eight minutes now."

It didn't take Rascal long to withdraw $500.00. He might have to help the others with their fines.

"Are you going back to Beech Tree with us, Jarvis?" Rascal asked.

"I was planning on it. Why?"

"Just that Mr. Hitchcock might like to know Jeters won't be in for work this evening."

"Okay. You stay here with Sheriff Burlock. I have just enough time if I run over to inform Hitchcock. I'll let your wife know also, Rascal."

Jarvis ran up the steps to Emma's office and she was standing in the window. "Are you taking them to jail, Jarvis?"

This kind of surprised him and then again it didn't, on second thought. "Sheriff Burlock is. Would you let Mr. Hitchcock know Jeters won't be coming to work tonight."

"I will. Maybe this will teach him." That last statement and her demeanor stayed with him all the way to the jail in Beech Tree.

"Court won't be until tomorrow morning, fellas, so you'll have to spend the night in jail," Burlock said and he closed the inner door.

Out in his office, "Lee, could I see that letter you received?"

"Sure, here it is," and he handed it to Jarvis.

Jarvis was intrigued where it said, "My husband is one of them!" There could not be any mistaking it. Emma had written the letter involving her own husband. He began feeling sorry for Rascal. He would never have guessed that Emma was so vicious. He was glad he didn't have to live with a woman like that.

"There's no sense of us putting up bail today, Sheriff. We'd just have to come back in the morning. Lock us up," Silvio said.

Jeters and Jeff just looked at him with their mouths open. Rascal was in agreement with Silvio, "Take it easy you two. One night in jail ain't all that bad. Plus we'll save train fare." Silvio and Rascal shared a cell and Jeters and Jeff shared another. "Too bad we didn't have one of those full Mason jars that we could pass around. I never tasted so fine a brandy in all my life," Jeters said.

"That was pretty good wasn't it," Jeff agreed.

"Even Burlock and Jarvis like it," Rascal said.

That night Silvio snored so loud the other three had very little sleep. After breakfast they were escorted over to the courthouse.

It was a slow morning. The cases for the day were the four of them. Rascal was hoping for a different judge, not Hulcurt. It was Hulcurt and he spotted Rascal right off. "I understand, Sheriff Burlock, that these four men were all involved in the manufacturing of an alcoholic beverage. Is that correct, Sheriff?"

"Yes, Your Honor."

"Mr. Antony, how old are you?"

"I'm seventy, Your Honor."

"What kind of liquor where the four of you making?"

"Brandy, Your Honor."

"What kind of brandy?"

"Your Honor, all that's left after the Sheriff busted things up is what is in that Mason jar in front of you. Have a taste, Sir, and see if you can tell."

"Well if I have to find you guilty of manufacturing liquor, I think I should at least taste it to be sure that it is liquor." Hulcurt took the lid off and took a sip and let his tongue savor the unique flavor. He took another taste. "This is indeed liquor. A very unusual taste. Very good, but I have never had a brandy with the same flavor. It's a little like rhubarb and just the hint of, I think, raspberries. The alcohol content is high also. Am I correct, Mr. Antony?"

"Yes, Your Honor. It is rhubarb with raspberry flavoring."

"It is indeed good. How much do you get for a quart jar of this fine elixir?"

"Your Honor, my granddaddy, my daddy and me have been making this elixir for many years and we have never sold a drop. We have given much of it to friends. But it was for our pleasure. The same as what we four were making for our pleasure. Not to sell."

"Mr. Antony, you said you are seventy. What's wrong with your feet? I noticed you limp."

"I worked for the C&A Railroad, Your Honor, and broke my ankle when I slipped while filling the engine with water."

"Ah, Mr. Ambrose, Mr. Daniels and Mr. Jeters have either of you made liquor before this?"

They all answered, "No."

"The law is very clear."

"Your Honor, may I say one more thing before you pass judgment?"

"Go ahead, Mr. Antony."

"It really saddens me when someone in this great country of ours can't make a little brandy for themselves, with no intention whatever of selling any of it. It saddens me, Your Honor." Jeters and Jeff were almost in tears. Jarvis was now feeling guilty for helping Sheriff Burlock.

"While I can sympathize with what you said, Mr. Antony, the law is very clear. There are no gray colors. You either manufactured brandy or you did not. I have no choice but to find the four of you guilty of the manufacturing of an illegal alcoholic beverage. Now what I do with this is up to me. I set my own guidelines here. I understand that the four of you spent last night locked up in jail. Is that correct Sheriff Burlock?"

"It is, Your Honor."

"Then I sentence each of you to one day in jail and time served. And $10.00 each for cost of court. But let me warn you gentlemen, if you appear in my court again for violating the Prohibition laws, I will not be so lenient. As soon as you pay the clerk you are free to leave." Judge Hulcurt disappeared in his adjacent office—with the mason jar of brandy.

"I ain't got $10.00 with me, let alone to my name," Jeters said.

"I'm in the same boat," Jeff said.

Rascal looked at Silvio, "I have $10.00, but that's about all I have."

"I'll pay it for all of us. I had a good year trapping."

Outside of the courthouse Jarvis said, "Silvio you almost had me in tears with that speech of yours, you made a lot of sense, though, and I think that is what swung the judge in your favor. I hope there aren't any hard feelings, boys, for me helping the Sheriff."

"None at all, Jarvis." Rascal said, "Maybe some time you can help me," and he left it at that, and left Jarvis wondering.

"Boys how about dinner before we go back. Since none of you have any money—my treat."

Chapter 10

They boarded the afternoon northbound and were home in time for supper. During the ride to Whiskey Jack, Rascal had decided not to let on that he knew or suspected that his wife had somehow told Sheriff Burlock what they were doing. And he was beginning to come up with a plan to give Emma some of her own medicine. It would take some planning and a lot of luck.

"See you tomorrow morning," Rascal said as he turned and headed for home.

Emma was home and cooking supper. "I didn't know if you'd be home tonight or not. I would have thought the judge would have given you and your friends some jail time."

"He did, one day—time served."

"I won't put up with you drinking whiskey with your friends, Rascal. You got what you deserved and you're not sleeping in my bed tonight. I didn't think you'd be home so I didn't cook much. You might want to get yourself something."

Rascal didn't answer. He found a jar of frog legs and a tin of biscuits, and he picked enough peas for a meal. He ate until his stomach wouldn't hold any more. Never saying a word to Emma.

He slept surprisingly good on the porch. He tried to stay awake as long as he could, listening to the loons and frogs, and the lightning bugs were putting on quite a display.

In the morning he awoke to the smell of coffee and bacon. The topic of drinking and liquor was not mentioned by either of them. In fact Emma was her usual loving self. "That doe deer is still hanging around, Rascal, and my lettuce is almost ready."

"I'll see what I can do."

"Starting Monday next week the mill is going to be shut down for repairs, and Mr. Hitchcock told me not to come in, so I'll be able to do a lot of canning."

Rascal walked with Emma to her office and then went to joint his friends. Silvio had yesterday's newspaper and on the front page was an article about Women's Suffrage. "According to this here article, Congress is expecting to pass the Women's Suffrage Act in the middle of next month. This country will never be the same again," Silvio said.

"I don't know, Silvio, why shouldn't women have the right to vote?"

"Well maybe," he grumbled.

"Do you still have a job, Jeters?" Rascal asked.

"I talked with Mr. Hitchcock yesterday before my shift started and he wasn't happy, but I still have my job."

"You know, fellas, we got off pretty damn lucky yesterday. We could still be in jail," Jeff said.

"Yeah, I guess we don't make any more booze," Silvio said. "Anita said enough is enough."

After coffee, Rascal went home and weeded the garden, hulled the potatoes, corn and green beans. There weren't any fresh deer tracks.

After lunch, Rascal loaded his .38-55 rifle, jacked a live round in the chamber and stood it up in the corner. Emma didn't have to ask what it was for. If she saw that pesky deer in the garden and even close to her lettuce, she would shoot it.

The next morning one row of peas had the tops clipped off so even it looked like someone had used shears. There were doe and lamb tracks in the row. For his plan to work, he decided against telling Emma about the peas. And to keep the deer away that day he spent a lot of time in and around the garden, knowing the deer wouldn't come close as long as his presence was there. But once in a while he could see a deer flicking flies with its tail just beyond the clearing.

He spent the afternoon tearing the old seat out of the outhouse and boarding over the hole in the floor and cleaning out the waste from underneath and dumping a bucket of wood ashes to cut the smell. It was a two holer and now without the seat there was enough room so he could use it for a storage shed or for wood.

He limbed trees around the property and piled the branches up in the clearing to burn once the ground was covered with snow. His reason for doing so much around the cabin was to keep the deer out of the garden. He didn't know how he was going to be able to time it so Jarvis would be here at the same time.

Emma went to church at the cafeteria Sunday morning and Rascal stayed home. He said, "I want to spade over more sod so we can have a bigger garden next year."

"My lettuce is almost ready, so you keep that deer out," she left and walked to church.

Rascal walked out back and the doe and her lamb were at the edge of the clearing. He would work for a while turning the sod over. Then he'd pull some weeds. It seemed as though there was always weeds to pull. He picked one small cabbage that wasn't doing well and he tossed it towards the deer.

Of course the deer ran off some, but still in sight. And it wasn't long before both deer were eating the cabbage.

Turning a garden spot over with a spade wasn't easy work and he wouldn't be doing it now if not for trying to keep the deer out until it was time. A fence would have been easier to erect, but he used the excuse that he had used all the fencing for peas, and Douglas didn't have any in the store.

When Emma was back from church she walked out back to see how Rascal was doing. "I see the deer has stayed away from my lettuce. And I don't see any of her tracks at all."

"No, I guess she has found better food in the woods."

"She'd better stay there or I'll shoot her. Why are you making the garden bigger?"

"Oh, I thought about putting in some strawberries next spring and another row of corn."

Emma went inside and made lunch for them both. A fish chowder. "No biscuits?" Rascal asked.

"No, I plan to do biscuits tomorrow morning."

After lunch Rascal continued turning over the sod and finished that late in the afternoon. Then he sharpened his scythe and started cutting the tall grass and bushes around the cabin toward the lake.

He was getting tired and running out of things to do to keep the deer away from the garden.

After supper he asked Emma to sit out on the porch and watch the sunset. Hoping their talking would keep the deer out of Emma's lettuce tonight.

* * *

At the breakfast table the next morning Rascal said, "You know it's really strange not hearing the mill whistle in the morning. Mr. Hitchcock has never shut the mill down for a week for repairs. Is there a special reason now, Em?"

"Business has been good and some of the machinery, Mr. Hitchcock said, is wearing and some of the saws need to be aligned. He expects to be even busier this coming year and he said he doesn't want a major breakdown when they do get busy. Most of the men will keep working on maintenance, so they won't lose any time or money. Me, I told him I would enjoy a week off."

"Now why don't you go have coffee with your friends at the cafeteria. I promised you biscuits this morning. And I'll bake an apple pie, too."

As he walked down the road toward the village he began wondering if Emma was being overly amiable. If she was, then why? Or was he being too suspicious? It was promising to be a beautifully clear day, although hot.

He stood on the dam and looked down at the pool below. He could see several large brook trout just lounging about in the shade.

The train had pulled in a few minutes early and Rascal could see Jarvis standing on the platform. He walked over, "Good morning, Jarvis."

"Good morning, Rascal."

"Are you here for any particular reason?" Rascal asked.

"Yes, I am." Jarvis noticed how Rascal's jaw was set firm. "I'm not after anyone. I was hoping you and I could go fishing up at the head of the lake. You know, at the mouth of Jack Brook."

"Is that all?"

"Isn't that enough. There's not much going on, on these hot days, and I'd like to take a mess of fat trout home for my family."

"Okay, but we might as well go have coffee first."

"I thought fishing would be better early before the sun was overhead," Jarvis said.

"It is mostly, except at the head of the lake."

They joined Silvio for coffee and donuts. Jeters and Jeff were on maintenance duty at the mill. "Good morning, Silvio."

"Jarvis."

"I hope you guys don't hold it against me for helping Sheriff Burlock. He had never been here and asked for my help."

"We don't hold nothing against ya, Jarvis. We know you were only doing your job."

Jarvis sipped his coffee and ate a donut and then said, "That was some speech you said in court, Silvio. If I'd been the judge I'd let you fellas off. As it was Hulcurt did what he could to help you."

"We understand that Jarvis. We ain't mad at no one. That was pretty good tasting brandy, weren't it, Jarvis."

"It was the best I have ever tasted. It's too bad it's all gone."

Silvio coughed and said, "Yeah, that's all." Maybe it didn't all get destroyed.

"What are you doing up here today, Jarvis?" Silvio asked.

"Going fishing," that's all he said.

Silvio stood up and said, "I told Anita I wouldn't stay long this morning."

Rascal and Jarvis got up also. "We'll have to walk up to my cabin to get my gear. Where's yours?"

"My fly rod is with my pack on the platform."

They stopped and picked up Jarvis' pack and started down the steps.

"Emma is baking biscuits and an apple pie this morning. Maybe the biscuits are ready now."

As they were crossing the tracks, Emma looked out the window and both deer were eating her lettuce. She picked up Rascal's rifle and quietly opened and closed the door. Leaning against the corner of the cabin she sighted in on the doe and pulled the trigger.

Jarvis and Rascal were midway across the dam and they both stopped. "That ain't good," Rascal said.

Jarvis turned and looked at Rascal. Rascal shrugged his shoulders. Jarvis didn't waste any time getting to the cabin. Just as Emma was coming out of the garden carrying Rascal's .38-55 rifle. Her hands were shaking when she saw Jarvis and Rascal. She said, "That damned deer was eating my lettuce. I told you, Rascal, I'd shoot it if I saw it eating my lettuce."

Jarvis reached for the rifle and Emma let him have it. He jacked out the empty shell and then he emptied the magazine. "You'd better go see if the deer is dead, Rascal."

Emma held out her bloody hands and said, "It is, I cut her throat."

"Jarvis, I need to go inside to take the biscuits and pie out of the oven."

They all three went in. The smell of biscuits and apple pie was overwhelming.

Jarvis said, "I'm in sort of a conundrum here."

"What do you mean, Jarvis?" Rascal thought he understood what Jarvis was saying.

"Well, do I arrest you, Emma, and take you to jail or not," Jarvis stammered.

"Jarvis," Rascal said, "If it were me, you'd take me to jail in a heartbeat." Emma was looking at Jarvis waiting for him to say something and Jarvis in shock looked at Rascal. Rascal nodded his head, ever so slightly.

"He's right Emma. I have no choice here."

"I'm shocked, Em. I won't have no poaching wife." Jarvis was really shocked now. But then suddenly he remembered the anonymous letter Sheriff Burlock had received. *My husband is one of them.* He understood now. Rascal knew all along who had sent him and his friends to jail for making brandy.

"I don't have any choice in this matter, Emma. You'll have to come to Beech Tree with me. You'll have to spend the night in jail and court will be Tuesday morning."

"Em, when you get to jail, ask for cell #1. It has a pretty good bed. And you'd better withdraw enough money also."

"Rascal, would you mind dressing that deer and dragging it down to the platform. I'll have to take that with us."

"Not a problem."

As they were leaving, Emma wouldn't look at Rascal. He wasn't happy, but she was getting her comeuppance. He dragged the deer out into the trees and dressed it. Then he brought it back to the cabin and sloshed water up in the cavity to wash the blood out. He kept the heart and some of the liver.

When he was ready, he dragged the deer down to the station house. Jarvis and Emma were sitting on the platform. "Can you leave the deer under the eves, in the shade, Rascal?"

"You going to wait all day here, Jarvis? I mean you could wait at the cabin," Rascal offered.

"I thought of that, but Greg said there was a special train out of Lac St. Jean. It appears there is a backlog of freight cars that need to be taken out to free up some space here."

"There's the whistle now."

Rascal waited on the platform until Jarvis and Emma were aboard. Then he left and went home. By now the entire village had heard that Emma had shot a deer and Jarvis was taking her to jail. The only question that some folks had was, why Rascal didn't take the blame instead of letting his wife go to jail.

* * *

There was no conversation between Jarvis and Emma on the way to Beech Tree. He was busy thinking about the whole thing. He was almost convinced that Rascal had set this whole thing up. But he would have to know that Jarvis would be in Whiskey Jack and at what time. And then the two of them walking across the dam just as Emma pulled the trigger.

He finally concluded that there was no way Rascal could have set the stage for his wife getting arrested for shooting a deer in July. He was also concerned that everything that happened were coincidences. But there sure were a lot of coincidences. Starting with him deciding to take the train that morning to Whiskey Jack and go fishing with Rascal. And then he was sure Rascal wanted him to take Emma to jail. Did he know or suspect who had turned him and his friends into the sheriff for making liquor? Was it only payback? If it was, then how did Rascal orchestrate everything? He didn't have an answer. Some day he would have to ask Rascal about it.

"Jarvis," Emma asked, "what brought you to Whiskey Jack this morning?"

"There usually isn't too much to do on hot sunny days like this, so I decided to go fishing in the lake. I have checked Rascal coming back from fishing many times and I asked him if he would go fishing with me."

"He didn't know you were coming to Whiskey Jack this morning?"

"No," that's all he could say.

Jarvis knew Emma too was wondering if Rascal had set this whole thing up, so she would get arrested.

For Emma the train ride to Beech Tree seemed very short. Time had passed so fast. There was no one else in any of the cells, and she was locked in cell #1.

Jarvis went home and poured himself a stiff drink. "I thought you were going fishing, Jarvis," his wife Rita said.

"Things changed. Mrs. Ambrose shot a deer."

"She what?"

"She shot a deer. Rascal and I were on the dam when we heard the shot."

He had to explain to his wife why he would arrest a woman and take her to jail.

* * *

After the train left the station, Rascal went home, cleaned the heart and liver. Then sliced the heart and fried it with onions and warmed up the fresh biscuits. After which he made a pot of coffee and sat on the porch. He didn't feel smug or happy about his wife going to jail, but he figured she had it coming to her after what she had done to him. He didn't consider what he had done as revenge or retaliation, he looked at it more as showing her some of her own medicine. He hoped she would be okay and not too angry with him when she was home.

For supper he fried the liver with onions and more warm biscuits and a slice of apple pie for dessert. Then after he cleaned up the kitchen he sat out on the porch long after the sun had set sipping the last of his brandy.

The next morning Rascal had breakfast at the cafeteria and one by one his friends joined him. But all during their coffee hour no one asked Rascal about Emma. But it was in their minds as it was with everybody's in the village. Had Rascal done this to his wife on purpose? And why had Jarvis really been in Whiskey Jack yesterday, to everyone his presence at the right moment seemed to be more than a coincidence.

Rascal took a newspaper home with him and sat on the porch reading it until noon. It was almost a sure thing that the Women's Suffrage Act would pass next month. Rascal believed that they should have the right to vote, but he was also uncertain whether things would change.

Emma would be coming in on the northbound train in the afternoon and he didn't want her to find the cabin in a mess. So he washed all the dishes and put everything away and swept the floors, and made the bed.

He made a pot of venison stew and picked some lettuce and put it in a bowl on the table.

There were no new deer tracks in the garden. The lamb, smelling death, had run off to be a deer and not a begger.

The stew was simmering on the stove and Rascal was on the porch with his feet propped up on the railing. The train whistle blew. Emma would be home soon. Now he was getting nervous. Would she be angry? Would she pack up and leave? And he was now wondering if he had done the right thing. But it wasn't over with yet either.

He saw her crossing the dam and went inside to stir the stew. It was ready and he moved it off the heat. When she walked through the door she was surprised to find the cabin so neat, and a hot supper ready to sit down to. There was no hugging and kissing. The two acted as if she had just come home from work. She didn't say anything about the bowl of lettuce, fearing that might upset things if she did.

Emma's real surprise came though when it was time to go to bed, and Rascal said, "I won't be sharing my bed with no poaching wife. You sleep on the porch."

This shocked her and later as she was by herself on the porch it finally dawned on her that all this, Rascal was giving her a little of her own medicine.

* * *

Emma didn't sleep at all that night. At first she wanted to be angry at Rascal. Then it began to sink in, the realization that Rascal had only shown her some of her own medicine. How she had treated him. But that wasn't the real problem either.

Then she began soul searching. When she confronted the real problem, she burst into tears. Ever since the death of their two children, Beckie and Jasper, she had been blaming Rascal because he was not here to help her with the children, to comfort her; he was away fighting in a war she knew little about. And he wasn't there because he wanted to be. The loss of her two children had changed her, hardened her against love and life. She had built a fence around her, to protect her from ever feeling that much hurt again. And up until now she had taken out all of her hate on Rascal.

Rascal had responded in the only way he knew how. To show her, her own medicine. And then the loss of her two children hit home again and she muffled her crying in her pillow. She cried for a long time. And when she had no more tears, she quietly went deep within herself where there was calm, strength and love. And little by little she began to feel better. Then suddenly it was like a new awakening that was surrounding her, and the barrier was no longer there.

She laid on her back for the rest of the night feeling better and more alive than she had for a long time. She was happy because she knew now the barrier was no longer there.

She made sure she was up before Rascal and after starting a fire in the kitchen stove, she put on a pot of coffee and started frying bacon. Bacon, hot biscuits and coffee brought Rascal out of bed. Neither one speaking tersely towards the other.

"Rascal when you come back from having coffee with your friends I would like to go fishing with you. It has been a long time since I have been."

"Okay, don't bother to put up a lunch; we'll roast trout over the fire. Bring some tea though. I'll get your fly rod from the shed when I get back."

"Did Emma get home okay, Rascal?" Silvio asked.

"Yes, she's fine."

Silvio was curious as hell about what had happened. Everybody in the village had their own theory. As much as he would like to know, he respected both Rascal and Emma enough not to ask. So they talked of fishing, hunting and Women's Suffrage. Silvio was even beginning to soften.

Rascal didn't spend as much time this morning at the cafeteria. Emma had asked to go fishing and it had been a long time since she had gone with him. He owed her not to stay at the cafeteria for long.

Emma had everything ready and already in the canoe. Rascal was seeing a new, younger Emma. As they paddled up the lake she carried on like she had when they were first married. And her happiness was having its effect on Rascal. He was happy to see Emma now so happy. Neither one of them saying a word about either of them having to spend a night in jail. There was understanding enough for them both, so not a word had to be spoken.

"If I remember correctly," she said in a quiet voice, "we have to sit still for a few minutes."

As they waited, neither one of them spoke. Then Emma looked at Rascal and he nodded his head. She cast out beautifully with a red wolf fly and no sooner did the fly hit the water and a huge brook trout came completely out of the water as it took the fly. Emma set the hook like a professional and played it until it tired. And without a net she reached down and grabbed it by the gills and brought it into the canoe.

"Wow! Look at that, Rascal. It's so large and so orange," Emma said excitedly.

Rascal was happy just watching her. "Do it again, Em."

She cast out in the same spot and began inching the fly back and another took it and headed for the bottom.

Rascal didn't have to tell her to play it, or keep a tight line. He knew she already knew what to do. And she did. When the trout was played out she landed it like she had the first one. Rascal was having more fun watching his wife with this renewed sense of being than fishing himself.

She turned to look at him and said, "Why are you smiling?"

"Oh, just watching you." She was back and he could not have been happier.

They caught a few more trout and Rascal said, "Let's go ashore, build a fire and roast a couple of these trout for lunch."

While Rascal cleaned the fish Emma started the fire and put a pot of water on for tea. While the trout were roasting Rascal and Emma made love on the ground. Dry spruce and fir needles as their only blanket.

Afterwards they sat naked on a log eating fresh trout. When they had drank all the tea and had their fill of trout, Emma said, "I want to make love again," and she smiled.

How could Rascal resist, seeing her smiling so serenely was more beautiful than her naked body.

* * *

From that day at the head of the lake, Emma was her old self. And everyone in the village noticed the change. She was always happy now and smiling. And she no longer held Rascal's coffee friends in contempt.

On August 8th, Congress passed the Women's Suffrage Act and women everywhere now had the right to vote. And in Whiskey Jack everyone understood and accepted it, but life continued on as it had without any great hoopla.

In early September, as Rascal was walking around the corner of the station house he saw Jarvis and another game warden step out of the passenger car. "Who are they after?"

He followed them into the cafeteria, "Jarvis, why don't you and your friend join Silvio and me."

"Where is Jeff Daniels? We wouldn't want to crowd him out," Jarvis said.

"Oh Jeff, he move on. Sit," Silvio said.

"I'm retiring at the end of this month and this is Marcel Cyr; and he will be replacing me. He speaks fluent French and will be more effective along the border than I was."

"Hello, Marcel, I'm Rascal Ambrose."

"And I'm Silvio Antony."

"Gentlemen."

"Marcel is brand new and I'm showing him the district."

"You'll have a big pair of boots to fill, sonny," Silvio said.

"Jarvis, even though you were always the law, the people in Whiskey Jack have always considered you family. Even when you took us to jail," Silvio said.

"Thank you, Silvio."

"What will you do now, Jarvis?" Rascal asked.

"Oh, I thought about moving to Whiskey Jack and selling deer to sports." That brought a laugh to them all except the new game warden, Marcel Cyr.

"Take my advice, Jarvis, be careful who you sell to," more laughter.

"My wife Rita and I are going to open a furrier shop. Page's Furrier. No sense in all the good furs being sold across the border.

"How's Emma? Did you two patch things up?" Jarvis asked.

"My wife is fine and there never was anything to patch up."

"Glad to hear that. You know you still owe me that fishing trip. To that special place at the head of the lake."

"Whenever you can make it, Jarvis, I'll take the time."

"What special fish hole is this?" young Marcel asked.

Jarvis spoke up and said, "I'd rather give you my wife than to tell you where it is."

About the Author

Randall Probert lived and was raised in Strong, a small town in the western mountains of Maine. Six months after graduating from high school, he left the small town behind for Baltimore, Maryland, and a Marine Engineering school, situated downtown near what was then called "The Block". Because of bad weather, the flight from Portland to New York was canceled and this made him late for the connecting flight to Baltimore. A young kid, alone, from the backwoods of Maine, finally found his way to Washington, D.C., and boarded a bus from there to Baltimore. After leaving the Merchant Marines, he went to an aviation school in Lexington, Massachusetts.

During his interview for Maine Game Warden, he was asked, "You have gone from the high seas to the air. . .are you sure you want to be a game warden?"

Mr. Probert retired from Warden Service in 1997 and started writing historical novels about the history in the areas where he patrolled as a game warden, with his own experiences as a game warden as those of the wardens in his books. Mr. Probert has since expanded his purview and has written two science fiction books, *Paradigm* and *Paradigm II*, and has written two mystical adventures, *An Esoteric Journey*, and *Ekani's Journey*.

Acknowledgements

I would like to thank Amy Henley of Newry for your help with typing and with the revisions and the backcover synopsis. I would like to thank Sarah Lane of Bethel for the front cover. And I would also like to thank Laura Ashton of Pinellas Park, FL for your help formatting the book for printing.

More Books by Randall Probert

A Forgotten Legacy   *A Grafton Tale*

An Eloquent Caper   *Paradigm II*

Courier de Bois   *Train to Barnjum*

Katrina's Valley   *A Trapper's Legacy*

Mysteries at   *An Esoteric Journey*
*   Matagamon Lake*

A Warden's Worry   *The Three Day Club*

A Quandry   *Eben McNinch*
*   at Knowles Corner*

Paradigm   *Lucien Jandreau*

Trial at Norway Dam   *Ekani's Journey*